DARK PRINCE'S DILEMMA

THE CHILDREN OF THE GODS BOOK 30

I. T. LUCAS

NOTE FROM THE AUTHOR:
Dark Prince's Dilemma is a work of fiction!
Names, characters, places and incidents are products of the author's
imagination or are used fictitiously and are not to be construed as real. Any
similarity to actual persons, organizations and/or events is purely
coincidental.

CAROL

*D*uring her drive to the village, Carol contemplated how to present her idea of rescuing Areana to Kian without him dismissing it out of hand before she could adequately articulate it.

The way she saw it, Kian would have two major objections. The main one was that he didn't trust Lokan and would never let him go with her to the island. The second one was the level of risk involved, which he might decide was unacceptable.

But that was because he was overly protective and risk-averse when it came to civilians and especially females.

Except, Carol was willing and ready, and she had to convince Kian that her plan was the only way to verify whether Annani's sister was being held captive by Navuh, and if she was indeed there, to get her out. Carol hadn't figured out the second part yet, but that could be done later, when and if Kian approved the first one, which was iffy at best.

She'd spent most of the night trying to come up with an

alternative to infiltrating Navuh's harem, with Lokan's help or without it, and then reporting her findings to him via dream-sharing. But then, Carol wasn't a strategist, and her imagination could carry her only so far.

Kian and Turner might come up with a different plan, one that didn't involve letting Lokan out of his prison cell or sending her to the island. If they did, Kian would undoubtedly choose that plan over hers.

If they failed to produce a viable alternative, though, Annani might pressure him into approving her plan.

The goddess wanted her sister back, and what the goddess wanted the goddess got.

Kian and Turner would still have to come up with the extraction plan, but Carol had faith in Turner. After the two incredible rescues he had already planned and executed, she had no doubt that he would think of something

"Come in," Kian called out when she knocked on his door.

This time, she entered his office without the anxiety that had accompanied her previous visits. For one, she'd texted him beforehand so he was expecting her, and secondly, she was now Lokan's official confidant and liaison, which elevated her status from a mere café manager to a spy in training.

"Good morning, Kian."

He waved at one of the chairs in front of his desk. "Take a seat, please."

"Thank you."

"How can I help you, Carol?"

She was in luck. Kian seemed to be in an amiable enough mood, which was a rarity for him. "I have an idea for how we can infiltrate Navuh's harem and find out whether he has Areana."

Kian shook his head. "I'm not letting Vivian and Ella go

on another risky mission. So, if that's what you came to talk to me about, we are done."

Ugh. Even when in a good mood, Kian was hard to talk to.

"That's not what I had in mind." She shifted in her chair. "Did Arwel tell you that Lokan and I can dream-share?"

"Yes, he did, and my first response was to put the bastard in stasis the moment I got the island's location from him. But then I reconsidered." He smirked. "I wanted to see if he was stupid enough to try it with anyone else, but apparently, he is not."

She nodded. "Lokan believes that he can do it only with women he is attracted to. He attempted to dream-share with human male acquaintances, people he wanted to influence, but it didn't work. It might not work on immortal males either, but I think it's worthwhile for us to find out."

"I'd rather not."

She shrugged. "It's not that important. If Ella managed to hide her thoughts from Lokan while they dream-shared, then I'm sure others could do so as well. It's mostly a useless talent, though, except for what I have in mind."

Taking a long breath, she continued. "If Lokan can get me into the harem, I can dream-share with him and tell him what's going on in there. It would effectively be the equivalent of what he wanted to do with Ella and Vivian. Dream-sharing is also an undetectable communication that goes both ways."

Kian leaned back and crossed his arms over his chest. "I'm not going to let Lokan out of his cell, let alone take you with him to the island. But I'm curious to hear how you thought to pull it off. In fact, I'm curious to hear how he planned on doing it with Ella and Vivian's involuntary help."

Curious was good.

She could whet Kian's appetite, and maybe then he would be willing to reconsider.

"Lokan is the one who compels the human pilots operating the island's transport planes. As we know, they are the only ones allowed to fly to and from the island. Also, other than Navuh and Lokan, no one knows the exact location of it."

Kian's eyes lit up with interest. "As long as it's nothing too big and it flies under his father's radar, so to speak, he can compel them to transport whatever and whoever he pleases."

"Precisely. And because he is Navuh's son, he doesn't have to go through the same checks everyone else does. He could have smuggled Ella and Vivian in."

Kian arched a brow. "Even if no one checked his luggage, how was he going to explain the two new humans? They must have records of everyone on the island."

Carol shrugged. "Lokan didn't elaborate, but he could have probably claimed that he brought his personal toys along. Again, as Navuh's son, he has more leeway than others. Besides, getting onto the island is less of a problem than getting off."

"How was he going to do that? And before that, how was he going to get one of them assigned to the harem?"

"Lokan says that the guy in charge of staffing the harem owes him some favors. Lokan could have pretended to tire of either Vivian or Ella, put one of them in the harem, and kept the other one for himself or assigned her to general housekeeping."

Kian nodded. "So far, the plan makes sense. A thousand things could have gone wrong, but if everything went smoothly, he could have pulled it off. Getting them out is another thing altogether, though. But I think he had no intention of doing so. After he got what he wanted from them, he would have just left Vivian and Ella to work on the island for the rest of their lives."

The thought had crossed her mind, but even if she was willing to accept that her mate was a heartless bastard, it would not have been prudent for him to betray his partners in crime because they could have betrayed him in turn.

"The plan was to fake their deaths or at least the death of the one in the harem. Since humans are in charge of burials, he could have compelled them to load the caskets onto a transport plane that he was flying off the island."

"A very ambitious plan. I still don't think that he ever intended to get them off the island, but I'm willing to give him the benefit of the doubt."

Carol shook her head. "He could not have just left them there because he would have run the risk of them telling on him. His options would have been to either get them out or kill them, and I don't think Lokan is that cold."

Kian arched a brow but wisely said nothing.

Not that Carol could blame him for believing the worst of Lokan, when she had nagging doubts herself. The fact that he was her mate didn't mean that he was good. In fact, he'd never claimed to be a nice guy.

"I assume that your plan is to follow the same scenario?"

"With modifications, of course."

"Not going to happen, Carol. Lokan is a liar, and he would say anything to get out of the dungeon. Half of what he told you might be lies. But even if everything is true, I'm still not letting him out, and you can't do any of it without his help. Case closed."

"What about Annani?" Carol used her one ace argument. "What are you going to tell her? That you are not willing to rescue her sister? She will never accept it."

Kian grimaced. "I'll think of another way."

"I spent all of last night trying to come up with an alternative, and there are none. Only a human can get into the harem or an immortal female impersonating one. And the only way to communicate with someone on the inside is through unconventional means."

Uncrossing his arms, Kian leaned forward. "With all due respect, Carol, you are not an expert. I'm sure Turner can come up with a better plan."

"By all means." She waved a hand. "Let him try."

LOKAN

"*A*re you surprised?" Lokan asked once Carol was done telling him about her meeting with Kian.

Pacing the length of the living room, she threw her hands in the air. "I thought that mentioning how much his mother wanted to find her sister would help, but Kian said that they would come up with a different plan, one that didn't involve you."

He snorted. "Good luck with that. I've been mulling over that for decades, and until I met Ella, I couldn't figure out how to get someone on the inside to tell me who was the important female Navuh was hiding in his harem. I never actually planned on getting her out."

"What if that mystery woman turned out to be your mother? Would you have just left her there?"

"I can't see how it is possible to get an immortal female out of the harem. She can't fake her own death."

As Carol resumed her agitated pacing, the sight of her enticingly swaying hips was affecting Lokan. With his focus shifting from planning and strategizing to his throbbing erection, all he could think of was the shortest route to getting her in bed.

Except, Carol wasn't doing it on purpose, and sex was the furthest thing from her mind.

She stopped and put her hands on her hips. "What if someone starts a fire? I'm sure your father will evacuate everyone. He wouldn't let his wives and concubines suffer, right? The immortals would survive, and he might not give a damn about the humans, but what about the babies? His babies?"

Shifting to relieve the pressure, Lokan forced his mind to get back on track. "Too dangerous and too obvious. He would know it was arson."

"Not if it's done right." Carol chuckled. "And believe me, we know how to stage things so they look authentic."

After the two rescues that the clan had organized for Ella, he had no doubt. "That still leaves the problem of actually getting her off the island. After a stunt like that, security will be at an all-time high."

Carol sauntered over to the bar and pulled out a bottle of water. "I'll leave it up to Turner. The guy is a freaking genius. He will figure something out. But first, I need to get in there and find out whether Navuh has Areana. Otherwise, there is no point in taking such a huge risk."

"Who is Turner?"

"The guy who shot you."

"Is he a clan member? I thought he was a sociopath human. He didn't emit any scents."

Carol sat next to him on the couch. "Turner was human before he transitioned, but even then he didn't emit any scents. He's an anomaly, not a sociopath. A bit cold, that's true, but he's awesome. Without him, Kian would have never found where Sebastian was holding me, and Ella's rescues would have probably failed."

Interesting. Lokan had thought that Kian was the brains behind Ella's rescues. Instead, it was the short, blond dude who reminded him of a younger Putin.

"What I don't understand is why they didn't kill Gorchenco. Why let him live so he could chase after Ella?"

Carol put her empty water bottle on the coffee table. "Ella refused. She claimed to have a gut feeling about Gorchenco still being needed for some unknown future purpose that he was supposed to fulfill. But I think she just didn't want him to die because the girl got soft-hearted."

"He treated her well. Not that I'm justifying what he did, but it could have been much worse for her. Perhaps that's the reason she had mercy on him."

Carol's expression changed, turning hard. "If it were me, I would have killed the bastard myself."

It was a chilling reminder that she wasn't as gentle as she looked.

Then she shrugged, and the viciousness disappeared as quickly as it appeared. "But who knows? Maybe Ella's other special talent is premonition, and Gorchenco will still prove useful in some way?"

Even though Carol was back to her usual self, witnessing the sudden change in her made Lokan uneasy. The momentary hardness went against her core nature, and he had a feeling that if life had been gentler on her, she would have never developed that hard edge necessary for survival.

Frustration came on the heels of an overwhelming need to shield Carol from all the ugliness. He wanted to create a cocoon for her, a place where she would be safe and free to be herself, soft and sweet and tempting. But he was in no position to pamper her, let alone protect her.

Besides, Carol was an independent and adventurous spirit, and she would not have appreciated him trying to coddle her.

He could, however, redirect the conversation.

Wrapping an arm around Carol's shoulders, Lokan pulled her closer to him. "The Russian can be useful for many things. He can arrange assassinations, and he can supply the clan with weapons they can't get their hands on legally. All for the right price or in exchange for keeping the dirt I have on him from reaching Putin."

She tilted her head. "Extortion?"

"Precisely."

Carol straightened her back and turned to face him. "I can think of another thing he could be useful for. He can get me on the island." Her eyes sparkled with excitement. "He can bring me along as his plaything. We then pretend to have a fight, and he leaves me there. I find a way to get myself assigned to the harem, and when I'm done with the investigation, the clan organizes an extraction, maybe even with Gorchenco's help. I can still dream-share with you from over there. It is not limited by distance, right?"

"It's not. But there is one big hole in your crazy idea. You are too beautiful to get assigned housekeeping work. You would get conscripted into the brothel, and to ensure your cooperation, an immortal will attempt to thrall you. Game over."

Huffing out a breath, Carol slumped back on his arm. "What if I have a disability? I won't be suitable for the brothel if I have a lame leg or if I'm deaf. I can pretend."

"Wouldn't work. We have doctors on the island, and every girl gets a thorough physical before being put into service."

"You are smart." She waved a hand. "How about you come up with some ideas instead of shooting down all of mine?"

She looked so disappointed, but he couldn't let her think her plan was actionable.

"They were all very clever and inventive, but you can't do it alone. With me, it was dangerous. Without me, it's suicide."

Carol shook her head. "I'm not giving up so easily. What if I can thrall the pilots? I just need them to cooperate with me for a little while, so a thrall might be enough."

"The compulsion makes them unsusceptible to thralling. I made sure of that."

"Crap, and double crap. What about shrouding? I'm better at that than thralling anyway. I can make myself invisible to them and sneak onto the transport plane."

"My instructions to the pilots were about not accepting orders from anyone they are not supposed to, and about not revealing any information about the island, so shrouding might work on them. But it will not work on the immortals who check all incoming planes."

"Well, I won't have to hide if I come with Gorchenco, right?"

"This is futile. We are going round in circles. You are not doing this, and that's it. Hell, I wasn't sure about this plan when the idea was for me to go with you, but I'm absolutely certain that you can't do it alone."

Palming the back of his neck, Carol pulled him down to her. With their noses almost touching, she looked into his eyes. "I'm not giving up. If you and Kian and Turner put your heads together, I'm sure you will come up with a solution."

Instead of answering, Lokan closed the rest of the distance and kissed her. "I can't think straight when I'm lusting after you. Let's go to bed."

KIAN

*A*fter Carol's visit, Kian had put in a couple of hours of work and then grabbed his pack of cigarillos and climbed up to the roof.

It was too early in the day for that, and he was well aware that he was going through the fancy little packs way too quickly, but Merlin had given him a great excuse for indulging.

While he and Syssi were trying to conceive, it was imperative that he kept calm. The biofeedback Merlin had prescribed had helped some in the beginning, but that was because of the novelty. It had become really annoying really fast, and Kian had dropped it, managing his stress the old-fashioned way. Making love to his wife, smoking, and drinking.

How did that mesh with his insistence on healthy eating?

It didn't.

Except for the lovemaking, which was a healthy and productive activity. The other two couldn't be justified. But then he had no aspirations to sainthood, and he was fine with sinning as long as it was done in moderation.

Right. Keep telling yourself that. It's lack of self-control.

Then again, Syssi had told him on more than one occasion that he was being too hard on himself, and that it was only adding to his stress. Perhaps she was right. Hell, he knew she was, but he didn't know how to be any other way.

Besides, how was he supposed to keep calm with his mother breathing down his neck about freeing her sister, and Carol coming up with crazy rescue plans?

He prayed to the Fates that Lokan's dream mother looked nothing like Areana, so he could put this whole insanity behind him and go back to the much less stressful routine of managing the clan's business empire.

And he wasn't even being sarcastic.

Making money for the clan wasn't emotionally demanding. No lives were at stake, and he enjoyed the game.

Hell, he thrived on it.

When his phone rang, Kian was tempted to let it go to voicemail and finish his cigarillo in peace, but regrettably, he was too anal for that. Pulling the phone out of his pants pocket, he glanced at the display and was glad he'd decided to answer.

"Andrew. What's up?"

"I talked with Tim. He can take a day off tomorrow and do both portraits. He wants six thousand for both and a gourmet lunch to be delivered to him while he works."

"Not a problem."

"You are aware that it's highway robbery, true? The going rate is no more than five hundred apiece."

"Yeah, but Tim knows that he is the best and can demand any price he wants. I have no problem with that."

In fact, after the big deal Andrew had made about Tim's outrageous demands, Kian was expecting to pay more.

"He'll be glad to hear that. By the way, I've been thinking about the order in which we should have the portraits drawn. I suggest that Annani go first, so we know what Areana looks like, but we don't show it to Lokan. Then when Tim draws the portrait from Lokan's memory, we can compare the two."

Kian tapped his cigarillo, watching the ash float down and disperse. "It doesn't really make a difference who goes first. What I'm worried about is Tim's residual memory of the first drawing when he draws the second. It might affect him subconsciously."

"The bigger problem is Annani getting influenced by the one drawn from Lokan's memory," Andrew said. "She wants his mother to be her sister, and after so long, she might not remember Areana's face so well. And as to Tim, we will have to thrall him before he goes to see Lokan. Which brings up another issue. The guy is crusty and suspicious. He might be immune. Which is a big problem given who he will be spending time with."

"Right. We need to test him before we let him see Annani. If he can't be thralled, she will have to tamp down her glow and pretend to be human."

"Does she have any normal everyday clothes? And she should put her hair up too." Andrew chuckled. "Not that anything is going to make Annani forgettable. Tim might be too stunned to draw."

"From what I've heard about him, your guy doesn't seem like the type who's easily shaken."

"True. Where do you want to do this? I don't want to bring him to the keep and then discover that he is immune to thralling, and I can't test him myself because I still can't thrall for shit."

"We can use the office building across the street from the keep. If Tim is immune, we will take him down to the underground parking and blindfold him before taking him to the dungeon. Is he going to be okay with that?"

"He will probably ask for more money. When do you want to meet up?"

"Ten in the morning tomorrow. I'll text you the address."

"Good deal."

4

LOKAN

$\mathcal{A}$s Lokan stepped out of the shower, the phone rang.

The only one who ever called him was Arwel, and the timing was not a coincidence. It was a reminder that nothing in his plush prison was private, including their lovemaking.

Carol claimed Arwel wasn't watching the feed or listening to it, relying instead on his empathic ability, but that wouldn't have told him when they were done showering. Thankfully, there were no cameras in the bathroom.

Perhaps from now on they should only have sex in there. Except, there was no hiding from Arwel's empathic senses. Lokan liked the guy, but he hated the intrusion. It was like having a mental threesome every time he and Carol had sex, and Lokan wasn't into sharing his woman with another male.

Wrapping a towel around his hips, he padded to the living room and picked up the receiver. "Were you waiting for me to be done?"

"In fact, I was. I have maps for you to mark the location of the island on. Tell Carol to get dressed."

Lokan's gut twisted. "Give us ten minutes."

He'd been wondering when Kian was going to collect on the promise, and had been vacillating between keeping his word or going back on it. The problem was that Lokan still wasn't sure that he was doing the right thing.

He felt like a fucking traitor. Hell, he was one. It didn't matter what excuse he used to ease his conscience. The bottom line was that he was about to reveal the Brotherhood's most guarded secret.

"Was Arwel asking about lunch?" Carol walked in with a towel wrapped around her body. "He must be hungry." She smiled and winked. "Someone didn't let me out of bed until way past lunchtime."

"He could have used the vending machines."

Lokan was hungry too, but he was perfectly fine with the trade-off. Two hours in bed with Carol were well worth the price of an empty stomach.

"Arwel is bringing in maps for me to mark the island's location on."

"Then I should hurry up. While you guys are busy with that, I'll go upstairs and make us lunch. In the meantime, you can snack on pretzels."

"Thank you."

She stretched up on her toes and kissed his cheek. "No need to thank me. That's how I show affection. I like feeding people. Especially you."

Cupping her bottom, he lifted her up and kissed her properly. "Snatching that towel off of you is way too tempting." He let her down. "Get dressed in the bathroom or the closet. I don't want Arwel to see you naked, even if he is your so-called cousin."

It still baffled him how the clan members could regard each other as closely related when in fact they were separated by many generations and had very little genetics in

17

common. Had it been drilled into their heads? Or was it something they felt instinctively?

Carol rolled her eyes. "Fine."

By the time the door to Lokan's jail apartment opened, Carol had not only gotten dressed but had also made coffee and put snacks on the table, one small bowl of mixed nuts and another of pretzels.

Walking in with an armload of maps, Arwel sniffed the coffee and smiled. "How did you know that I needed a caffeine boost?"

Carol shrugged. "I'm a good hostess."

Arwel dropped the maps on the table and walked over to the bar. "Are you going to make lunch? Or do we skip straight to dinner?"

"I'm making lunch, and later I'll make dinner." She patted his arm. "See you later, boys." She kissed Lokan's cheek. "Play nice while I'm gone."

"What's with the paper maps?" Lokan asked when the door closed after Carol. "It would have been much easier on a screen where I could have enlarged the picture. You are aware that the island is tiny, right?"

"I've printed close-ups of satellite images. I had no idea that there were so many islands in that area of the ocean that were not marked on any of the official maps."

"That's because most are insignificant in size." Lokan lifted one rolled-up map and spread it over the dining table.

The size was so blown up that it was difficult to figure out what he was looking at. There was no major landmass, just a lot of ocean dotted with scattered rocks.

He spread out another one. "You could have at least included the coordinates. These satellite photos are useless without them."

"You said that you didn't know the coordinates but could recognize the island by sight. That's why I brought you these.

I didn't think you would have a problem pinpointing the island."

"I need to piece them together." Lokan gathered the photos and went into the bedroom.

Spreading them over the bed, he matched them up like a puzzle, and once he had the entire map of the area, finding the island was easy. "That's it." He pointed.

Arwel pulled a red marker out of his shirt pocket and circled the island. "How do you fit so many people on it?"

"The warriors live underground, and it goes deep. We have eleven floors going down."

"Impressive. Who built it?"

"It was a joint effort. My father brought in human crews, but he also put the warriors to work."

Arwel grimaced. "What happened to the humans?"

"I ensured their silence. What did you think, that we killed them all?"

The Guardian shrugged. "Doomers show no regard for human lives."

"That's true to an extent. My father believes that the goal justifies the means, but he is also averse to waste. Unless killing off humans benefits him in some way, he doesn't condone it."

Arwel snorted. "A true humanitarian."

"It is what it is." Lokan walked over to the bar and pulled out a bottle of whiskey. "Do you want some?"

Arwel shook his head. "I'm good for now." He started collecting the printouts from the bed. "What I don't understand is how you managed to keep the island hidden in this day and age. What about satellites and airplanes and drones?"

"It's not that people don't know that the island is there. They just don't know that it's populated, and it's not interesting enough to investigate."

"You have a resort. I'm sure you don't keep it dark at night. Any ship or plane can detect the lights."

Lokan smirked. "The island is privately owned, and it does not belong to any country. And just to be on the safe side, we also spread rumors that the island was used for nuclear testing and is still unsafe."

"There are ways to check those things."

"We make sure that no one bothers."

5

CAROL

"*P*erhaps we should invite Arwel to dine with us." Carol put two paper cups on the table. "I feel bad about him eating alone in his room."

Lokan grimaced. "He is with us in spirit, and unfortunately, it is not just an expression."

She sat down and put a napkin over her lap. "Does it bother you so much?"

"Of course it bothers me."

Carol waved a dismissive hand. "It's not so bad once you consider the alternative. A different Guardian would have watched and listened to the feed. At least Arwel only senses our emotions."

Lokan cut into his steak and speared a chunk with his fork. "That's what he tells you. I'm inclined to accept that he mutes the audio and dims the video when we are having sex, but he is not doing that at other times. Otherwise, how would he have known to call right as I stepped out of the shower?"

Frowning, Carol glanced at the surveillance camera. "I'll have a talk with him."

"It won't help. That's what he was told to do. He's doing his job."

"His job is not to spy on you." That job was hers. "And he doesn't have to listen to everything we say to each other. He is here to make sure that you don't escape and that I'm safe."

"Right." Lokan attacked the steak with renewed vigor.

The way he was going at it with the knife, he was going to cut through the plate along with the tabletop.

As soon as Carol had entered the cell, she could feel Lokan's agitation crackling like an electrical current. She'd smiled, kissed him, and had tried to chitchat about this and that, but if anything, her efforts had only made it worse.

Perhaps once Lokan was full he would feel better. She'd noticed this about men. Because most were not attuned to their own feelings, simple things like hunger and fatigue irritated them. But since they didn't make the connection between the physical discomfort and their mental state, they instead looked for objective reasons for the agitation, and if there weren't any, they made them up.

To have a pleasant time with a guy, it was prudent to make sure that he wasn't tired or hungry or thirsty, and if he was human, that he wasn't ill.

"How is your steak?" she asked, to start a conversation.

Lokan shrugged. "It's okay."

Talk about grumpy.

Perhaps giving up the island's location had upset him?

Was he blaming her?

It wasn't her fault. In this, she was just a bystander. In fact, Lokan had probably been spared a much harsher treatment because Kian was mindful of her feelings for him.

He'd get over it. What was done was done, and there was no point in dwelling on it or reassessing the merit of his decision or lack thereof.

She decided to give diversion another go. "Do you want to watch a movie after lunch?"

He looked at her as if that was the dumbest suggestion ever. "I'm not in the right mood for watching a movie."

Great. Prince Charming was starting to show his true colors.

"Don't be angry at me just because you did as you promised and gave Arwel the island's location. It had nothing to do with me."

"I know, and I'm not angry at you. I'm angry at myself. I shouldn't have given it up so easily."

She snorted. "Would you have preferred to get tortured first?"

He put his fork down. "At least I would have felt like less of a spineless traitor."

For a smart guy, Lokan was really dense, and he was talking out of his ass.

"Have you ever been tortured?"

"I've gotten beaten up pretty bad, but I don't know if that counts as torture."

"How badly? Were you in excruciating pain, bleeding from multiple wounds? Did the torment continue the next day, and the day after that, and the next, and the next, until you prayed for death to release you from your suffering?"

"No."

"Then you have no freaking clue what you're talking about. Thank the merciful Fates that you were spared that, and that Kian convinced you to talk instead of torturing it out of you. Besides, it was the right thing to do if you ever want to find out whether your mother is still alive."

Raising his hands, Lokan pressed his palms to his temples. "You're right, and I'm sorry for snapping at you. I just feel like such a failure right now. And I'm not at all convinced that I did the right thing."

Carol sighed. "Life is full of compromises, and things are seldom black and white. Stop agonizing about your decision and learn to live with it because there is no going back. What's done, is done."

"Precisely. That's why it's eating at me. The word traitor is playing on a loop in my head."

Carol pushed her plate away and got up. "I have a cure for that." She offered him a hand up. "Let's go to bed."

He shook his head. "I can't believe I'm saying it, but sex is not a cure-all."

"No, it's not. But I guarantee that it will make you feel better."

6

LOKAN

*L*okan took Carol's hand, but he didn't get up. Instead, he kissed the back of it. "Can you go ahead without me? I need a moment to gather my thoughts."

She arched a brow but then nodded. "Don't take too long. I might take a nap." The teasing tone didn't match her apprehensive scent.

"I won't." He forced a smile. "I just need a moment."

The woman had healthy instincts.

He was angry, mostly at himself but also at Carol, and Lokan had a rule against getting in bed with a woman unless he was in full control of his emotions.

Aggression ran in his veins, and reining it in required effort even when he was in the best of moods. When angry, he was dangerous.

But then, Carol wasn't human, and he couldn't accidentally break her. He might hurt her, though, or scare her. A nasty voice in the back of his head whispered that it didn't matter. After all, he was her fated mate, so it wasn't like she was going to leave him because he'd gotten too rough with her.

Perhaps she would even like it.

They still had a lot to learn about each other, and testing limits was part of that exploration.

Pushing to his feet, Lokan walked over to the bar and poured himself a shot of whiskey.

Carol was right. Disclosing the island's location was a done deal, but at least he could justify it by getting her into the harem and finding once and for all who Navuh was holding there.

This could be his only ticket to freedom.

If Areana was indeed his mother, then he was Annani's direct nephew, and the goddess would not let her son keep him imprisoned forever. Especially if they somehow managed to get Areana out.

The problem was his overwhelming need to shield Carol from danger, and there was no way to reconcile these two contradicting needs.

He tried to reason with himself that Carol wanted to do it, but every fucking instinct he had was rebelling against letting her out of his sight, let alone leave on a dangerous mission.

Shaking his head, Lokan emptied the drink down his throat and then poured himself another shot.

It wasn't like him to be so concerned with another person. He was an opportunist who had never had qualms about using others to further his agenda. What had happened to him? Why couldn't he get himself under control and think with his brain instead of his gut?

Damn. He hated the compulsory component of the whole fated mate thing. As a compeller, he was supposed to be immune to that. His entire life had been about being in control, and he hated that this thing, whatever it was, controlled him to such an extent.

How could he even be sure of his feelings for Carol?

What if the intense need to be with her was chemically induced?

And the thing was, he could not help but blame Carol for this even though she was a victim of this crazy compulsion as much as he was.

The irony wasn't lost on him. The fucking Fates were paying him back and giving him a taste of his own medicine.

Except, he didn't believe in that nonsense. So, where did it leave him?

Pouring the second shot of whiskey down his throat, he forced himself to think logically. What could be responsible for the inexplicable change in him?

Getting captured and imprisoned was the simplest explanation, but he knew that was not it. Something else was involved, and it wasn't the fucking Fates.

The clan had always invested in the latest cutting-edge technologies, so it was possible that they had access to advanced medicine as well. What if Carol had been putting some kind of drug in those tasty dishes of hers, a type of aphrodisiac or some other substance that was making him addicted to her?

Because that was how it felt. Like an addiction.

That made much more sense than the nonsense she'd fed him about the Fates and true-love mates.

Clever. Coming up with a story that explained his sudden bonding with her was a smart move. Had she come up with it on her own or had she been coached?

The puzzle pieces suddenly fell into place.

Carol showing up in his prison cell and claiming that she was there to see to his needs, bringing him gourmet meals that he now suspected hadn't even been prepared by her, getting him addicted to her, and explaining it away with a story he had no way of proving or disproving because he knew nothing about immortal matings.

The problem was that the only way to test his hypothesis was to stop eating the meals Carol brought him, but if he did that, she would get suspicious.

Besides, he couldn't go hungry. He needed to stay sharp.

But why keep up the charade after he'd given Kian the island's location?

Well, that was obvious.

The goddess wanted to get her sister out of there, but they couldn't do it without Lokan's help, and the only way to ensure his cooperation and keep Carol safe was to make him believe that he was protecting his fated mate.

Those stories about Dalhu and the other Brother had been meant to brainwash him into believing that his mate was more important than anything else he valued in his life, and that defecting for love was perfectly acceptable.

There was only one hiccup with this theory. What could they possibly gain by pretending that Kian was against the plan?

Well, that was quite obvious too.

If Kian had agreed right away to free him and send him with Carol to the island, Lokan would have suspected something wasn't right.

Carol was a great actress, he had to give her that. The way she'd pretended to come up with the idea herself, and then pretending that Kian had refused and trying to find a different solution.

It was the perfect setup.

In a few days, Kian would pretend to succumb to pressure from his mother and agree to Carol's plan.

The big question was what Lokan was going to do with the information. Despite all the underhanded subterfuge, his goals aligned with the clan's in the matter of possibly freeing his mother, whether she was Annani's sister or not.

And then there was his gut, refusing to believe even one word of the perfectly logical conspiracy theory his brain had devised.

7

CAROL

*N*aked under the blanket, Carol waited for Lokan with an uneasy feeling churning in her gut.

She could understand his agitation and his guilt over revealing the island's location, even though it was illogical, but not why he was directing his anger at her. Lokan hadn't said anything offensive, and he'd tried to be polite, but she could sense the turmoil simmering just under the surface.

It upset her.

He was supposed to be her fated mate, putting her above everything and everyone, but obviously, he didn't. Otherwise, he wouldn't have cooled toward her like that. Lokan was distraught over his decision, and for some reason, he was blaming it on her.

Perhaps she should get dressed and leave?

With her gone, he would have time to process what he had done and hopefully make peace with it.

Throwing the comforter off, she was about to get out of bed as he entered the room.

He leveled a hard stare at her. "Where are you going?"

"Home. I think you need some time alone."

He rubbed a hand over his jaw. "Please stay."

Despite the please, it had sounded more like a command than a request.

"I'd better go." She pushed to her feet and padded to the bathroom.

He followed. "Am I scaring you?"

She cast him a glance over her shoulder. "No. But you need time alone to think things through, and your anger makes me uncomfortable."

"Please, don't go."

That still sounded like a command, but it had a pleading undertone, and Carol wasn't looking forward to spending the night alone. She'd gotten used to sleeping in Lokan's arms, and going back to an empty bed was a depressing prospect.

Turning around, she sauntered up to him and wrapped her arms around his neck. "Do you promise to be nice?"

He smiled, but it was forced. "I can't promise that, but I can promise to make it good for you." Cupping her bare bottom, he lifted her and pressed her against his erection. "I'll never be all sunshine and cheer, baby doll. Do you want me to put on a mask for you or promise you falsehoods?"

She shook her head.

"I didn't think so. If we are indeed fated to be together, you should get to know me in all my forms, the sunny and the stormy, the playful and the combative. What I can promise you, however, is that I'll never hurt you." His protruding fangs made him look evil as he slowly leaned and nipped her earlobe, sending a zing of arousal straight to her core. "At least not more than you want me to," he whispered into her ear.

Ugh, he was such a sexy devil, knowing precisely what to say to get her all hot and bothered.

"Okay," she murmured.

Lifting his head, Lokan regarded her with his nearly black eyes, the red embers glowing inside them making him look dangerous.

But Carol believed his promise.

On a visceral level she'd known all along that she was in no danger from him. He might get a little rough, but she wasn't averse to rough play as long as she was a willing participant and he didn't cross the line.

Still holding her up by her bottom, Lokan carried her back to the bedroom and dropped her unceremoniously on the bed.

She scooted back, propping herself on her forearms to watch him take off his clothes. Her eyes remained riveted on his handsome face, though, his dark almost menacing expression and glowing eyes tantalizing even more than his muscular body.

His smile was conceited, his fully elongated fangs and the red glow in his eyes making him look vampiric. "You like what you see, don't you, baby doll?"

"You know that I do. You're gorgeous." She smirked. "I now know how the vampire myth started. It was because of you."

Lokan hissed, getting into the role play and raising goosebumps on her arms. Fully nude and very aroused, he put his knees on the bed and palmed his erection. His eyes never leaving hers, he pumped his fist up and down the rigid length as if contemplating his next move.

She could help him with that.

Leaning up, Carol dipped her head and licked the very tip, just an experimental swipe of her tongue.

With another hiss, Lokan cupped the back of her head and pulled her closer, then brushed the head of his shaft over the lips, gently teasing them apart.

But as he threaded his fingers through her hair and fisted

it, Carol knew that the teasing part was over and opened her mouth, ready to take him.

"Hands behind your back," he hissed out a command.

If she'd had any doubts where this was going, they were gone now. It was going to be a taking, and Lokan wanted complete control.

It didn't scare her. It excited her.

She'd always had a thing for commanding men, and she was an expert on fellatio.

With a nod, he cupped her jaw, locking her in place for his pleasure, and thrust his length into her welcoming mouth.

Relaxing her throat muscles, she looked up at his lust-suffused face, hoping he could read the challenge in her expression.

Except, Lokan didn't take her up on it. Instead of surging all the way in, he started with short, shallow thrusts, making sure she could take it before going deeper a fraction of an inch at a time.

When his fist tightened in her hair, she groaned around the thick length, and he thrust all the way in, reaching the back of her throat and pausing. He was blocking her air supply, but it lasted only for a second. Then he withdrew, letting her suck in a breath, and followed with several shallow thrusts before once again surging in all the way to the back of her throat.

Adjusting to the rhythm Lokan dictated, Carol ached to touch herself, but he'd told her to keep her hands behind her back, and she didn't want to disobey.

With everything else in his life spiraling out of control, Lokan needed her to yield to him. She could hold off her own gratification for a little longer, knowing that he would reward her for it later.

8

LOKAN

*H*is mate was incredible. A beautiful, lustful angel. His gut hadn't lied. His brain had. To realize that, all Lokan had to do was gaze into Carol's eyes and see the adoring way she looked at him. A look like that couldn't be faked.

Except, Lokan found it difficult to trust anyone beyond a shadow of a doubt, especially given how quickly he had gotten attached to her. As much as he struggled against it, her hold over him was unbreakable.

As he rhythmically thrust in and out of her mouth, hitting the end of her throat and then withdrawing nearly all the way, he was keenly aware of how misleading the scene looked.

Seemingly, he was in the driver's seat, having his way with Carol and using her as he pleased, but it was an illusion.

She was yielding to him physically, but she was choosing to do so, and her eyes, which had never left his, were challenging him to let go of his restraint and take everything she had to offer.

Except, he was not going to accept her challenge.

First of all, because it wasn't in him to just take from a woman without giving anything in return, and secondly, because every instinct in his immortal body demanded that he pleasure his mate first.

Carol might not be aware of that, but he was struggling to keep this going and not push her back onto the mattress and dive between her legs. Given the strong scent of her arousal, she was soaking wet, and he hungered for a taste.

Except, her intensifying aroma and the sounds she was making made it obvious that she was enjoying this. Seemingly under his complete control, Carol was nevertheless running the show. He was so attuned to her, his body so responsive to her cues that he felt as if she was directly connected to his nervous system and manipulating it as she pleased.

Elation warred with despondency as Lokan realized Carol had won, and that he was utterly ensnared by her. His will and his body were no longer his own, and it didn't even matter whether this was the work of some chemicals she might have been feeding him or the machinations of the mythical Fates. The result was the same.

Like a conjoined twin, his life was irrevocably entwined with hers, and if the connection was ever severed, he wouldn't survive on his own.

The question was whether Carol felt the same.

Unable to wait any longer, he pulled out and leaned down, replacing his shaft with his tongue and devouring her mouth. It was just a quick stop on the way to his desired target, but then Carol wound her arms around his neck and kissed him back with just as much fervor.

As she pulled him on top of her with surprising strength, Lokan hesitated for a brief moment, wondering if she would let him feast on her nectar first, but then she licked at his fang, wresting the decision away from him. He penetrated her with one swift thrust, gliding into her moist heat.

"Yes!" Carol murmured into his mouth. "Show me what you've got."

Responding to her challenge, he captured her wrists and pulled her arms over her head, pinning both with one hand while fisting her hair with the other and tilting her head back to expose her neck.

Carol shuddered, the muscles in her sheath contracting around his shaft and urging him to up the heat. He knew what she wanted, but he wasn't going to bite her yet.

Instead, he licked and sucked the spot he'd chosen, while driving into her forcefully, daring her to retract her request to give her all that he'd got.

The bed rattled and shook, banging against the concrete wall and threatening to fall apart, but Carol's excitement only climbed higher.

She was taking everything he was dishing out and begging him for more.

Her moans and groans spurring him on, Lokan let loose. The last of his restraint snapping, he erupted inside her and sank his fangs into the soft flesh of her neck.

9

CAROL

*A*s Carol came down from the venom-induced trip, she was snuggled against Lokan, her head resting on his bicep and her arm draped over his torso.

Awake, he was staring at the ceiling, his dark brows furrowed, and his mouth pressed into a tight line.

Not exactly the picture of post-coital bliss.

The awesome sex had helped at least one of them to relax, but not the one who'd needed it most.

"What's the matter?" She turned sideways, resting her head on his chest. "Still worried over what Kian would do to the island?"

"That too." He wrapped his arm around her and started absentmindedly caressing her back.

Carol stifled a relieved breath. Things seemed to be back to normal between them. "What else?"

"I was thinking about your idea to use Gorchenco to get you to the island."

That was a surprise. Suddenly, Lokan was okay with her going without him?

On the one hand, Carol was glad he was no longer

fighting her on this, but on the other hand, she wondered about his change of heart. "What do you have on Gorchenco that you are so sure he is going to cooperate?"

"A nuclear submarine."

"What?"

"He stole one. Getting some of the senior officers to cooperate in exchange for a big payoff, they staged a fatal malfunction, evacuated the crew, and sank it somewhere deep. Except, they didn't. A skeleton crew remained, and after a time, they stealthily delivered the submarine to a prearranged location."

"How do you know that?"

"Because he tried to sell it to the Brotherhood and took me to see it. I was one of several interested parties, or at least I pretended to be. Not that my father wouldn't have loved to put his hands on an awesome weapon of destruction like that, but the Brotherhood couldn't afford Gorchenco's asking price."

Carol had no idea how much nuclear submarines were selling for, so there was no point in asking Lokan what Gorchenco wanted for it. Regardless of the cost, though, she was sure the Russian would find interested buyers who were willing to pay any price for it. A nuclear submarine was a strategic weapon that they couldn't get their hands on any other way.

She waved a dismissive hand. "He's probably sold it by now, and besides, how can we use it as leverage? Are you even sure that Gorchenco wasn't acting on behalf of the Russian government? I wouldn't be surprised if they manufactured the whole story. It's a clever way to raise capital by selling off their arsenal without appearing desperate."

"That is true, but not in this case. The submarine has a lot of top-secret Soviet technology that Putin would never allow to fall into foreign hands. If he discovers what

Gorchenco did, he will feed him to the sharks, and I mean it literally."

Carol lifted her chin. "Why would Gorchenco do that, then? He has enough money and he has Putin's unofficial support. Why risk it?"

"First of all, the sub is worth a shitload of money, more than all of Gorchenco's assets put together. And secondly, for a man like him, it's not only about the money. It's about power. And if he can swindle Putin out of a nuclear submarine, then he feels like he bested the most powerful man in the world."

"I thought that was the President of the United States."

Lokan chuckled. "The American President is not free to do as he pleases. There are checks and balances in place to ensure that whoever is holding office can't gain absolute power. The Russian, on the other hand, is not encumbered by the legislative and judicial branches. So even though his country as a whole can't compete with the United States, militarily or economically, he is much more dangerous than your President."

"Gorchenco has balls, I have to give him that. Although personally, I would have loved to cut them off." She smiled evilly. "Maybe once this is over, I will. Ella is my best friend, and I want to avenge her."

"If you want to pretend to be his toy, you have to shelve this attitude." He looked into her eyes. "Can you fake adoration for him even though all you can think about is castrating him?"

Carol waved a dismissive hand. "Of course I can. I'm a pro."

"Putting on a face won't be enough. Immortals would smell your resentment toward him."

"So what? I won't be the first pretty thing with a sugar daddy, pretending to adore him and secretly plotting to take his money. All they are going to do is snicker behind his back and call him an old fool."

"It would be more convincing if you could make yourself like him for real, or at least feel attracted to him. To pull this off, your act needs to be above suspicion."

"Right. You have a point." Carol sighed. "I'm a good actress, but I'm not that good. I can't fool myself."

For some reason, her answer amused him instead of worrying him.

Smiling, Lokan kissed the tip of her nose. "Then you'll have to use your sugar daddy idea and act it up all the way, making it obvious to everyone. You can roll your eyes when he's not looking or murmur nasty retorts that he is not going to hear but the immortals will."

She propped herself on her forearm. "That's an awesome idea. I will not look suspicious because my behavior will match my aroma."

"Precisely. And that could be a good setup for your lovers' spat. He hears something you said, or catches you making faces at him, and storms off, leaving you behind."

"I can do better than that. I can flirt with someone else, pretending like I'm looking for a better sugar daddy. With all the rich guys visiting the resort, I will have no problem finding plenty of men to hit on. I know how to manipulate those types."

Fortunately, Lokan was too busy plotting and scheming to notice her slip. Otherwise, he might have wondered how she'd acquired that particular expertise.

"If I could meet with Kian and Turner, we could brainstorm ideas. Can you suggest it to Kian?"

"I can try. Is it okay if I tell him about Gorchenco's submarine?"

"Not yet. This entire plan depends on the Russian's cooperation, and the only way he will do that is if we have leverage over him. I want to use this information to get something out of your boss."

"Since Kian is adamant about not letting me go to the island, I'm not sure you have anything to negotiate with. The stolen submarine might be good only as leverage for getting the Russian off Ella's back, but the question is how much her freedom is worth to Kian."

"He'll change his mind. Annani is going to pressure him, and he will have no choice. It's only a matter of time. That's why I think you shouldn't tell him just yet. Let him stew in his own juices for a while. Then when you approach him again, he will be more inclined to listen."

KIAN

*a*s Andrew entered the room with Tim by his side, Kian stood up and offered his hand.

"Good morning, Tim. Thank you for coming."

The guy was short, pudgy, and had thinning hair. Not exactly what Kian had imagined given what he'd heard about the forensic artist. But then the calculating gleam in Tim's smart eyes was exactly what he'd expected. Apparently, an extraordinary talent and strong spirit were housed in a misleadingly average shell.

Tim looked up at him with a crooked smile lifting one corner of his mouth. "My pleasure. When Andrew told me that his friend Ken needed a favor, I didn't realize that he was talking about Barbie's boyfriend." He glanced at Brundar and Anandur. "Did all of you guys go to the same spa?" He chuckled. "Is there a Barbie convention in this building? Because I'd rather see some girl Barbies."

Kian lifted a brow, not sure whether he should laugh or punch the guy in his smug puss. Tim was like a Chihuahua, posturing and barking as if he was a bulldog.

Behind them, Andrew snorted. "No, Tim. We didn't all go to the same spa."

Tim looked at Andrew over his shoulder. "Where is that damn place? Didn't they rebuild already?" He waved a hand over his torso. "I know this is awesome, but there is always room for improvement."

"I haven't checked," Andrew said.

"Then what are you waiting for? I'm not getting any younger."

"Gentlemen, please take a seat." Kian motioned to the two chairs facing the desk and went back to the other side. "I'm told that you are the best in the field."

Tim dipped his head. "I am." He looked at Brundar. "Did you find that lady you were looking for?"

Brundar nodded.

"That's proof of my talent. My portraits come out so accurate that they can be used in facial recognition software. No one else I know of can do that."

Leaning forward, Kian looked into Tim's eyes. "The spa that you mentioned. Is it an inside joke between you and Andrew?"

"No joke." Tim waved a hand at Andrew. "When my buddy here came back from vacation two inches taller and looking marvelous like he does now, he told me that he received special treatments in an exclusive spa. Unfortunately, the place burned down. I would have loved to get the same treatments."

"I see." The memory was old, so it wasn't the best candidate for thralling away, but on the other hand, Tim had no visuals of it, only a verbal mention.

"Why are you looking at me like that?" Tim asked.

Kian leaned even closer. "I thought that you had something in your eye. But it's just an eyelash." He made quick work of suppressing the memory of Andrew telling Tim

43

about the spa and replacing it with a story about a spine operation.

Tim rubbed his eyes. "Is it still there?"

"I don't see it now. It must have fallen out. By the way, did Andrew tell you how he regained the two inches in height that he lost?"

Tim frowned, then lifted a hand to his temple and rubbed it. "A spine reconstructive operation? Is that what it was? My memory is getting really shitty. He couldn't have had an operation and recuperated in the time he took off. His vacation wasn't long enough."

Damn, Kian hadn't thought of that. He waved a dismissive hand. "It's a new type of minimally invasive procedure. It's not approved in the States yet, so he had it done in Switzerland."

"Oh, yeah. I remember he told me something about doing it abroad."

It seemed that Tim wasn't as difficult to thrall as they had feared.

Kian pushed to his feet. "Let's go to the next room."

Tim looked around. "Yeah. I wanted to tell you that the lighting in here is crap, but we got sidetracked." He got up and lifted his artist's bag off the floor. "Which one of you gentlemen am I going to work with?"

Kian walked toward the door. "The lady you are going to draw the portrait for is waiting for you over there."

Tim's eyes brightened. "Oh, a lady. I like working with the fairer sex." He looked up at Kian. "No offense to you and your bodyguards, but as pretty as you all are, I still prefer the ladies."

"So you are in for a treat. A word of warning, though." Kian stopped with his hand on the handle. "Anna is a foreign dignitary, and you need to treat her with the respect afforded to a queen. Can you do that?"

Tim waved a hand. "Don't worry. I'll be on my best behavior."

Kian opened the door and walked in. "The forensic artist is here, Anna. Can I let him in?"

Annani rose from the chair. "By all means. I was awaiting his arrival with bated breath."

It was still a shock to see his mother in a pair of jeans and a silk button-down blouse, her long hair braided and twisted into a large knot on top of her head. She was also suppressing her glow.

Except, nothing but a shroud could diminish her beauty, and as Tim walked in behind Kian, he took a step back, bumping into Andrew.

"Holy crap. Which country produced this? I need to move there."

Ignoring Tim's crass language, Annani smiled. "I am afraid this will have to remain a secret." She looked up at the ceiling. "Is the lighting in this room conducive to your artistry, Tim?"

The guy shook his head. "Your beauty is enough to illuminate the darkest spot. I shall lack for nothing in your presence."

Frowning, Annani lifted her hand and looked at it. "Oh, good. For a moment there I was worried that I was still glowing."

"My comment must have been lost in translation," Tim said. "I meant it figuratively."

Annani smiled again. "You are most charming, Tim. Thank you for the compliment. Shall we begin?"

Kian stayed in the room for several more moments, observing Tim work. The guy didn't stop talking, asking Annani question after question, showing her what he drew and then correcting it according to her input.

It was a long process, and after ten minutes they were still working on the eyes, which Tim had said were the most important feature.

"Are you going to be okay here without me?" Kian directed the question to his mother.

Tim answered. "Leave, your hovering is distracting."

Annani smiled. "You can go, Kenneth." She added a wink.

The room they were in was an inner office, and the only entrance was from the main room where the brothers and Andrew were waiting.

The only thing that bothered Kian was the windows, but Tim insisted he needed the blinds off for the natural light. The glass wasn't bulletproof, but it had a reflective coating on the other side. During daytime, even immortals couldn't see the inside of the office.

Besides, there wasn't much he could do about it even if he stayed.

"How is it going?" Andrew asked as Kian entered the room.

"They are still working on the eyes."

"Yeah, it takes a long time. I should have warned you. I can get us coffee while we wait."

"Maybe later." Kian sat behind the desk and flipped his laptop open. "I should get some work done."

An hour later, Tim came out. "Can we get something to drink and eat in there?"

Kian glanced at his watch. "Lunch should be delivered in about fifteen minutes. How is it going?"

"Good. Do you want to take a look?"

"Naturally."

"Spivak." Tim waved at Andrew. "Get us a couple of bottles of Perrier. The lovely Anna is thirsty, and so am I." He clapped his hands. "Chop chop."

"No problem." Grumbling under his breath about Tim's lack of basic manners, Andrew walked out.

In the next room, the artist's work in progress was propped on a portable easel, and Annani was staring at it with misty eyes.

"Is that how you remember her?"

There wasn't much, just a pair of sorrowful, blue eyes, a contour of a face, and an outline of a mouth, but it was enough to give Kian a general idea of what Areana looked like, and it was nothing like Annani.

Areana was a gentle beauty, while Annani was pure fire. There was no mischief in those pale blue eyes, no burning curiosity and superior intelligence like in Annani's. But there was compassion in them, the kind that only those who had suffered greatly could feel for the suffering of others.

ANNANI

*T*ears blurred Annani's vision as Areana's face slowly materialized on the canvas, her delicate features drawn with such precision by Tim's nimble fingers.

He cast her a questioning look. "I gather that the drawing is accurate?"

"It is. You are a true artist, Tim. I do not know how you translate what I say into lines. It is as if you can look into my mind and see what I see. But it is even more than that. Your questions force me to remember things I have forgotten. They bring her back."

"How long has it been since you saw your sister?"

"Thousands of years."

He nodded. "It must feel this way when a loved one has gone missing."

"Yes, and yet I remember parting with her before her journey as if it were yesterday. I remember every word we exchanged, and how brave she was. But most of all I remember how guilty I felt for letting her take my place."

"Your sister joined the armed forces? Did she go missing in the Middle East?"

The alarm in his voice touched Annani's heart, and although technically Areana had gone missing in that specific region, what Tim was imagining was a completely different situation.

Hopefully, her sister had not been violated or abused by Navuh, but it was possible, and Annani shuddered to think of the never-ending torment her sister had endured and was still enduring.

All because of her.

Everything Areana had suffered was Annani's fault. Her sister had sacrificed her peaceful, secluded life to allow Annani several short moon cycles of happiness.

"My sister did not join the army, but she fought a brave personal battle." She reached for the canvas. "Can I have the drawing?"

"Let me just spray it with a protective coating."

When he was done, Tim carefully placed the sketch on the desk. "The spray needs to dry for a couple of minutes. I'll tell Ken that we are done."

"Thank you. You have no idea how much this portrait means to me. I do not have any pictures of my sister. I am going to hang it up in my bedroom so I can look at her beautiful face and remember her."

Looking uncomfortable, Tim slunk away to the other room, and a moment later Kian entered.

"Are you okay?" He closed the door behind him.

Annani shook her head and pointed at the picture. "Take a look. This is your aunt, Areana."

"She looks nothing like you." He stood next to the desk and gazed at the portrait. "Her eyes are so sad, so full of compassion."

"Areana is a pure soul, and she suffered greatly because of me."

Kian turned around and leaned against the desk, blocking

her view of the sketch. "Stop doing that. Your father did not force Areana to take your place. He asked and she agreed. It was her choice."

"I know, but poor Areana wanted our father's approval so badly that she would have walked into a fire if he had asked her. And in a way she did." Annani wiped a stray tear away, then took a shuddering breath. "Can we go see Lokan now? I want to show him the picture."

Kian shook his head. "Tim is going to work with him first, and draw from his memory. After he is done, we are going to compare the two portraits. For obvious reasons, I don't want Lokan seeing Areana's picture before that. He will just say that this is the woman from his dreams."

"But you will have Andrew there. Lokan cannot lie with him present."

"He can if he convinces himself that this really is the woman he saw in his dreams. Besides, I suspect that the guy is a pathological liar, and that Andrew can't detect his lies any better than the machine could. Lokan has been lying for nearly a thousand years and even managed to fool his father, which means that he has perfected his craft and knows how to hide all the signs that give less professional liars away."

"Perhaps."

Annani didn't share Kian's opinion of Lokan, but she just didn't have the energy to argue about it right now.

"Would you like me to take you back to the village? There is no reason for you to wait. Tim is going to take just as long with Lokan as he did with you, and you'll be bored. I'll bring both portraits when I come back."

Annani shook her head. "I am not letting this picture out of my sight, and I am coming with you. I want to see the second portrait as soon as Tim is done with it, and then I want to show both to Lokan and watch his reaction."

"I don't want you there while Tim is working with Lokan.

Before we leave, I'm going to erase you from his memory, along with the sketch he made, so that he isn't influenced by it when he draws the other one."

"I do not mind waiting in Arwel's quarters."

"Very well." Kian walked over to the door and opened it. "Tim, can you please come in and collect your things?"

As the forensic artist rolled up the portrait and handed it to Annani, she gently hugged it to her chest. "Thank you again."

She wanted to add that she would cherish it forever, but in a few moments, Tim was not going to remember her or Areana's portrait.

KIAN

*A*s Annani entered the Lexus with the brothers, Kian walked Andrew and Tim to Andrew's car.

He offered Tim his hand. "I want to thank you again for the great work you did in there."

As the guy shook what he'd been offered, Kian looked into his eyes, entering his mind and manipulating the memory of the last several hours.

Instead of Annani, he planted a different woman in Tim's head. For some reason, the first female that came to mind was Edna's human secretary, Lora. Perhaps his brain had made the connection because of Lora's sister and how guilty Lora still felt about not stepping in to help her.

The woman had been abused by her ex-husband to the point of sustaining neurological damage, and by the time Lora had intervened, the damage had become permanent. Feeling guilty, Lora had been volunteering in a shelter for abused women ever since. The similarities were obvious. Just like Annani, Lora blamed herself for her sister's misfortune, and just like Annani, she was looking for ways to atone for her perceived sins.

The problem was that Kian had never seen a picture of Lora's sister, so planting a memory of Tim drawing her portrait was challenging. Improvising on the spot, Kian changed several of Lora's features and created a look-alike image to put in Tim's head.

When it was done, Kian nodded at Andrew. "I'll see you later."

The keep was just across the street, but the plan was for Andrew to drive around, stop somewhere, and put a blindfold on Tim before heading back. That way, once the forensic artist was done with Lokan, he wouldn't have to be thralled again. Hopefully, Lokan wouldn't blurt out anything that would later require erasing.

Walking back to the Lexus, Kian motioned for Anandur to open Annani's window. "I'm in a mood for a walk. Would you mind going without me?"

Annani frowned. "I would not mind that, but I do mind you going alone without your bodyguards. We can all walk together to the keep."

"Are you sure? It's a good twenty minutes' walk."

"I am not averse to a little stroll." She smiled. "But please be mindful of my much shorter legs. It will take a bit longer than if you were walking alone."

"That's fine." Kian opened the door for his mother. "Do you want me to carry the portrait?" He reached for the tube that she had tucked under her arm.

"I cannot part with it even for a moment. Not yet."

Offering her a hand, he helped her down from the tall vehicle. "I can make you a copy, several in fact. And I can also scan it and send you a photo for your phone."

"That would be wonderful. Thank you."

After entering the tunnel through the hidden door inside a storage unit, the four of them walked in contemplative silence, with Kian and the brothers forcing their strides to match Annani's pace.

Without her long gown to hide her legs, her gait lost some of its gliding effect, but it was still smooth and graceful, her tiny ballet flats barely connecting with the concrete floor.

"I was thinking," Annani said after several moments. "Lokan might indeed be an excellent liar, and he can fool Andrew, but he cannot fool Edna. You should bring her to probe him."

"I'm planning on doing so. But Edna has her own limitations. She can assess intentions, deep-seated resentments, and malevolent intent, but she can't discern truth from lies or read thoughts."

Annani shrugged. "It is worth a shot, right? It cannot hurt to let her give it a try."

"Absolutely. Maybe her insight would help shed light on his personality. If Lokan is rotten to the core, Edna would know that."

"He is not." Annani huffed. "I might not possess Edna's probing talent, but I have been around for quite a while, and I know people. Lokan is not a bad man. He might have done despicable things for the Brotherhood, but so did Dalhu. And being Navuh's son did not make it any easier. Lokan grew up under his father's close scrutiny. That is why he is such an accomplished liar and manipulator. If Lokan had grown up in a nurturing environment, I have no doubt he would have been an honest man."

Kian wasn't so sure. Even if Lokan's mother was a pure angel, his father was as close to the devil as it got, and Lokan must have inherited many of his father's traits, which had gotten reinforced by Navuh's tutelage and Mortdh's teachings.

The question that bothered Kian was how much of what Lokan had said was lies and how much was truth.

He doubted Lokan's purported noble plans for the island and for his people. The Doomer had said what he believed would make him more likable and harder to torture or kill. So, all of that was probably a load of BS.

What about his bond with Carol, though?

It was less likely that he could have faked it, and that was something that Edna could easily verify.

Just for that one thing, it was worth dragging her over to the keep and probing Lokan. Having a fated mate was a game changer even for a Doomer. He would be compelled to keep her safe and happy, which translated into shifting his loyalties to her and her people.

If Lokan wasn't who he was, Kian might have released him from his cell just based on that.

But Lokan wasn't a simple soldier. He was sharper, far better informed, more powerful, and more talented than most immortals.

Navuh's son might be the unusual immortal male who could choose his own agenda and his quest for power over his true-love mate.

13

LOKAN

*L*okan had spent the morning thinking over the new plan to get Carol onto the island using Gorchenco. But it was a no-go, and it had nothing to do with his instinctive resistance to sending his mate into danger.

Without him using his compulsion to ensure the cooperation of several key humans, it wasn't going to work. He even considered having Gorchenco bribe them instead, but that was likely to work only on some. The pilots' compulsion would prevent them from accepting bribes, and without their cooperation there was no way to get Carol off the island, alone or with his mother.

But perhaps that was the part that the clan could handle. A blitz commando attack of grab and go, somehow swooping down and plucking Carol and his mother up on the wings of dragons, or rather their mechanical counterparts.

Like Guardians wearing jet packs.

He didn't know much about the technology, though. Was it possible to carry another person? And what was the range of those things?

Perhaps they could parachute in and jet out? It would

save on fuel consumption going in, but it precluded a stealth approach.

Damn. He was a well-trained soldier and had led many commando units on secret missions, but that had been a long time ago, when none of those new technologies existed yet. The scenarios he was coming up with were based on movies.

Without talking to Kian and that Turner guy, who Carol claimed was a genius at those kinds of operations, it was like trying to put a puzzle together blindfolded and with half the pieces missing.

When the phone rang, Lokan was relieved to have an excuse to stop the frustratingly futile mental exercises.

Arwel was probably calling to let him know that the forensic artist was on his way.

"Is he here?"

"ETA fifteen minutes. Kian and his bodyguards might get there sooner."

"Thanks for the heads up."

For some reason, Kian didn't want Carol to be there while the artist worked on the sketch, and she had been instructed to leave.

He must have his reasons. Perhaps he didn't want the artist to see her?

That could be it.

Carol's beauty and sex appeal could be a distraction Kian wished to avoid.

Walking up to the bar, Lokan pulled out a bottle of Snake's Venom and popped the lid. When the door mechanism activated several minutes later, he emptied the last of it, tossed the bottle into the trash, and sat on the couch.

As Kian walked in with his two bodyguards, Lokan draped his arm over the sofa's back and crossed his legs. "Good afternoon, Kian, gentlemen."

"Good afternoon." Kian sat on one of the armchairs and his guards pulled out chairs from the dinette.

"A few things we need to go over before Tim gets here," Kian said. "The name we are going to use is Logan. If Tim asks why you are kept locked up, don't answer him. The less he knows the better."

Lokan arched a brow. "Aren't you going to thrall him when he is done?"

"I'd rather not. I already thralled him to forget seeing the goddess and drawing the portrait of her sister. Thralling him so soon after that might cause him brain damage."

"Two consecutive thralls are harmless. Especially when the memories thralled are recent."

"We are not as cavalier with humans as you are. Tim's talent is too precious to ruin by carelessness."

"Nevertheless, he shouldn't be left with memories of me, or you for that matter. Secrecy and anonymity are crucial for both of us."

"I'm touched by your concern. By the way, Tim knows me as Ken."

Lokan shrugged. Kian had much more to lose than he had. This was his town, wherever it was.

When the door opened again, Andrew the lie detector walked in with a short human who was holding an artist bag under his arm.

The guy paused at the entry and shook his head. "This must be the twilight zone. Five pretty Kens in one fancily decorated prison cell? Am I in a Barbie movie?" He walked in and put his bag on the table and then turned to Lokan. "But this one has cuffs on as accessories. How interesting."

Lokan had no idea what the guy was talking about. Maybe there was something to what Kian had said about thralling causing brain damage. Especially if they'd let someone with no finesse do a hatchet job on the artist.

"Okay, pretty boy. Come sit over here where the lighting is not as crappy as in the rest of this bird cage they've stuck you in. What did you do? Fuck big Ken's sister?"

As Kian grimaced, Lokan stifled a chuckle and glanced at the portrait hanging over the couch. He hadn't, but another Brother had, and it must have taken a couple of centuries off Kian's immortal life.

"I didn't have the pleasure," he said as he joined the human at the table. "But a woman was involved."

"Aren't they always." Tim pulled out a large sketch pad. "They say money turns the world around, but I say it's pussy."

"Watch it, Tim," Andrew warned.

The artist raised a brow. "What? We are all men here. And I'm right. Guys chase money and power to get more pussy. That's how things work. God knew what he was doing when he created Eve and made Adam lust after her." He pulled out a pouch containing pencils and unfolded it next to the sketch pad. "She told him that the snake gave her a forbidden apple, and then she asked Adam how he was going to top that. That's how human civilization was started."

"I didn't know you were a religious man," Andrew said sarcastically.

Tim shrugged. "So what if I am? It's a free country."

"Gentlemen, we don't have all day," Kian said. "Let's concentrate on the sketch."

"You're not paying me by the hour, buddy. You'll get your portrait. And I would appreciate you all leaving me alone with Mr. Ken number five. I need to concentrate."

Lokan was amazed that Kian was allowing the human to talk to him like that. On the island, rude Tim would have been dead already, but not before his tongue had been cut out to teach the other humans a lesson in manners.

"One of my guards will have to stay. You can choose which one."

Tim didn't hesitate for a moment. "The blond. He's unobtrusive like a statue."

"Very well."

As Kian pushed to his feet, Andrew and the tall redhead followed him to the door.

"Call me when the portrait is done."

The blond nodded.

When the door closed behind them, Lokan offered the artist his hand. "My name is Logan, not Ken number five."

Tim smiled. "Nice to meet you, Logan. So, who are we drawing today? I assume it's a lady?"

"Yes."

"Let's start with the eyes."

14

CAROL

"Something is burning," Ewan said as he entered the apartment. "I smelled it all the way from the elevator."

"Oh, crap." Carol grabbed the pan of charred onions and dumped them in the sink.

Sometimes even cooking wasn't enough to calm the storm, and she hadn't been so confused and distraught in a long time. Thinking about Lokan's strange mood swings and wondering what was going through his head had distracted her and ruined her dish.

Pulling three new onions from the fridge, she started chopping a new batch.

After he'd given Arwel the island's location, Lokan had been angry and remote. At first, she'd thought he was blaming her for it, but then he'd started talking about getting her to the island with Gorchenco's help, and she'd thought of another possible reason for his change in attitude.

As her mate, Lokan would have a hard time with her going on a dangerous mission like that, but since it was crucial that she go, perhaps he was trying to distance himself from her emotionally?

After making love several times last night and again this morning, he was back to his old self with her. If she had stayed a little longer, she could've coaxed the truth out of him, but then Arwel had called, telling her that she needed to leave. Kian's orders.

Why the hell couldn't she have stayed and watched the forensic artist at work?

It wasn't as if she had any idea what Areana looked like and could have whispered clues in Lokan's ear. If she did, would she have done it, though?

It would have been tempting, that was for sure. Because if the woman in Lokan's dreams was Annani's sister, Carol's chances of getting to the island would have improved significantly.

When the new batch of onions was ready, Carol scooped them up on top of the asparagus and closed the lid.

She'd planned on making dessert, but at the rate things were going, she'd better stick with ice cream. Chocolate syrup and some crushed walnuts on top would dress it up, making it look fancy.

Besides, her time would be better spent catching up with friends. She hadn't talked to Ella since the wedding.

Taking the phone with her, Carol stepped out onto the balcony, sat on a lounger, and called her friend.

"Hi. You must have read my mind. I was about to call you."

"Oh, yeah? Any new gossip? Are you or your mom transitioning?"

"No, not yet, and I hope it doesn't start for me for another week."

"Why?"

"I'm wrapping up the videos, and I want it done before I

start transitioning. The fundraiser is going really well, and we don't need any more recordings, but I want to have four more ready in case the original videos become stale."

"I'm glad to hear that. So, what's next for you, any college plans?"

"I'm going to do it online, and in my free time I plan on working in the café. Wonder is practically begging me to help her out, but I told her that it doesn't make sense for me to start before I transition."

"That's true. But with you busy doing other things, who is going to manage the fundraiser?"

"With the videos done, I don't expect there will be much to do, and my mother offered to help."

"It seems you have everything figured out."

Ella chuckled. "I wish. What about you? Are you ever coming back to run the café?"

"Probably, but I don't know when. Everything is up in the air right now."

"Can you talk about it, or is it classified?"

"I'm not sure. I have to clear it with Kian."

"How are things going with Lokan? Is he treating you right?"

Carol sighed. "He's a complicated fellow. Sometimes he seems to worship the ground I walk on, and other times he seems distant. I don't know what to think."

"You should test him like we talked about."

Carol switched the phone to her other ear and looked over her shoulder into the living room to make sure that Ewan hadn't come back. "I'm not bringing him a stripper."

"Hmm, maybe that won't be necessary. Julian and I want to visit Lokan. I can dress up provocatively and come on to him, see if he reacts to me."

Carol chuckled. "Right. With Julian there. Don't be ridiculous. He'll see right through you."

"Not necessarily. Lokan doesn't really know me. What if I'm the kind of girl who needs every male's attention on her?"

"He'll know you are not attracted to him."

"Right. I keep forgetting about the smell thing. It's a real pain in the butt. Can we come anyway? Julian wants to meet Lokan."

"Hopefully not because he wants to pick a fight."

Ella snorted. "He might issue a threat or two. He's worried about Lokan visiting my dreams before I transition."

"I have a newsflash for you. Lokan can enter the dreams of an immortal female as well. He entered mine."

"Oh, wow. That's not good. I thought that once I transitioned, I would be safe from him."

"I don't think you have anything to worry about. Lokan knows how precarious his position is, and he's not going to do anything stupid. If it makes you feel better, Julian can do some chest-thumping and threaten retribution. But you'll have to clear the visit with Kian first. Without his authorization, Arwel is not going to let you and Julian into Lokan's cell."

"I'll tell Julian to ask Kian. As Bridget's son, he is more likely to get permission."

"Let me know when. I will prepare a nice dinner for the four of us."

"I will, but maybe you should do it for five."

"Why? Do you want to bring your mom along? If she comes, then Magnus will want to be there too."

"I wasn't thinking about my mother. What if I ask one of the single ladies to come along and try to work her charms on Lokan?"

"Who do you have in mind?"

"Ingrid. She is a big-time flirt."

That could work. Ingrid was blond and curvaceous,

which Lokan claimed was his type. Except, he might have been lying about that.

"You'll need to tell her what the deal is, and you'll also need to come up with a good excuse for her coming along."

"Simple. She either wants to redecorate the cell or ask Lokan's opinion about what should be changed. And if he doesn't buy it, she might claim curiosity, which I'm sure is true."

Carol didn't feel right about this at all, but on the other hand, it was a way to put her insecurities to rest once and for all.

"Julian will have to clear Ingrid's visit with Kian as well."

"Naturally."

15

LOKAN

*T*im leaned back in his chair and shook his head. "I'm good, but even I can't work with practically nothing." He waved a hand at Lokan. "Did you consider hypnosis? Maybe if Ken number one brings a hypnotist to ask the questions, we can milk your memory for more."

"I'm afraid that it's not possible. I'm not susceptible to hypnosis."

The artist wasn't the only one disappointed. As Lokan had feared, the memory of his dream mother had faded over the years, until a very vague impression remained. He'd hoped that the right questions would bring back more, but that hadn't happened.

The forensic artist threw his hands in the air. "That's a shame. You don't remember the lips, you don't remember the shape of her face, all we have are eyes and maybe a nose." He turned to Kian. "You're not going to find your lady from this sketch. But I did the best I could, so don't think to skim from my payment."

"Wouldn't dream of it," Kian said. "You did your best, and I thank you for your effort." He walked up to the guy and offered a handshake. "Andrew will take care of your fee and drive you back to the agency."

Shaking Kian's hand, Tim grinned. "I'm not going back to the office. I took a day off." He patted his pocket as if he'd already been paid. "A very profitable day." He turned to Lokan. "Good luck, my friend."

"Thank you."

The artist collected his supplies. "If you need another portrait drawn, give me a call." He walked up to the door. "For what you are paying me, I'll drop everything and come running." He winked as the blond bodyguard opened it for him.

Out in the corridor, the artist was met by Andrew, and Lokan watched them leave together as the door closed. He wondered where the other guard who always accompanied Kian had gone.

A few moments later, when the door opened again and the tall bodyguard walked in with Arwel and the goddess, his question was answered.

Clutching a rolled-up sheet of paper to her chest as if it was her greatest treasure, Annani seemed distraught, which was startling given how regal she'd appeared the other time he'd seen her. But that wasn't all. The only living goddess, and the most powerful being on earth, was wearing skinny jeans and flat-soled shoes, looking at first glance like a very beautiful high school girl.

Except, her skin was glowing, and her eyes shone with ancient wisdom. Her disguise wasn't very effective at hiding her otherworldliness.

Lokan bowed his head. "Greetings, Clan Mother."

"Yes, good afternoon, Lokan." She walked up to the dining table and looked at the portrait Tim had drawn. "It is her. This is my sister."

Kian shook his head. "You are seeing what you want to

see, Mother. There is hardly anything in this sketch."

"I disagree." She unrolled the tube and placed the rendering next to the one drawn from Lokan's memory. "Look at the eyes. They are the same color and they bear the same expression."

Gazing at it, Lokan felt like he had seen the woman before, but that could have been a reflection of his yearning. He wished for the beautiful, sorrowful female to be his mother. She looked gentle, a pure soul, and this was precisely how he had imagined his mother as a boy. Then again, that had been wishful thinking as well.

"But not the same shape," Kian said. "A lot of people have that shade of eyes. It's not unique."

"What about the expression?" Annani insisted.

Kian shrugged. "It's sad, but that isn't unique either. Bottom line, this proves nothing."

The goddess turned to Lokan. "What do you think? Does she look familiar to you?"

"She does, but it might be self-delusion. Who would not want a gentle beauty like her to be his mother? And you are right about the expression. That's what I remember most vividly from my dreams."

Annani tapped her lip. "Would you be averse to me taking a peek inside your head? Maybe I can dig out that memory?"

Even if that was possible, Lokan didn't want anyone inside his mind. Luckily for him, he didn't need to lie about her inability to do so.

"Because of my compulsion ability, I'm immune."

"Would you mind if I tried?"

Annani was a pure-blooded goddess and probably more powerful than his father, so there was a small chance that she might be able to do what Navuh's compulsion couldn't, but refusing her would cast suspicion on him that Lokan couldn't afford.

"Go ahead."

When the goddess walked around the table to where he was sitting and stood in front of him, her eyes were level with his. She was such a tiny female, and yet so incredibly powerful.

Reaching with her small hand, she brushed his hair away from his forehead and looked into his eyes.

Lokan couldn't have looked away even if he wanted to. He'd expected Annani's gaze to be unnerving, intrusive, but all he felt was warmth and love.

How could she have those feelings for him?

Even if he were her nephew, he'd wronged her clan, harmed humans who'd been her protégés, and done numerous other things that she must have considered atrocious.

Kian was well aware of that, and Lokan was sure he hadn't kept it a secret from his mother, the head of his clan.

And yet, she found it in her heart to regard Lokan with love. He didn't know whether to revere her for it or ridicule her.

"I cannot enter your mind." Annani cupped his cheek. "Which means that I will have to trust my intuition. You are my nephew, Lokan, my sister Areana's son."

Behind her, Kian rolled his eyes.

Ignoring him, Lokan focused on the goddess instead. "Can I keep Areana's portrait? I'll trade your daughter's for it." He pointed at the one hanging over the couch.

"It's not yours to trade," Kian barked.

Annani shook her head. "I cannot part with it. But Kian promised to make several copies for me. I can have him make one more for you."

Lokan bowed his head. "That would be greatly appreciated. I didn't get to know my mother. I can start by gazing at her lovely face. "

"Kian will have it for you later today." She looked at her son over her shoulder. "Right, dear?"

"Your wish is my command, Mother."

Turning back to Lokan, Annani winked. "If only it were true." She patted his shoulder. "We will find a way to make it all work. I promise."

KIAN

*A*s Kian followed his mother out of Lokan's cell, he braced for the inevitable confrontation.

"Do you keep any office equipment in the keep?" Annani asked. "In particular, I am interested in a copy machine that can handle a drawing this size." She lifted the rolled-up tube with Areana's portrait.

"I have one in my old office, but the paper quality is not going to be as good. I used it to copy and print blueprints, not artwork."

"Can we stop somewhere on the way and make copies? I want Lokan to have one as soon as possible. I feel guilty for not leaving him his mother's portrait, but I just could not part with it."

Here we go.

The campaign had started.

"I can send someone to do it later. I want to get you to the village first."

"No." She looked down at her jeans and smirked. "I am dressed appropriately for a visit to a store. If there is one nearby, we can make the copies, come back, and Brundar can drop one off at Lokan's while we wait in the car. It will make me feel better knowing that it is done."

There was no point in arguing.

Kian sighed. "Fine. But you can stay in the car while Brundar is in the store."

She nodded. "That is an acceptable compromise."

He wondered how much time this small capitulation would buy him.

As he'd expected, not long at all.

As soon as he joined Annani in the backseat of the Lexus, she turned to him. "I want to get Areana out as soon as possible."

"It's impossible, Mother."

She waved a dismissive hand. "There is no such thing. What about using Vivian and Ella to infiltrate the harem?" Before Kian could voice his objections, she pushed on. "Lokan's idea has merit, and neither of them has transitioned yet. If we hurry up, we can put his plan in motion."

To suggest this, his mother must be losing it. "They could enter transition at any moment now. Besides, they are done. I'm not sending either on another risky operation. And even if I was willing to do that, it involves letting Lokan out and that's not an option."

Crossing her arms over her chest, Annani slumped into her seat and let out a breath. "You are right. Any other ideas?"

He didn't want to tell her about Carol's, but to keep it from her didn't feel right either.

"Carol had a suggestion, but it also involves letting Lokan go free. I can't do that."

"Tell me."

"Carol and Lokan can dream-share, so theoretically they can communicate with each other mentally like Vivian and Ella can do telepathically. If he can get her into the harem, she can tell him what's going on in there."

As he'd feared, Annani perked up. "That is a wonderful solution. And Carol is much better suited for that kind of a mission."

"True, but she is an immortal, and only human servants are allowed in the harem. Then there is Lokan. If we let him go with Carol, we are putting her life in his hands."

"Is he not her mate? He will do everything to keep her safe."

Kian sighed. "That's the thing. I'm not sure he is. Lokan is a master manipulator and an exceptional liar with a thousand years of practice at hiding things from Navuh. I wouldn't be surprised if he can fool even Andrew. And as for Carol, this is something she wants to believe in, so convincing her that he is her true-love mate is not that difficult. Especially not for a good-looking, charming fellow like Lokan, who can lie with a straight face and without emitting any incriminating scents."

"Is there a way we can test it?"

"Maybe Edna can try to probe him, but since he is immune to compulsion, he is probably immune to her type of intrusion too. You tried and couldn't get into his head. And besides, even if Lokan is Carol's mate, he is not an ordinary immortal. His ambition might overpower the instinct to put his mate first."

Annani shook her head. "Even if you are right about this, it is illogical for him to do so. Lokan wants to find out if his mother is in the harem. What would he gain by betraying Carol?"

"His freedom. His ambitious plans. He can have Carol report what she finds and then leave her stuck there. If he helps her escape, the Brotherhood is lost to him, and so are his future plans. He will be completely dependent on us and our goodwill. Frankly, if I were in his position, I would be conflicted."

Annani arched a brow. "You would sacrifice Syssi for your ambitions?"

"No. Not for that. But if I had to choose between her and the lives of my clan, I'm not sure what I would do."

"Yes, that is understandable. But Lokan is not going to have to choose between Carol and the lives of his people. His choice will be between leaving the Brotherhood and leaving Carol."

"Yeah, and I'm not sure which one he will choose."

"Then find a way to test it."

"There is a small chance that Edna's probe will work. But even if it does, it won't be conclusive either. If he is as good of a liar as I think he is, he might fool her as well."

"I think you are overestimating Lokan's abilities."

"Underestimating him could lead to disastrous consequences. I can't afford to do that. *We* can't afford to do that."

"On the other hand, my dear son, you might be overlooking a great opportunity. If we can bring Lokan over to our side, he can be a great asset to the clan."

Kian nodded. "I'm aware of that. But my first priority is always safety. The reason we are still around is the extreme caution we practice. Without it, Navuh would have wiped us out of existence a long time ago."

Annani shuddered. "That is unfortunately true. Talk it over with Turner. And maybe with Carol. She might have some ideas about how to test Lokan's devotion to her."

17

CAROL

*T*he phone call from Arwel arrived more than three hours after Carol had been told to leave. "The coast is clear. You can come down."

"Thanks. I need to warm everything up."

"What did you make?"

"Nothing fancy. I was too stressed out for that. It's roast beef with mash potatoes and a side of asparagus. There is ice cream for dessert, though. Do you want me to bring you some, or are you coming upstairs?"

"I can't leave right now and I'm hungry. So, if it's not too much trouble, I would appreciate a plate."

"No problem. I'll be down in ten minutes."

"Thanks."

Carol chuckled. She should write a new book about winning friends and influencing people by feeding them tasty meals. She could be the new Dale Carnegie, but instead of calling her book *How to Win Friends and Influence People*, she would call it *Feed Them Well and They Will Come*.

Perhaps she should reread Carnegie's book, though.

Maybe it would provide insight into whether Lokan was indeed her fated mate or if he was doing something to manipulate her into believing that.

Shaking her head, she started loading the carrier. The nagging suspicions were killing her, but she couldn't ignore them. Lokan's mood swings combined with his change of mind about her going to the island without him were two red flags. A true-love mate would not have done either.

Then again, Lokan wasn't an ordinary immortal. He'd been raised to be a leader and to think big. He'd also learned to put his own needs and wants aside while pursuing a larger agenda.

Except, Lokan didn't share Navuh's world domination ambitions, and his own were still an enigma. He talked a big talk, but that could have been a smokescreen. He knew what the clan's goals were and what to say to make himself look good in light of those goals.

Hefting the carrier, she slung the strap over her shoulder and headed out.

Down in the dungeon, Carol found Arwel's door open and walked in. "Do you want me to leave your dinner here, or do you want to join Lokan and me?"

"I wouldn't dream of intruding. I'll have it here."

She didn't want to point out that he was intruding whether he was in the same room with them or behind the concrete wall separating the cells. "Here you go." She put two containers on his table. "You may want to put the ice cream in the fridge. It's going to melt by the time you finish the main course."

He took the smaller container and put it in the tiny freezer compartment of the under-counter fridge. "Do you want to talk about it?"

"Talk about what?"

"I can sense your disquiet. What's troubling you?"

She waved a dismissive hand. "Oh, you know, girly stuff. He loves me, he loves me not, sort of thing."

"Lokan?"

"Who else?"

"Isn't it too early to be pondering the L-word?"

"Yeah, it is. I guess I'm just anxious to find out how the portrait drawing went." She slung the strap over her shoulder. "Can you open up for me?"

He reached for the carrier and took it from her. "You should commandeer one of the rolling food carts from the kitchen instead of carrying everything in a bag."

"Not a bad idea. Can you get one for me? You can leave it outside Lokan's door."

"Will do."

As Arwel put the code in and the door started to open, Carol took the bag and pushed inside through the narrow opening.

Lokan was at the door, waiting for her. "Oh, good, I'm starving." He reached for the bag and carried it to the table.

"That is it? I'm starving?" She followed. "No 'I've missed you' or 'I'm so glad to see you?'"

He put the bag down, turned around, and pulled her into his arms. "I missed you." He nuzzled her neck. "And I'm glad to see you." He tightened his arms around her and kissed her.

Loads of nervous anxiety melted away as if Lokan's body was a furnace and Carol had just come back in from the cold.

"That's better," she whispered against his lips. "Everything feels right when we are in each other's arms."

He cupped her bottom and gave it a squeeze. "It would feel even better on a full stomach. Let's eat."

And that was it. The romantic moment lost.

Except, Carol knew men, and Lokan's behavior was typical. He needed to be fed. It was true that lust was a stronger hunger, but then she'd made sure that Lokan was thoroughly satisfied in that regard. They'd had a quick romp in the shower that morning, then they'd somehow ended up in bed again, which had necessitated another shower.

So, yeah, the sex was great. But what about the rest?

As Carol set up the table, Lokan opened a wine bottle and poured some into the two plastic flutes. "Cheers." He handed her one.

She clinked it to his. "How did the portrait drawing go?"

He grimaced. "Kian had the artist work with Annani first and then with me, so he could compare the two versions. The only similarity was the eye color and the sad expression. Not very convincing. But it was enough for Annani, so that's encouraging. She also promised to make me copies of the portraits."

"Good. I'm curious to see what Areana looks like."

A dreamy look crossed Lokan's eyes. "She is beautiful, of course. But what I found most appealing was the gentleness and the compassion in her expression. She looks like a pure soul."

"What does it even mean, a pure soul?"

"Someone who will never harm anyone intentionally and will always try to help as much as she can. A giver."

More like a pushover, but Carol wasn't about to throw mud on Lokan's dreams.

From all that she had heard about Areana, the goddess had no sense of self-preservation. In Carol's experience, selfless pleasers like Areana often sought approval and recognition because they didn't get any from their parents.

Carol was a pleaser too, just not a selfless one. She loved feeding people and making them feel good in any way she could, but only as long as her giving was reciprocated in one way or another. She would never throw love and attention at someone who gave her the cold shoulder.

Then again, her drive to accomplish an impossible feat like infiltrating Navuh's harem wasn't all that different from Areana agreeing to take Annani's place. Just as Areana had sought to gain her father's approval, Carol sought the same from her clan.

18

LOKAN

*A*s Lokan dug into his ice cream, the cell door opened.

"Sorry to interrupt." Arwel walked in. "I'm just dropping off the portraits." He produced a roll of clear tape from his pocket. "For putting them up on the wall." He tossed it at Lokan.

"Thanks."

Arwel put the two portraits side by side on the coffee table.

"Would you like to join us for ice cream?" Carol asked.

"Thank you, but I have a date with the dumb box."

"Oh, yeah? What are you watching?"

"Harry Potter."

"Really? Why? I thought those were kids' movies."

Arwel shrugged. "It's fun. Goodnight."

"It was probably just an excuse," Lokan said as the door closed behind Arwel. "He didn't want to intrude."

Carol got up, walked over to the coffee table, and gazed at the renderings for a long moment. "I agree with Annani. The eyes are the same."

"The shape is not."

"That's because you don't remember the details. The expression is the important part. Even if you didn't get the color just right, that would have been enough for me."

Joining her next to the coffee table, he wrapped an arm around her waist and looked at the two portraits, his eyes drawn to the one Tim had made from Annani's memory. "Thank you. I appreciate your vote of confidence, but I'm trying to look at this as an impartial observer. If I had no stake in these portraits, I would have estimated the chances of them being of the same woman as less than five percent."

She leaned her head against his side. "That's because you are a pessimist."

"I'm a realist."

"Let's put them on the wall and then step back. Looking at them from different viewing angles might reveal something."

"Should I take Amanda's picture down?" he asked.

Carol looked behind her shoulder at the large screen television. "How about you tape them to the screen? That way we won't damage the paint on the wall, and we can then sit on the couch and look at them while eating ice cream."

Lokan was more concerned with damaging Areana's portrait by attaching tape to it, but without a frame there was no other way to put it up.

Once he was done, he joined Carol on the couch and lifted his ice cream bowl. "I love her face."

Carol leaned against him. "Of course you do. Every boy loves his mother."

"I wish I could share your confidence that Areana is indeed my mother. But it's doubtful. I look nothing like her. Not even a single feature."

"What about the lips? Yours are fuller than Navuh's. I think they look a little like Areana's."

He chuckled. "Nice try. I look exactly like Navuh. The only difference is that my face is a little rounder and less angular than his. I have his eyes, his nose, his lips, and his coloring. In fact, I look more like him than any of my brothers. Maybe that was the reason he favored me for a while."

"When did he stop?"

Lokan rubbed a hand over his jaw. "I guess he always favored me a little, but that was because of my compulsion ability. I was valuable to him. That's also why I got the cushy post in Washington. I could achieve more with less money spent on bribes."

For the next few minutes, they gazed at the portraits while eating their ice cream in silence. It was top quality, and the chocolate syrup and nuts added pleasant flavors, but Lokan could no longer enjoy the tasty treats Carol was making for him without wondering what else she was putting in them.

His gut and his brain were at constant war, with his gut urging him to forget his suspicions and accept that he'd been granted an incredible gift, while his brain insisted that he had to be smart about it and not let his raging hormones blind him.

If he had access to the internet, he could research whether pheromones could be added to food, or what kind of drugs created an addiction to another person.

Or maybe it wasn't in the food at all? What if Carol had put on a special kind of perfume or lotion and that was the culprit?

Except, what was the point in dwelling on conspiracy theories when he had no way of proving or disproving them?

It was easier to focus on the motive.

The benefits to the clan were obvious, and the method was ingenious. Whoever designed it should get a medal.

Instead of trying to torture information out of him,

which had been proven ineffective even on a civilian like Carol, the clan adopted a modified version of the coercion interrogation technique used by the Chinese. Convincing prisoners that they were doing the right thing for the right reasons worked better.

If Lokan accepted and internalized all that nonsense Carol was feeding him about fated mates and how devoted they were to each other, he would be more inclined to coop- erate and disclose information he otherwise would not. And by showing him examples of two Brothers who had suppos- edly crossed over for love, they sought to reinforce his conviction.

Not only that, suggesting that Areana was his mother might be just another ploy to lure him into crossing over.

That seemed less likely though, mostly because of Kian's attitude. He'd dismissed the similarities Annani had claimed to see. Then again, he might have been playing the bad cop to her good one.

What a mess.

Right now, the only way he could think of testing his theories was to meet up with Dalhu and get him to talk about his bond with Amanda.

Hopefully, the guy wasn't an accomplished liar.

The question was how to get Dalhu to visit him, prefer- ably together with Amanda. Observing them together could provide him with the answers he needed. Because if they behaved in the way Carol claimed true-love mates did, and if he was convinced that they weren't acting, it would be proof that she hadn't been lying about it.

"You seem transfixed by her," Carol said.

While thinking, he'd been staring at Areana's portrait, but he hadn't been really looking. Nevertheless, it provided a good excuse for his prolonged silence.

"I was trying to jog my memory, but it's no use. I want to

believe that she is my mother, so I'm not objective." He rubbed his chest. "In here I feel she is. But in my head I know it's wishful thinking and that I don't recognize her."

Carol reached for his hand and clasped it. "Maybe we are looking at it the wrong way. What you've inherited from her were not your looks, but your goodness. We know that it couldn't have come from Navuh, so it must have come from Areana."

He arched a brow. "My goodness?"

"Yes." She looked into his eyes. "The things you want for your people, those are not selfish or self-promoting. You want to give them a better life. That's goodness."

19

CAROL

*A*s Carol waited for Lokan's answer, she gazed into his eyes, seeking to distinguish truths from lies.

Lokan smiled. "That's a nice way to think about it, but my motives are not entirely selfless. Without my father's compulsory hold over the Brotherhood, it couldn't have existed in its current form. There would have been too much resentment. A different ruler, one who doesn't rely on compulsion and scare tactics, will have to offer his people a good reason to stick around."

That was an honest answer. "Meaning you, of course."

He nodded. "Ultimately, democracy is the best form of governing people. Not that the Brothers are ready for it, but in time and with better education they might be. Changes like that cannot happen overnight."

"Yeah, but you have a problem. Without taking your father out, change is not possible. And if he's eliminated, you don't have time for the gradual transition you described."

He sighed. "I didn't claim to have a solution. I have a vision for the end result but not the means of getting there."

"Unless you can find a way to influence your father."

"Right. But after five thousand years, I doubt he can change."

Carol tucked a curl behind her ear. "What if he doesn't have a choice?"

"What do you mean?"

"Leverage. What if the clan threatens to nuke the island if he doesn't capitulate to our demands? We could start by demanding that he allow the dormant females to transition."

Lokan pinned her with a hard stare. "Did Kian tell you that this is what he plans to do?"

Ugh. Apparently she wasn't the only one with suspicions on her mind.

"No, of course not. I'm just thinking aloud and throwing ideas around. You said that you didn't have the means to achieve your vision, so I'm trying to be creative here."

The red embers glowing in his dark eyes indicated that he didn't believe her. "Kian gave me his word that he would never nuke the island or even attack it with conventional means."

Exasperated, Carol threw her hands in the air. "He won't! I was talking about threatening, not actually doing it. And besides, it's not like Kian is going to listen to my ideas and immediately run to implement them. Why are you so suspicious?"

Pushing to his feet, Lokan walked over to the bar and pulled out a bottle of beer for himself. Not asking her if she wanted anything to drink, he popped the lid and took a long swig.

"Wouldn't you be suspicious in my position?"

She crossed her arms over her chest. "I wouldn't jump to conclusions, that's for sure. I was just trying to help."

One hell of a fated mate he was.

Except, he probably wasn't. If he were, he wouldn't be okay with sending her alone to the island, he wouldn't attack her for every stupid thing she said, he wouldn't blame her for things she had nothing to do with, and he would offer her a drink when he took one for himself.

As tears gathered in the corners of her eyes, Carol got up, strode into the bathroom, and locked the door behind her. Not that it would hold Lokan out if he wanted to get in, but at the moment she had a feeling he needed some time alone just as much as she did.

Sitting on the edge of the tub, she wiped her eyes with the back of her hands and took a deep breath.

Perhaps she was overreacting.

Being her mate didn't mean that Lokan was the perfect partner. He had his own issues, and she couldn't expect everything to always be great between them. After all, people came in all varieties, and she was sure that the other mated couples had their own problems and issues to deal with. Syssi had to deal with Kian's stress, Wonder was mated to a joker, and Brundar was not an easy guy to deal with either.

But what if it was more than that?

Usually, Carol was confident in her ability to have any guy wrapped around her little finger with hardly any effort, but Lokan wasn't any guy.

For the first time in her life, Carol felt outclassed.

Lokan was a powerful immortal, and he might possess other hidden talents besides compulsion and dream-sharing. Perhaps he could make himself irresistible, evoking emotions designed to convince her that he was her true-love mate.

She'd been stupid to tell him about the fated mates phenomenon, giving him a weapon to use against her.

How could the Fates be so cruel to her? Dangling two possible mates in front of her with neither being the real deal? After what she'd suffered, she deserved a reward, not further punishment,

And why would they punish her? What wrongs had she committed?

Were they angry at her because she'd sold her body for money and favors?

It was a chilling thought.

Carol had never felt guilty about her courtesan days. She'd had fun using her feminine wiles to lure rich men who'd been more than willing to pay for her favors. It had been a turn on, a power game that she'd enjoyed tremendously, but maybe it had been morally wrong, and that was why she was being punished?

Her people didn't have a religion, and the only moral compass they used was universal decency. Not to do harm, to promote freedom and equality, and to help humanity make life better for as many people as they could. Sexuality and promiscuity were not frowned upon like in the human religions.

On the contrary, they were celebrated.

Still, as far as Carol knew, she'd been the only one who had taken it as far as selling her sexual favors, so maybe she'd erred after all.

One thing she was sure of. Lokan could never find out about her past.

"Are you all right in there?" he asked from the other side of the door. "Can I come in?"

"I need a moment."

"You've been in there for almost an hour."

She hadn't realized it had been so long.

"I'm sorry if I upset you. My reaction was uncalled for."

Well, that was something. At least he'd apologized.

Pushing to her feet, Carol opened the door and let Lokan pull her into his arms.

"I'm used to suspecting everyone. It's hard to turn it off."

She rested her cheek on his chest. "I only want what is

best for you, Lokan. That is what mates do. They support each other to the best of their abilities."

He sighed. "I wish it were as simple as that. But nothing about our situation is simple."

"Making love is."

"That is true." He kissed the top of her head. "Am I forgiven?"

Carol looked into Lokan's dark eyes and smiled. "You'll have to earn it."

"What can I do?"

"Make love to me, and I'll consider it."

20

KIAN

*K*ian's walk from his house to the office was usually uneventful. Seven o'clock in the morning was too early for most clan members to be out and about, but this time he had company, and it wasn't coincidental.

He heard Ella jog up behind him and then slow down when she reached him.

"Good morning, Ella."

Since her regular running route didn't go by his house, he figured she wanted to talk to him and preferred to do so outside the office.

"Good morning." She smiled. "Julian and I want to go visit Lokan, but Carol said that we need to clear it with you first."

He stopped and turned to her. "Why would you want to see him after all that he did to you?"

She shrugged. "Lokan and I had a relationship. It was unconventional, and it ended abruptly without proper closure. There are some things I want to say to him, and I think he owes me an apology. Julian is curious about him too."

"You are still human. He can grab hold of your mind and thrall you."

"Not likely. First of all, I know how to shield my mind, and secondly, Julian is going to be there to keep me safe. Lokan won't dare do anything with him around."

Kian regarded Ella for a long moment before cracking a smile. "You want to gloat, don't you? Show off your handsome mate."

"Guilty. Wouldn't you?"

If Lokan had done to him what he'd done to Ella, his retaliation would have been much more severe.

"I guess you deserve your little revenge. I'll tell Arwel it's okay to let you in. When do you want to go?"

"Is this afternoon okay?"

"I don't see why not."

Thinking they were done, he resumed walking, but Ella kept pace with him.

"One more thing. Can we take Ingrid with us to visit Lokan?"

Kian stopped again. "Ingrid? Why the hell do you want her to accompany you? Did she ask to go?" He narrowed his eyes at her. "I'm not a fan of Lokan, but he is not an animal on display in a zoo."

Ella lifted her hands in the sign for peace. "That's not it. Carol and I were talking, and we wondered what would be a good way to test whether Lokan was indeed Carol's fated mate. We figured that bringing in an attractive single immortal lady was a good test. If he reacts to her flirting, then he is not Carol's mate for real."

Interesting. Apparently Carol had doubts as well.

"It's not a bad idea, but Lokan is too smart to fall for that. Besides, with his dream-sharing ability, I don't want another immortal female to get exposed to him. Ingrid might not be as good at shielding her thoughts as you are."

Ella's shoulders slumped. "I hadn't thought of that, but you're right. It was a silly idea. I just wish there were a way to test it, if only to put Carol's mind at ease."

"There might be. I'm going to ask Edna to probe him. There is a chance she can tell whether he loves Carol or not."

"Love?" Ella arched a brow. "They are not there yet. Carol doesn't claim to love Lokan, and I don't think he's told her that he loves her either."

"That's why I didn't do it yet. Edna can sense feelings and intentions. The mating bond is neither of those. Eventually, though, if the bond is there, love will come."

"Right. But we know that under normal circumstances, once the bond is created, mates desire only each other. So that was why Carol and I thought to dangle Ingrid in front of his nose and see if he got aroused. If not for Julian, I might have done a little flirting myself, but I can't do that to him. I've put him through enough already."

Kian nodded. "I'll think of something. But Ingrid is a no-go."

Ella shrugged. "I thought it was worth a try. Thanks for allowing Julian and me to visit Lokan."

"Have fun."

She smirked. "Oh, I will. Have a great rest of your day, Kian."

"You too."

He watched Ella jog away and then kept on walking, thinking over their conversation. Apparently, Carol was not convinced of Lokan's devotion to her and wanted to test it.

Perhaps he shouldn't wait for a love test. He could ask Edna to do a general reading of Lokan's intentions, or at least attempt to. That way he would know if the option of using her talent was at all available to him. If Edna was successful in this first attempt, he could always ask her to do it again later.

When Kian reached his office, he sat at his desk and fired off a text to Edna. *I need to talk to you.*

He knew the judge to be an early riser but didn't want to assume.

She called right back. "Good morning, Kian. What can I help you with?"

"Good morning. I was wondering whether you are free to probe Lokan today."

"And I was wondering when you'd get around to calling me. There is only so much Andrew can help you with. It's about time that you brought out the big guns. Let me check my schedule."

As he waited for Edna to come back on the line, Kian rapped his fingers on the surface of his desk and wondered the same thing. He shouldn't have waited with the probe. He'd made an assumption that Lokan was probably unreadable, but as the saying went, assumption was the mother of all fuckups.

"I can be there at two-thirty this afternoon," Edna came back. "Does it work for you?"

"I'll make it work. Do you want to come here first so we can carpool to the keep, or do you want to go there straight from your city office?"

"I'm working from home today, so I'll take you up on your carpooling offer."

"Very well. Meet me at the parking garage at two."

"See you there."

Kian disconnected the call and texted Ella. *I need you and Julian to be out of there by two-thirty. I decided to bring Edna to do an initial probing of Lokan.*

Ella's return text came a moment later. *Excellent idea.*

E L L A

*E*lla hadn't expected the cloak and dagger operation that visiting Lokan proved to be. The clan's old keep was a maze, with cleverly hidden entry points and underground tunnels. It was quite exciting, and she didn't need to worry about getting lost because Julian knew the way.

"It wasn't always that hard to get in," he said after they entered a storage unit in a nearby office building's garage. When Julian punched in a code to its back door, it swung open into a wide tunnel. "After most of us moved out and the security was fully entrusted to humans, we had to find a walk around to get into the keep's underground."

"Is it a long walk?"

"About ten minutes."

"That's not so bad. Do you know that Carol doesn't have her phone with her when she is in Lokan's cell?"

"Makes sense. He can take it away from her and call for help. How did you get in touch with her?"

"Arwel answered my text and then used the house phone to call Carol. That's how they communicate. She had to come to his room, which is next door to Lokan's."

"I know. Your mother and brother stayed in the apartment Lokan is in, and Magnus was in the one Arwel is using now."

She nodded. "It wasn't that long ago, and yet it feels as if years have gone by. I guess time feels different when a lot is happening."

When they reached the end of the tunnel, Julian entered a code into another door, and they exited into another parking garage.

"This is the clan's private parking." He led her to a bank of elevators. "And these are only used by us."

"Are we going down?" Ella asked when he pressed one of the buttons.

They were marked with letters instead of numbers, but other than G for garage, she didn't know what the others stood for.

"Yes. The keep's underground is many stories deep."

The dungeon level looked similar to the village's underground complex. Same wide corridor with concrete floor and concrete walls, and the same metal doors with small windows on top. The difference was the additional small window on the bottom and the thickness of the doors.

They were built with immortal prisoners in mind.

"Right on time." Arwel stepped out of his room and walked to the next door over. "I hope you are hungry. Carol is waiting for you with lunch."

"Yeah, she told us not to eat. Are you joining us?"

He glanced at Julian. "Do you need me there?"

Julian shook his head. "I think I can handle him."

"I'm going to lock you in, so it's not like he can escape. When you are ready to leave, call me on the house phone. Just press zero." He punched the code into the keypad. "I will need you to leave your phones with me. And if you have smartwatches, those too."

As Ella handed him her phone, Julian removed his watch. "I left my cell in the car. I only have this." He handed it to Arwel.

When the door opened, Carol walked out and pulled Ella into a hug. "I missed you, girl."

"I missed you too. You should come to the village every other day or so instead of spending all your time here."

Carol arched a brow. "Would you?"

Ella glanced at Julian and smiled. "Maybe only for a short visit. I hate it when we need to separate for longer than an hour."

"That was what I thought. Come on, the food is getting cold."

"Thank you for inviting us to lunch," Julian said.

He looked tense, which was understandable. After hearing so much about Lokan, he was finally going to meet him face to face.

As they stepped inside, Lokan rose from the couch and offered his hand to Ella. "It's good to see you."

"You too." She shook his hand, thinking that she really meant it. "Lokan, this is Julian, my mate." She made the introduction. "Julian, this is the infamous Lokan."

Side by side, there was no comparison. Lokan was handsome, but he couldn't hold a candle to Julian. Carol might disagree with her, but for Ella, Julian was the winner hands down.

Lokan smiled. "No wonder I had such a hard time luring her." He offered his hand to Julian. "I heard that you are a doctor."

"You heard right."

"Congratulations to you two. You fit together perfectly. Is Ella going to pursue a nursing career, or did you convince her to go for medicine?"

"She is still considering different options." Julian shook his hand.

"Whatever she decides on, I'm sure she's going to do well."

Ella stifled a chuckle. Lokan was laying the charm on Julian, and her sweet mate was eating it up.

"To the table," Carol said. "We can continue chit-chatting over pasta primavera."

The conversation wasn't nearly as awkward as Ella had feared it would be, and pretty soon Julian's animosity toward Lokan was replaced by his usual easy-going demeanor.

It wasn't hard to figure out why. Julian had no reason to be jealous because Lokan had eyes only for Carol, which made Ella wonder about Carol's suspicions.

Lokan was treating Carol the same way the other mated immortal males treated their mates. He kept touching her whenever he could, his eyes softened when he looked at her, and he listened attentively to everything she said.

What could have caused her insecurities?

Was it possible that Carol was not as confident as she appeared?

Or maybe Lokan was different with her when they were alone, and he was putting on an act to impress his guests.

22

LOKAN

*L*okan's neck hairs were prickling like crazy, much worse than they had in Kian or Arwel's presence. In fact, Arwel no longer triggered the alarm, and Kian did so only slightly.

It was strange given that Julian wasn't a threat to him. He was tall, and looked in shape, but he wasn't a Guardian. His chosen profession implied a compassionate nature and a soft heart.

Perhaps it was a remnant of the rivalry they'd had going on over Ella? Or was the trigger Julian's initial animosity?

In an effort to put the guy at ease as fast as possible, Lokan had been laying on the charm thickly. He needed the young immortal to relax and act naturally so he could observe his interactions with Ella. Supposedly, the two were true-love mates, and this was a priceless opportunity to study the mysterious bond Carol had gone on and on about.

He waited for an opportune moment in the conversation to steer it in that direction. "I heard that you two have moved in together. Any plans for a wedding?"

Ella and Julian exchanged glances, and then Julian

wrapped his arm around her shoulders and kissed the top of her head. "There is no rush. In our clan's tradition, for a union to be official it is enough that we pledge ourselves to each other in front of two adult witnesses. A ceremony is for the benefit of our friends and family who want to share in our happiness and celebrate with us."

Ella chuckled. "The goddess wants a wedding, but she understands that I'm not ready yet. I want to finish college first." She gazed into Julian's besotted eyes. "My mate is an educated man. I have some catching up to do."

Julian clasped her small hand between his two large ones. "You know that it doesn't matter to me. I know how smart you are. I don't need you to have a college degree to appreciate you."

The two appeared lost in each other's eyes, oblivious to their company.

If Arwel had been there, he would have rolled his eyes and said that he needed to take notes. To an outside observer, the sentimentality seemed saccharine sweet and looked quite silly, but Lokan could tell that the two were deeply in love.

He cleared his throat. "Is it true that you fell in love with Ella's picture?"

After gazing for hours at Areana's portrait, Lokan could believe that. He'd moved it to the bedroom where he could look at it from the bed, and the longer he gazed at Areana's beautiful face, the more he yearned for her to be his mother.

Tearing his eyes from his mate, Julian smiled. "I don't know if love is the right term. It was more like an obsession. I fell in love with Ella after I met her and had the privilege of getting to know her. But someone was creating interference." He pinned Lokan with a hard stare. "Confusing my Ella."

Lokan dipped his head. "My apologies. I was selfish, chasing my own agenda, but to ease your mind, I was never really interested in Ella romantically."

"Why not?" Unexpectedly, Julian's eyes started glowing with aggression. "Ella is the most beautiful woman I've ever met, and she is smart and kind and lovely to talk to."

Aha, the boy was offended on behalf of his mate.

"Ella is an amazing young woman, and if I were a young man like you, I would no doubt have fallen head over heels in love with her. But I'm nearly one thousand years old. Ella is too young for me." He turned to Carol and took her hand. "At my age, I appreciate a woman with maturity and experience." Mimicking Julian, he wrapped his arm around Carol's shoulders and kissed the top of her head.

That seemed to mollify the young buck. "I'm just glad that this is over. As long as Ella was gripped by your compulsion, she wasn't sure of our bond, but as soon as you lifted it, there was no doubt in her mind that I'm her true-love mate."

Carol sighed. "Young love. How sweet."

"I was wondering about it." Lokan took the opportunity to keep his investigation going. "How do you know that what you are feeling is that magical bond you guys believe in? I would imagine that infatuation and lust could be mistaken for true love."

Julian shrugged. "For me it was quite obvious. Ever since seeing Ella's picture, I couldn't even think of touching another female. And that was very unusual for me. Like most immortal males, I used to bed a different one nearly every night, and I have never had a problem moving on to the next one."

Blushing, Ella shifted in her chair. "I don't like it when you mention other women you've been with."

"I know, love." He leaned and kissed her cheek. "But Lokan is new to all this, and I wanted him to understand what it means to have a true-love mate." He turned to Lokan. "From the moment Ella entered my life, I knew she was the only one for me and that I would never want another."

Next to him, Carol huffed out a breath. "Everyone experiences this differently, Julian."

For some reason, she seemed annoyed.

Julian shook his head. "I think that this is universal for all bonded couples."

"How about Vivian and her Guardian mate?" Lokan kept pressing. "They are an older couple. Was their experience different than yours?"

Ella chuckled. "Not really. They are like a couple of teenagers, kissing and necking every moment that they think no one is watching. And don't start me on the giggling. Do you know how awkward it is to hear your mother giggle like a schoolgirl?"

"Since I grew up without a mother, I wouldn't know."

Ella's smile wilted. "Right, I forgot about that. I'm sorry if I touched a sore spot."

Her embarrassment was the perfect opportunity to peek into her mind. As Carol's friend, Ella might know if Carol was doing something underhanded to him to mimic the effect of a mated bond.

Lokan leaned forward and looked into her eyes. "No need to feel bad. I understand."

Damn, Ella's shields were up and as strong as ever. He should have known. If she could maintain them in her sleep, an awkward moment wasn't going to weaken them.

Ella and Julian seemed to genuinely believe in their true-love bond. They hadn't been putting on an act, and even though Julian was an educated man, a scientist, he seemed to be even more sure of it than Ella, who as a young girl might have been prone to flights of fancy.

Lifting the bottle of wine, Lokan filled everyone's glasses. "Let's drink to our good fortune and to the wise Fates for gifting us with such perfect mates."

23

CAROL

"That wasn't so bad," Carol said once the door closed behind Julian and Ella. "I was afraid Julian would be nasty to you, but you managed to charm him."

"He's a nice, mellow guy." Lokan got up and started clearing the table. "I think he was relieved to hear my apology. I don't think he was comfortable with puffing out his chest and thumping it in warning." He put the containers in the carrier.

Carol chuckled. "It's a stretch imagining Julian pulling the gorilla act."

It had been an interesting visit. On the one hand, Julian had spilled the beans on fated mates desiring only their partners, which ruined any chance of testing Lokan by bringing in a sexy lady to tempt him and watching his reaction. But on the other hand, Lokan's many questions about the special bond between fated mates could mean that he was just as suspicious of it and what had caused it as Carol was.

One hell of a couple they made. A match made in heaven.

Two jaded, mistrustful people, carrying too much baggage on their backs.

The question that bothered her, though, was what Lokan could possibly imagine she had done to make him feel the powerful bond snap into place, tying them to each other like a thick rubber band.

Pheromones? Those could induce lust but not that special feeling of belonging together. No chemical could do that, natural or manufactured. It was a meeting of the souls.

If anyone had a reason to be suspicious, it was her. Lokan's known special abilities were in the metaphysical realm, influencing the mind, so he was more likely to induce artificial feelings.

When the table was clear and all the dishes had been collected into the carrier, Carol called Arwel. "I need to take stuff upstairs. Can you open up for me?"

"I'll be there in a moment."

Taking her hand, Lokan pulled her into his arms. "Don't take too long." He dipped his head and nuzzled her neck, kissing the spot he'd bitten earlier. "I'm ready for another round."

She rolled her eyes but smiled. "You're insatiable, but so am I. So it's all good."

As the door started opening, he took her lips in a quick kiss. "Your Fates are savvy matchmakers. We are a perfect fit."

She pushed on his chest and reached for the carrier. "I told you so."

"Yes, you did."

Outside, Arwel was waiting with a rolling cart. "How is that?"

"Great." She put the carrier on top. "Now I can go for fancy presentations. What do you say, can I start using real plates and utensils?"

"Not a good idea."

She waved a dismissive hand. "Like beer and wine bottles

cannot be turned into weapons, and yet you allow those. Come on, Arwel. Be sensible."

"I'll think about it. By the way, Kian is on his way with Edna. They should be here in about half an hour."

Carol grimaced. "Do I have to stay away again?"

"Let me check with Kian. I'll let you know." He put her phone next to the carrier.

That was probably going to be a yes, and she should tell Lokan that she wasn't coming back right away. "Can you open the door for me? I need to tell Lokan that I might stay away longer than I planned on."

"Why?" Arwel started pushing the cart toward the elevators. "Kian might agree for you to be there. And besides, my instructions were not to warn Lokan ahead of time. Kian doesn't want him to shore up his defenses in preparation for her visit."

That made sense.

"I'm going to prepare a few snacks and bring them down to you. If I'm not allowed in, you can take them inside once Edna gets here."

Arwel chuckled. "As a way to improve the mood?" He rolled the cart inside the elevator.

"You got it." Carol followed in. "Little treats can have a big effect on mood, and a good mood is more conducive to cooperation, which in turn puts people in a friendlier disposition toward each other."

"You are truly devious, Carol."

"Thank you."

24

LOKAN

*W*hen the door opened, Lokan was expecting Carol, but instead, Kian's bodyguards walked in, followed by Kian and a woman in a man's suit.

There was nothing remarkable about her. In fact, she was quite plain for an immortal female, except for the eyes. Pale blue and wise, they captured his gaze and didn't let go. He couldn't look away even if he wanted to.

Talk about misleading appearances. The woman was powerful.

"Good afternoon, Lokan. Let me introduce our judge, Edna. Edna, this is Lokan."

She smiled, but it was a sad excuse for one, and offered him her hand. "I've heard a lot about you, Lokan."

He took her hand gently, mindful of her long, fragile-looking fingers. "I hope not all of it was bad."

Her smile got a little brighter. "Not all of it."

"Am I going on trial?" He let go of her hand but was still staring into her eyes like a deer caught in headlights.

"In a way. I'm here to examine your intentions and motives."

He chuckled. "Good luck with that. At this point in my life I'm not sure what they are."

"Understandable. Maybe I can help you with that. Let's sit on the couch."

As he joined her on the sofa, the door started opening again, and a moment later Carol entered with a rolling cart.

Relief washed over him. If he were to stand trial, he wanted her to be there. Someone who was on his side.

Or so he hoped.

"Hello, everyone. I hope I'm not interrupting. I brought hors d'oeuvres and coffee."

"Wonderful," Edna said. "I could use a cup of coffee and a bite to eat." She turned to Lokan. "If you're hungry, I suggest that you snack too. This can be a very draining experience."

"Thank you, but I just had lunch."

What he wanted was a tall glass filled to the brim with good whiskey, not coffee.

After Carol made the rounds, distributing coffees and small paper plates with appetizers, Edna helped herself to a little of each and then turned to him.

"I'm going to enter your mind, but I'm not going to read your thoughts. That's not what I do. I assess feelings and intentions. Resisting will make it more difficult for you and will make the process take longer. I suggest that you relax and cooperate to the best of your ability."

"I might be immune."

She nodded. "I'm aware of that. Give me your hands, Lokan."

There was no way out of this. If he refused, it would be like an admission of guilt, but if he complied, Edna might see more than he wanted her to see. His past was far from clean.

Reluctantly, he offered her his hands.

"Relax. I know that you are an old warrior and that your past is tainted with blood. That's not what I'm after."

Easier said than done, but he tried, taking in a deep breath and loosening his shoulders. "I'm ready."

As Edna looked into his eyes, the room and everyone in it receded into shadows, and all that remained were those two blue glowing pools of light. One moment they were on the outside looking in, and the next they were inside his soul, looking around, probing, touching.

It was the most unnerving experience he'd ever been subjected to, and it seemed to be going on and on with no end in sight.

When Edna finally let go of his hands and looked away, Lokan slumped against the couch's cushions and closed his eyes. "What the hell was that?"

"We call it the alien probe," Kian said. "What do you think, Edna?"

She lifted the cup of coffee that must have gone cold and drank until there was nothing left. "Carol, could you please refill my cup?"

"Sure." Carol rushed forward with the carafe and refilled both their cups.

After taking a few sips, Edna patted Lokan's knee. "You are a complicated fellow. Good and bad wage war inside you, but I think good is winning."

Carol let out a relieved sigh. "I could have told you that."

"Yes." Edna smiled at Carol. "The power of a good woman's faith should never be underestimated."

That was a cryptic remark. What had she meant by that?

"Meaning?" Kian asked.

Good. Lokan was glad that he wasn't the only one who didn't get it.

"The bond is there. I had no trouble finding it. It's still a fledgling, but it's the real deal." She lifted her cup and took several more sips.

"I still don't understand," Kian said.

Neither did Lokan.

Edna sighed. "When someone you care about has faith in you and thinks that you can do better, it reinforces your own faith in your ability to do so. Furthermore, you are more inclined to rise to the occasion because you don't want to disappoint that person. Lokan's intentions are almost equally balanced between wanting to do good for others and self-serving. But I believe that with Carol's encouragement, the scales can tip in the right direction."

That was news to Lokan.

In his opinion, self-serving and doing good for others were not mutually exclusive. By helping the island's population, he would be helping himself. Win-win, which was the best scenario.

"What I want to know is, can we trust him?" Kian asked.

Edna took a moment to contemplate his question. "I can't answer that. Perhaps when the bond between Lokan and Carol grows stronger, his loyalty and devotion to her will supersede all others. She is his mate, I can vouch for that, but they need more time for the bond to solidify and extract its full power. It needs to reach the point where nothing will matter to him more than her."

Lokan couldn't fathom a life that revolved around a woman. Carol was amazing, the best there was, and an immortal, which he hadn't dreamt of ever having the privilege of joining with, but Lokan's loyalty was and always would be first and foremost to himself.

Could it be that this was an elaborate setup to convince him the bond was real?

First they had staged Ella and Julian's visit, with the two of them gazing adoringly into each other's eyes. Then the judge showed up and did her probe. He'd felt it, so he couldn't deny what she had done, but her revelations could have been bogus.

Edna had the face and eyes that could convince Eskimos that it was sunny enough to wear swimming trunks and take a dip in the ocean, and for a moment there she'd managed to eliminate the last of his doubts, but he wasn't there yet.

As all eyes turned to him, Lokan deflected their attention by planting a smile on his face and turning around to glance at Amanda's portrait. "Now I'm really curious about the Brother who mated this gorgeous lady. I would like to meet him."

"Why?" Kian narrowed his eyes at him.

"From what Edna said, I understand that the bond between fated mates is so powerful that it overrides all other loyalties. Am I right?"

Kian nodded. "I don't know what I would do if I had to choose between my wife's welfare and that of the clan. Fortunately for me, there is no conflict. By keeping the clan safe, I'm safeguarding her as well."

"But that wasn't the case for Dalhu, was it?"

"I don't think he cared about the Brotherhood all that much." Kian put his elbows on his knees and leaned forward. "Dalhu admitted to being entirely self-serving. When he met Amanda, he had no problem switching sides. He didn't do it for the love of the clan, he did it for her and for himself."

"But to do that, he had to overcome Navuh's compulsion."

"I asked him about that. He said that the longer he stayed away from the island, the easier it became for him to shake it off. Meeting Amanda was probably just the last push he needed."

"That could be true. But I have another hypothesis, and that's why I would like to talk to him. What if the bond between fated mates is powerful enough to overcome compulsion?"

Carol shook her head. "It didn't work for Ella. As long as

she was under your compulsion, she couldn't feel the full power of her bond with Julian."

"Yes, but that was because my compulsion was very specifically aimed to prevent her from having a relationship with another man. Navuh's compulsion is general loyalty and devotion to him and the cause."

Pushing to his feet, Kian walked over to the fridge and pulled out a couple of beers. "Anyone want a cold drink?" He popped the lids and handed one to Lokan.

When Carol and Edna shook their heads, he took a sip from his and returned to his seat. "That's an interesting hypothesis. I would love to test it." He pinned Lokan with a hard stare. "Is that why you came up with it? A prelude to asking me to allow you to accompany Carol to the island?"

Lokan chuckled. He and Kian had a lot in common, including a suspicious nature.

"It didn't even cross my mind. The implications are far more significant than my particular predicament. If the bond between immortal true-love mates is powerful enough to override Navuh's compulsion, that might be another reason behind his policy of segregating the dormant females from the immortal warriors and not allowing them to transition. It's another way for my father to control his people and ensure their loyalty."

Edna nodded. "And he would know about the bond because he was there when the gods were still around. Although from what I understand, it wasn't common back then. Very few were lucky enough to find their true-love mates."

"The Fates have been very kind to us," Carol said. "For millennia we were alone, with no prospect of finding lifelong partners, let alone true-love mates. I wonder what has changed."

For several long moments, no one talked, each mulling over Carol's statement.

"Perhaps it was just the right time," Edna said. "Or maybe the Fates have some grand new plan." She looked at Lokan. "Maybe you and Carol are it. The machinations that have brought you two together were like a complicated chess game, with many moves preceding your meeting."

Lokan arched a brow. "For what purpose?"

Edna smiled her sad little smile. "Peace. Maybe you were meant to unify our people."

Out of respect for the judge, Lokan stifled a chuckle. "Then it is good that we are immortal because I don't see that happening for many more centuries to come."

SYSSI

*A*s Syssi and Kian left the Perfect Match board meeting, she let out a long breath. "That was stressful."

"You did well in there." Kian wrapped his arm around her waist.

Brundar and Anandur had been left to wait in the lobby, which they hadn't been too happy about, but Kian had been adamant about them staying out.

Anandur cast Kian a reproachful glance and then smiled at Syssi. "How did it go?"

"Okay, I guess."

"That's it?" The Guardian arched a brow. "From what I could hear you were leading the meeting." He opened the door for her.

Syssi's cheeks heated up and she was grateful for the evening air cooling them down. "I felt like a fish out of water. I thought that my minor in business was going to come in useful, but instead I got carried away designing futuristic cities."

They walked up to the Lexus, which was parked in the

first row of the office building's parking lot.

"Your input was much appreciated. They loved your ideas." Kian offered her a hand up into the back seat.

She scooted in, making room for him. "I thought they were just humoring their largest stockholder."

He wrapped his arm around her. "I'll make you a deal."

She rolled her eyes. "You and your deals."

"Do you want to hear it or not?"

"I'm listening."

"When they are done designing the new sci-fi adventure, we will test run it together. I bet that you will find that many of your suggestions were incorporated in its design. You have one hell of an imagination."

"Thank you."

All she had done was provide several rudimentary sketches of how she envisioned cities would look five hundred years from now. She had no clue how the Perfect Match team was going to translate those sketches into something that felt real in a virtual experience.

Still, it had been exciting to go back to her creative roots. Syssi had forgotten how much she loved architecture, especially when her imagination could run wild with designs that weren't limited by current building material constraints and didn't have to conform to building codes.

If Amanda didn't need her help in the lab, Syssi would seriously consider switching over to the design department of Perfect Match.

"Do you want to stop for a late dinner somewhere?"

"I would love to."

"Where?" Anandur looked at them through the rearview mirror.

"The Cheese Place." She looked at Kian. "If it's okay with you."

"Whatever pleases you, my love."

At the restaurant, the four of them squeezed into a corner booth, which was as private as it got in the place.

"Bottom line. It seems like you had fun in there," Anandur said. "And you were so worried."

"I have to admit that I enjoyed myself tremendously. A lot of creativity goes into designing those fantasies. The way it works, they have a pool of environments to choose from, and they use them in the various adventures people request. I just helped with the initial design of a futuristic city."

"Well, you are an architect." Anandur waved a hand.

"Not certified because I didn't intern."

Kian took her hand. "It doesn't matter. It's obvious that this is what you enjoy doing the most. Your eyes shone when you were drawing those sketches, and you sounded so excited when you explained your ideas. This is what you should be doing. You are wasting your time in the lab."

"I love working with Amanda, and what we do is important. Even if we don't find new Dormants, we are making progress toward legitimizing paranormal talents. It's about time that the scientific community accepted the paranormal as normal phenomena that are just rare and at the moment inexplicable. I'm sure future research will discover some kind of brain waves that make them possible."

"I'm not saying that it is not important, but Amanda can manage without you. She might not like losing you, but she can find a replacement." He leaned closer and lowered his voice. "I couldn't help thinking that with your foresight, the things you were drawing were not imaginary but a glimpse into the future."

She rolled her eyes. "Right. I'm the new Jules Verne. Maybe he also saw the future."

Her so-called gift was annoying. Instead of showing her cities of the future, couldn't it tell her whether she was pregnant or not?

The emotional turmoil she'd been experiencing for the past week was not conducive to conception. She should woman up and buy a freaking pregnancy test kit, or ten of them, and find out one way or another instead of obsessing over it because she was afraid of disappointment.

Her gut churning, Syssi's appetite went out the window, and when the waiter came to take their order, she just pointed at the first salad on the list.

"What happened?" Kian asked after the guy had left.

She couldn't tell him, not yet, and certainly not with Brundar and Anandur present.

"You didn't tell me much about Edna's impression of Lokan, only that she'd said he was complicated."

Kian grimaced. "She said that he was evenly balanced between self-serving and actually wanting to help his people."

"That doesn't sound too bad. What did she say about his feelings for Carol?"

"She is certain the mate bond is there, but it's new and needs time to mature."

"You don't seem convinced."

"I'm not. I wouldn't put it past Lokan to possess the ability to deceive even Edna."

"Andrew thinks he is okay, and frankly, I think so too."

Kian's brows dipped. "Then he has all of you fooled."

"And I think that you are prejudiced, and that no matter what proof you get, you are not going to trust him enough to send him to the island with Carol."

"You are right."

Stubborn man.

"Do you see a way around it? Because Annani is not going to let it rest."

Across the table, Anandur nodded in agreement.

"I'm going to brainstorm it with Turner. If anyone can come up with a plan to get Areana out it is him."

"He is not a magician, Kian."

He chuckled. "He's as close as it comes. Besides, maybe he can think of a better test for Lokan. I will not risk Carol based on hunches and feelings. I need a fail-proof way to test him."

"You didn't have one for Dalhu or Robert."

"I disagree. Both left the Brotherhood voluntarily."

"And still, you didn't trust them for a long time."

Across the table, Brundar and Anandur's heads were moving from side to side as if they were watching a tennis match.

"Precisely." Kian turned to her. "Are you willing to gamble with Carol's life on a gut feeling? What would you do if the decision was yours?"

Syssi swallowed. "I don't know."

"That's what I thought."

26

LOSHAM

*I*n his backyard, overlooking the San Francisco Bay, Losham opened a cigar box and pulled out a *Short Story*. The small cigar was a perfect companion to the fine whiskey he was sipping, and as its name implied, it wasn't going to last for hours like some of the larger ones did, but it was still an excellent cigar.

He cut off the cap but didn't light up.

The call he was expecting should come at any moment, and he decided to wait to light it after it was done.

His phone rang precisely at nine o'clock as scheduled.

"Good evening, detective. What do you have for me?"

"Still nothing, sir. No one went in or out of the penthouse apartment today."

"Very well. Keep watching and call me again tomorrow. If you see any activity, call me right away."

"Yes, sir."

It had been a week since Lokan had left his Washington residence, and he hadn't returned yet.

After their dinner meeting almost three weeks ago,

Losham had contracted a human detective agency to keep an eye on his brother's apartment.

Nothing too elaborate, just around the clock watching of the coming and goings from the rooftop of a nearby building. Planting surveillance equipment would have been too risky and so would following Lokan around.

All of Navuh's sons were trained to look out for tails and bugs. Lokan would've caught either right away, and it wouldn't have taken him long to figure out who was spying on him.

What was he up to, though?

Losham had hoped to discover a conspiracy. If any of their brothers or other immortals that the Brotherhood had planted in Washington were visiting Lokan, it would have suggested that he was cooking up something against their father. Delivering that information to Navuh could have restored their leader's faith in Losham.

But all he could report was that Lokan had been gone for a week, and there could have been legitimate reasons for that. He could have traveled to South America to meet up with crooked politicians and negotiate arms deals there, or to visit a senator in his or her state.

The thing that bothered Losham, however, was that Lokan still hadn't returned his call.

Wishing to coax more information from his brother, Losham came up with an excuse for visiting Washington, and he had called Lokan to arrange another meeting. But Lokan had never called him back, which was odd.

Their phones worked just as well in South America, or wherever Lokan was on the globe, and it was rude of his brother not to return his call.

"Sir." Rami stepped out through the living room sliding doors. "You've requested an update on our latest shipment."

"Oh, yes." Losham lit up his cigar. "Please, take a seat."

Things were going well with the new trafficking system he'd established. They'd already had five successful deliveries, which was astounding given that the operation had started a mere month ago. In most cases, the warriors had to thrall their victims only once it became evident that the travel plans had changed.

A promise of a romantic weekend in Europe turned out to be the perfect bait.

"I talked with Herpon's assistant, Borgan, and they are just as happy with the last two as they were with the previous three. Their indoctrination went smoothly, and the original three are already serving clients."

"Are they satisfied with their performance?"

"Borgan voiced no complaints."

"Splendid."

"Indeed, sir. May I offer a suggestion, though?"

"Naturally. What's on your mind?"

Rami was a sharp guy, and Losham liked having him around not only as an assistant and a sounding board for his ideas, but also for the occasional good suggestion.

"All five girls were picked up from the same university. When their families discover that they didn't return from their vacations, an investigation will inevitably start. If only one or two girls were missing, the police would have done nothing about it, but five disappearing around the same time and under similar circumstances is a different story."

"You are absolutely right. Make a list of all the colleges in the Bay Area. We will limit the abductions to one per institution and then move the operation to a different city. I was contemplating Washington."

"The Los Angeles area has several hundred, sir, and since it's only a short flight away, we won't have to move." He glanced at the view. "I like it here."

So did Losham.

The only reason he'd thought about Washington was that it provided an excellent excuse to spy on Lokan, but that was a secondary consideration. The capital wasn't as populous as Los Angeles and its neighboring cities, and most likely had fewer higher learning institutions.

The problem with Los Angeles, however, was the clan.

Losham was certain that their headquarters were there, and that meant Guardians. If he were still tasked with hunting clan members, he would have considered moving his entire operation there. Surely he could find a nice house with a great view in Los Angeles as well.

But that was no longer his concern, and snatching up girls on Guardian turf was asking for trouble.

27

CAROL

*A*fter dinner, Lokan leaned back in his chair and rubbed his stomach. "At this rate, I'm going to get fat. You are too good of a cook, and I haven't exercised in days."

"I beg to differ. You've had plenty of exercise." Carol cast him a suggestive look.

That got a smile out of him. "If sex were enough, no immortal would have to bother."

She spread her arms. "That's all the exercise I need. Speaking of which, do you want to go to bed?"

Surprising her, Lokan shook his head. "I'm afraid Edna's probe exhausted me, and then your fabulous jambalaya delivered the knockout. I need a little time to recuperate."

Talk about disappointing. She'd thought that her guy was invincible.

"How about a cuddle, then?"

"In bed?"

"Or on the couch. To feel that everything is right with my world, all I need are your arms around me."

His eyes softened. "That's the nicest thing anyone has

ever told me." He pushed to his feet and offered her a hand up. "Come here." He pulled her to his chest.

Clutching his shoulders, Carol lifted on her toes, feathered a chaste kiss on his lips, and then let go. "Let's sit on the couch and watch a movie."

Lokan arched a brow. "That's it? A tiny little kiss?"

"You said that you needed time to recuperate." She pulled on his hand and led him to the sofa. "If I kissed you like I wanted to, we would have ended up in bed."

With a light shove, she pushed him down and then sat in his lap. "Am I squashing you?"

His arms wrapped around her. "You're tiny."

"No, I'm not. I have a big butt, and I'm not exactly lightweight."

His hand reached under her and squeezed the aforementioned body part. "You have the most perfect ass I've ever seen. It's not too big or too small, it's just right."

He could be so charming when he wanted. But then he could also go cold in the blink of an eye and for no apparent reason.

Even Edna couldn't decipher him, and she could look into a person's soul.

Resting her head on his chest, Carol inhaled his special scent and felt her entire body go loose. It was better than smoking pot, and much more addictive. The question was whether it was healthier.

She was bonded to an enigma, falling for him hard despite all the flashing red warning lights.

If only the Fates could send her a sign that she was doing the right thing, or conversely give her a definitive warning so she could walk away while she still could.

If she could beat her addictions to drugs and alcohol, she could beat this one as well.

Maybe. She wasn't sure about that at all. No drugs or alcohol had ever made her feel as good as Lokan did.

He rubbed her back, his hand feeling warm and soothing. "What are you thinking about so hard?"

She blurted out the first thing that popped into her mind. "How to get to the island, of course. That's all I've been thinking about lately."

He chuckled. "You mean other than sex and food?"

"Well, those are necessities." She lifted her chin and cast him a coy smile. "And since I'm a pro at both, I don't need to think very hard about either."

"That is true. So, what were you thinking about the island?"

Crap. She had no new ideas. "I was wondering how we could use Gorchenco to get Areana and me out."

"I already explained why it's not possible."

"Yeah, you did. I was trying to come up with creative ideas. By the way, did Kian ask you about the dirt you have on Gorchenco?"

"Not yet. With everything that's going on, it must have slipped his mind. If his mother is stressing him half as much as my father stresses me, then it's perfectly understandable."

"Maybe you should remind him about it."

Lokan shook his head. "I need him to ask, so I can get something in return. If I just volunteer the information, I lose my one bargaining chip."

"What do you want to ask for?"

"There are many things I want, but none that he would grant."

"You should figure it out before he asks."

"Maybe I should ask him for something for you? What would you like to have?"

There were only two things Carol really wanted. One was security in the knowledge that Lokan was her true-love mate, but that wasn't something Kian could give her. And the second one was Kian green-lighting her mission to go to the freaking island and find out who Navuh was hiding in his harem. Except, that wasn't easily grantable either.

She went with her third and much less important wish. "I would have liked us to have an apartment with a kitchen, so I would not have to leave every time I want to cook. And windows. Living underground is oppressive. But he is not going to give us that."

"I prefer it this way. As it is, I don't know where I am, so I can't tell anyone where to find your clan. That leaves a tiny chance of Kian changing his mind about letting me go with you to the island."

"I don't think it's on the table."

"I agree. We have to figure out how to do it with Gorchenco's help."

Carol let out an exasperated breath. "Yeah. Maybe the freaking nuclear submarine can come in handy. Can a submarine be used to drill under water? Maybe we can dig out an escape tunnel straight from the harem."

28

LOKAN

"*I* love the way your brain works." Lokan wound a lock of Carol's hair around his finger, then let it spring free.

She narrowed her eyes at him. "I know people think I'm just a ditsy blond, but I'm much smarter than I look."

He chuckled. "Anyone who thinks that is a moron. I suspected you were an evil mastermind from the first moment I saw you." He pushed to his feet with her in his arms.

She clung to his neck. "Why evil?"

"Because you look like an angel, so of course you have to be evil."

She laughed. "That's some warped logic."

He kicked the bedroom door closed and laid her on the bed. "Not at all. When my enemy sends a beautiful temptress into my cell, the most logical assumption is that she is up to no good."

"Well." Carol scooted back on the bed. "It depends on what you define as no good." She reached for the hem of her shirt and pulled it over her head.

His eyes zeroing in on her lacy bra, he reached behind him and flicked the light switch off. Hopefully, Arwel would get the hint and give them privacy.

"Following your logic, I should assume that you are pure goodness."

"Hardly." Lokan unbuttoned his shirt only halfway and then pulled it over his head.

Carol's throaty chuckle and the sound of her bra clasp releasing sent an electrical bolt straight to his groin.

"With those red glowing eyes you look like a demon, so you must be an angel on the inside."

Her leggings hit the floor.

Unbuckling his belt, Lokan pulled down his pants together with his boxer shorts. "In my case, what you see is what you get."

As he leaped on the bed, covering her with his body, he found her as naked as he was.

She wrapped her arms around his neck. "My beautiful demon prince."

"Close your eyes, my angel." Dipping his head, he brushed soft kisses across her eyelids.

Carol smiled. "I like that."

"The kisses?" He brushed his lips across her cheeks.

"That too. I like it when you call me your angel." She pouted. "I don't like it when you call me evil."

He had to kiss those pouty lips, but first he had to set the record straight. "I was teasing. You are my sweet angel."

As a soft sigh left her mouth, he felt her melt under him and realized that he'd meant it. She was his angel, pure and good with just a splash of naughty and adventurous, the best thing that had ever happened to him.

His suspicions of her had been the result of a lifetime of intrigue, subterfuge, and mistrust, but his gut had known all along that his mind was steering him astray.

As he claimed her mouth, her arms slipped around his shoulders and then his back, pulling him to her, her hands caressing, kneading.

He groaned as she nipped his lip, his eyes rolling back in his head when she licked one fang and then the other.

Reaching down, he parted her wet folds and stroked them with just his fingertips, teasing her until she moaned into his mouth.

"You want more, my sweet angel?"

"Yes."

He gathered her slickness and slid his fingertips up to the apex of her womanhood, stroking gently.

She writhed under him, trying to get more friction, but he kept teasing her with just the pads of his fingers while kissing his way down her throat.

After a few more moments of sweet torment, he took pity on her and thrust two fingers inside her, scraping her neck with his fangs at the same time but careful not to draw blood.

Slipping a third finger into her wet heat, he continued kissing down the column of her neck, along her collarbone, until he found her straining nipple and took it in his mouth.

As Carol arched beneath him, he nipped it with his blunt front teeth, then licked the small hurt away and suckled on the stiff peak.

"Stop teasing me, Lokan," she hissed. "I want you inside me."

His angel came with sharp teeth, but that was what he liked about her the most. Carol was the perfect combination of yielding and yet demanding, carnal and yet sweet, soft and yet possessing a core made from titanium.

As he retracted his fingers from her sheath, they were slick with her juices, and he used that lubricant to coat his shaft as he aimed it at her entrance.

Always mindful of how much smaller she was, he pushed just the tip inside her, then moved his fingers to her clitoris, stimulating the little nub as he pushed a little further and then a little more until he was seated all the way in.

They both groaned.

Carol's small hands clutching his bottom, she spread her legs wider, getting him to go as deep as he could.

Swiveling his hips, he pulled back a couple of inches, then pushed back in, fucking her with quick shallow thrusts that were meant to tease.

When she scored him with her fingernails, he grabbed her hands, pulled them over her head, and kept the slow plunge and retreat.

"You're evil," she hissed.

He chuckled. "But you love me anyway."

Her eyes popped open, their blue glow intense as she regarded him in stunned silence.

He didn't expect her to confirm. She wasn't ready to admit it yet. But he knew it to be true.

29

CAROL

*D*id she love him?

Right now Carol wasn't sure.

Lokan was arrogant, infuriating, and the sexiest man she'd ever been with. She felt like biting and scratching him until he fucked her like she wanted to be fucked, and that wasn't love.

It was carnal lust.

And yet, it was true. Maybe. She still wasn't sure.

But she'd be damned if she said those words before he did. Until he got over his suspicions and surrendered to the bond, she was going to treat him as a lover and not as the one she loved.

She bucked up hard, nearly toppling him over. "I'm not one of your human playthings, Lokan. Give me what I need."

"Shh." He let go of her hands. "Don't fight me, little tigress. I know what you need."

Infuriating male.

She could play along.

Forcing herself to relax, Carol went still, feigning detachment. "Do you need to be in charge, lover boy? Is that how you like it?"

His smile was evil as he grabbed her hair and tilted her head back. "Yes, I do like to be in charge, and you like it as well." He scraped his fangs over the column of her neck, for sure drawing blood this time.

Carol hissed, but it was because of her inner burn and not the one blooming on her neck. He licked the twin scrapes, cooling her skin but not the inferno blazing in her core.

Pulling almost all the way back, he plunged forcefully inside, hitting the end of her channel and holding there. "Is that what you want?"

"Yes."

His fingers tightened in her hair, causing pinpricks of pain. "Like this?"

"Yes."

As he retreated and plunged again, she lifted her hips to meet him. Again and again, her core tightening as her orgasm neared.

"You are mine, Carol."

"Yes." It was true and easier to admit that than to fess up to loving him.

"I'm your man. The only one who is going to fuck you for the rest of your immortal life." He surged inside her.

His possessiveness excited her. She wanted that, which was still quite a shocker. Carol had never thought she would be satisfied with just one man, but then Lokan wasn't like any of the men she'd been with.

He was a powerhouse, perfectly capable of satisfying her in every way.

Even though he was bossy, and arrogant, and believed that he knew what she needed better than she did, Carol knew that she would never tire of him.

Well, maybe he did know better.

He was incredibly skilled and just as attentive, paying attention to what drove her crazy and filing it away for later use. Not to mention so handsome that just looking at him scrambled her brain.

Riding her hard, his groans soon turned into growls, and combined with the red glowing eyes and fangs, he looked more like a demonic creature than a man.

An angel and a demon, a match made in heaven, or in the twisted minds of three bored Fates.

As Lokan threw his head back and hissed, a climax rippled over Carol, and as he struck, hitting her neck and sinking his fangs into the soft flesh of her neck, she climaxed again.

Riding the euphoria cloud, she remained tethered to reality by clutching Lokan's broad shoulders and listening to the rapid beat of his powerful heart.

Drenched in sweat, he was still panting as he snaked his arms under her and flipped them over, holding her tight as if afraid that she might float away.

"I'm not going anywhere," she whispered into his chest.

"I know."

"You can let go."

"I don't want to."

She felt his shaft stir under her and chuckled. "Already? I need a moment to catch my breath."

"Take as long as you want. Just don't go anywhere." Using his foot, he flung the comforter over her back.

It was a small gesture, but it spoke volumes.

She knew Lokan was still hot and sweaty, but he'd thought about her comfort first.

"Thank you."

Listening to the strong beat of his heart, she drifted off wondering if he loved her too.

30

KIAN

A paper cup of steaming coffee in hand, Turner walked into Kian's office and closed the door behind him.

"Good morning." Kian got up and walked around to the other side of his desk. He pulled out a chair for Turner and sat in the other. "What's on the agenda for today?"

"Several things." Turner popped his briefcase open and pulled out a large aerial photograph. "Our satellite was finally in position over the island at around three o'clock at night our time." He handed the black and white to Kian. "It looks like the right one, but you should verify it with Lokan."

As Kian looked at the picture of the tropical island, he understood why it hadn't been detected from the air. The vegetation was dense, and the resort was built in a way that blended with nature. He had to focus to see the thatched roofs of several bungalows. The shapes were round, and from the air they looked like the tree canopies surrounding them. He suspected that there were many more hidden from sight.

Straining his eyes, Kian searched for visible signs of the

airstrip, but it was expertly hidden. According to Dalhu, the island's transport operated only during the night, and its single runway was camouflaged during the day.

"Impressive. It was a brilliant move to choose a tropical island for their base. Not only is it isolated, but it also provides excellent natural camouflage. With the sparse vegetation here in Malibu, we had to rely on technology to achieve a similar level of concealment."

Turner nodded. "And by building the warriors' quarters and other facilities underground, they also solved the heat problem. It is much easier to cool subterranean accommodations than those housed in structures built above ground."

"It solves the space constraints as well. This island is what? Forty acres? Fifty? Some of Malibu's private estates are that size."

"I contracted an operator to snoop around with a fishing trawler. I want to find out how close he can get and what they will do to turn him away."

"Have him try to land a small drone on the island. I want to see if we can land a miniature drone unnoticed. If that's possible, it will solve the communication problem."

Turner nodded "I thought about that. I don't trust Lokan any more than you do, and I don't want us to be dependent on his dream sharing with Carol for communication. Once she is there, he can blackmail us into releasing him in exchange for the information."

Kian hadn't thought of that. It wasn't a stretch to imagine Lokan choosing his freedom over finding his mother. "Good point. Any ideas on how it can be done?"

Turner shook his head. "A tiny drone the size of a large bug can go unnoticed, but it doesn't have the range, and a larger drone will be spotted by their security even if it manages to evade the radar. We need something custom made. I'll ask my guy to work on it." He reached into his briefcase and pulled out a printout. "On a different subject, I want you to take a look at this."

"What is it?" Kian took the page. It was a missing persons report filed with the San Francisco Police Department.

"As of last weekend, three female students went missing. All were undergrad students at UCSF."

Kian frowned. "Are you suspecting more Doomer murders?"

"I don't think so. One of the girls is the niece of an old buddy of mine from my Special Ops days. When she didn't return from a weekend off with her new boyfriend, her parents panicked, and he called me. I did a little digging, and apparently two more girls went missing under similar circumstances. All three are good students who also happen to be very good-looking. I suspect a trafficking ring specializing in college girls."

"Those are not their usual targets."

"My thoughts exactly. That's where things get interesting. I checked their travel itineraries. All three bought plane tickets to places around the Doomer island, using their debit cards. One booked a trip to the Maldives, another to Sri Lanka, and the third to Agatti. Curiously, cash funds matching the costs of the tickets were deposited into their accounts several days prior to the booking."

"Interesting."

"I'm having William and Roni hack into the San Francisco airport security network to find out who they traveled with, and then match the pictures to passports. I'm sure we will find that the identities of the boyfriends are fake. I think Navuh has eliminated the middleman and is collecting girls for the island one by one."

"That's much less efficient, and I'm not sure that it's less costly."

Turner nodded. "That is true. But then traffickers don't

supply college girls. If Navuh wants educated women for his brothel, he has no choice but to do it himself, using his warriors to lure the girls into going with them."

"Why would he want educated women?"

Turner shrugged. "His clients must favor them. Some men like to talk as well as have sex with their paid company, and rich clients can afford to be choosy."

Kian handed the printout back to Turner. "Especially nowadays that human contact has been replaced by text messaging and following celebrities on the internet. People are lonely and hungry for companionship."

Shoving it into his briefcase, Turner took a sip from his cup and grimaced. "It's lukewarm. I like your thermos idea." He put the cup down on the desk. "We should have a talk with Lokan about this. See what he knows."

Kian looked at the yellow pad and his to-do list, then shoved it aside. This new development was more important than what was on his agenda for the day.

"This afternoon work for you?"

"I have a couple of meetings. Can you make it by five-thirty?"

Kian glanced at the yellow pad again and sighed. "Yeah. My wife is not going to be happy about it, but so be it. I'll make it up to her later."

31

LOKAN

*L*okan looked at the transformed bedroom and shook his head.

Carol was a force of nature.

Once she decided something, she made it happen, charming any guy into doing her bidding. She'd managed to cajole his jailers into moving equipment from the gym into their bedroom, so he could release some of his pent-up energy on an activity other than sex.

Arwel clapped him on the back. "Do you know why this is good?"

"It's going to keep me in shape?"

"I don't care about that. What I care about are the waves of nervous energy you are bombarding me with day in and day out. Hopefully, this is going to put you in a better mood."

"I doubt it. I'm still a prisoner, and my mate is adamant about leaving me to go on a dangerous mission. The only way I can relax is if someone knocks me out."

Smirking, Arwel dipped his head. "I'm at your service. Call me when you need me." He arched a brow when his phone buzzed in his pocket. "Already you are calling me? You didn't even try the treadmill yet." He chuckled at his own joke and pulled out the device. "Yes?"

"Tell Lokan to expect visitors today at five-thirty," an unfamiliar voice said. "Kian and Turner want to talk to him."

Finally. Lokan had wanted to meet that Turner guy that Carol was hailing as a strategic genius for a while now.

"I'll let him know." Arwel closed the phone.

"Who was that?"

"Shai, Kian's assistant."

"What time is it?"

Arwel glanced at the phone. "Two-twenty. You have plenty of time." He waved a hand at the treadmill and the punching bag swinging from a hook that they had attached to the ceiling.

"Thanks, Arwel."

The Guardian clapped him on the back. "You're welcome."

As the Guardian opened the door to leave, Carol came in with a vacuum cleaner and a mop.

"Do you know how to use it?" She handed him the strange-looking vacuum device.

"I can figure it out."

"It's the latest Dyson handheld. You're gonna love it. Just pretend it's a gun, point and shoot."

"Got it."

He took it to the bedroom where debris from the drilling covered the floor and dust bunnies floated from moving the furniture around. The dresser went into the closet, making room for the treadmill, and the bed was shoved against one wall to make room for the punching bag, which Arwel had assured him was designed for immortals and could take a serious beating.

"Point and shoot." He pressed the trigger and the device roared to life, sucking in the dirt. It was a surprisingly satisfying task, and he was disappointed when there was nothing more to clean.

"Good job." Carol entered with the mop. "Vacuum the living room as well. The guys dragged dirt over there with their shoes."

He was happy to comply but then stopped at the doorway. "By the way, Kian's assistant called Arwel and asked him to inform me that Kian and Turner are coming to talk to me. Do you know what it is about? Did you arrange this?"

"I didn't." She leaned on the mop. "He didn't say?"

"I'm afraid not. Just that they are coming at five-thirty."

Carol glanced at her watch. "I'd better hurry up and prepare dinner. Whatever they want to discuss with you will go smoother with food in everyone's bellies."

Leaning the vacuum against the doorjamb, Lokan reached for Carol's hand and pulled her into his arms. "You are too good to me." He took her mouth in a crushing kiss.

She laughed when he let go. "If I knew the Dyson would have such an effect on you, I would've let you vacuum days ago." She glanced at the device. "I have to admit that it is kind of sexy."

"Thank you for looking after me. I just want you to know that I appreciate the exercise equipment that you so thoughtfully arranged for me to have, and the effort you put into the meals you prepare for me and for the others, making sure that everyone is in a good mood so they treat me better."

She waved a dismissive hand. "I like feeding people. It's my way of showing affection. Besides, if I bring the food, Kian will feel bad about kicking me out again and will have to let me stay."

CAROL

*B*y five-thirty, Carol had a buffet-style dinner arranged on the table, with a stack of paper plates, plastic utensils, and napkins ready for however many people Kian might bring with him.

Brundar and Anandur would be there for sure, and maybe Andrew as well. It depended on what they wanted to talk to Lokan about.

Perhaps Turner and Kian had come up with a better plan for getting Areana out? One that didn't involve her?

The prospect of abandoning her quest was bittersweet. Sweet because she dreaded leaving Lokan for an extended period of time, but at the same time bitter because she'd miss her one opportunity to do something monumental, something that could forever enter her into the clan's hall of fame, and not as its only courtesan or even the survivor of torture.

Lokan entered the living room, his hair still damp from the shower, looking like the suave handsome devil he was, and calmer than she'd ever seen him.

The two hours of intense training he'd put in had been transformative, getting rid of his nervous energy and restoring him to what she imagined was his natural state. Confident, powerful, and exuding vitality.

Fates, the man made her hot just by being in the same room with her.

He cast her an appreciative look. "I like seeing you in a dress. You are beautiful and so perfectly feminine." He made the hourglass shape with his hands.

"Thank you." Smiling, she smoothed her hands over her sides in a practiced move.

The dark green dress was form-fitting but not clingy, and it reached below her knees. It was one of the more conservative pieces she owned, accentuating her figure but not making her look slutty. Three-inch black sling-backs and dangling earrings completed the look.

Carol hadn't had a chance to play the part of hostess in a long time, and she was looking forward to showing off her skills.

As the door mechanism engaged, she took in a deep breath, plastered a smile on her face, and joined Lokan on the couch.

The brothers entered first, with Anandur immediately bee-lining for the table and checking out the selection. Kian and Turner followed with Andrew closing the procession.

Just as she'd anticipated. "Good evening, gentlemen." She pushed to her feet. "I figured none of you had dinner yet, so I prepared a little something to tide you over." She motioned to the table "Help yourselves."

"Carol, you are the best." Anandur grabbed a plate and started loading it.

Kian and Turner each sat in an armchair and Andrew joined the brothers at the table.

"May I prepare plates for you?" she asked. "You can talk over dinner."

With a sigh, Kian got back up. "Syssi is waiting for me

with dinner, but I don't want to be rude and refuse after you went to all this trouble." He motioned for Turner to join him. "Come on, Victor. Humor the lady and grab a plate."

On the couch, Lokan stifled a smirk.

Kian looked at him over his shoulder. "You too."

"Don't mind if I do."

Once their plates were loaded, Turner sat back on the armchair, took a couple of obligatory bites, and then put his plate on the coffee table.

"We haven't been properly introduced. I'm Turner."

Mimicking him, Lokan put his plate on the coffee table as well. "I know who you are. You are the guy who shot me."

Turner nodded. "I did my best to minimize the damage."

"I'm aware of that. You are a good shot and an even better actor. Because of your lack of emotional scents, I was sure you were a sociopath human."

Turner didn't seem offended. "I'm an anomaly. I also didn't trigger your immortal alarm."

Lokan frowned. "That could be a very handy trick. You can easily pass for a human, which means that you can get onto the island undetected."

The same thought was probably passing through everyone's heads, and there was a long moment of shocked silence. Lokan wondered how come no one had thought of it until now.

Instead of involving Gorchenco, who was a wild card, Turner could impersonate a rich guy and take Carol to the island instead.

Turner was the only one who didn't look surprised. "I'm aware of that, but at the moment I don't see any tactical advantage in doing so. We came here to discuss a different issue. What can you tell us about the abductions of young women from the Bay Area to serve in your island's brothel?"

33

LOKAN

*T*he question took Lokan by surprise, and he wondered how to answer it. He could claim to know nothing about it, but the lie detector would know he wasn't telling the truth. He could talk in generalities, though, without divulging any particulars unless asked directly.

Rubbing a hand over his jaw, he nodded. "From what I understand, the tastes of the resort's clientele are changing, and there is a rising demand for English-speaking service providers who can also carry on an intelligent conversation."

"That's what I thought," Turner said. "Who are you using to lure the women, your warriors?"

"Since this is not something I'm involved in, I'm not using anyone, but I've heard that choice warriors have been selected for this task."

From the corner of his eye, Lokan could see Kian's jaw muscles clenching, but Turner's expression was as impassive as if they were discussing commodities. The guy either didn't care or was just as emotionless as his lack of scents suggested.

"Isn't it a waste of manpower?" Kian asked.

"As you are well aware, as of late there aren't that many military opportunities for us. The Brotherhood has less income and an excess of men who have nothing to do. It has been decided to use them in more creative ways."

"Selling drugs and trafficking," Kian said. "I'm sure your father is not happy with that state of affairs. What are his plans for the future?"

"He didn't share them with me."

Kian leaned forward and offered him a chilling smile. "Come on, Lokan. You are a smart guy. I'm sure you have some idea where things are going."

Lokan crossed his legs and draped his arm over the couch's back. "As much as things change they also stay the same, and this lull is not going to last long. Humans are restless and aggressive by nature, and there will always be wars. Progress and technology only mean a larger body count."

With a sigh, Kian leaned back in the chair and crossed his arms over his chest. "Regrettably, I have to agree. Hoping for everlasting peace is naive. It doesn't take much to start a new war."

"Why college students, though?" Turner ignored the entire philosophical discussion, going back to the reason for his visit. "From the information I gathered about them, all three were excellent students."

Lokan shrugged. "If they are looking for smart ladies, it is easier to find them in colleges. It beats running them through intelligence tests before snatching them up."

From the corner of his eye, he caught Carol shaking her head. Seated between the lie detector and the tall redhead, she wasn't even trying to hide her displeasure from them.

Apparently his comment hadn't been as humorous as he'd intended.

Touchy people.

"Who is running the operation in the Bay Area?" Kian asked.

Damn, he didn't want to give Losham away. Except, he could talk in generalities, and if they pressed, provide them with the name. Hopefully, they were not going to ask him for more.

"One of my brothers."

Turner arched a brow. "For your father to assign the task to one of his sons, it must be important to him. I would have assumed a lesser commander would have been good enough."

"In time, when the operation is streamlined, I'm sure that will be the case. My brother's job is to set things in motion and standardize the procedures."

Kian snorted. "Not going to happen if we can do something about it."

Turner was still eyeing Lokan with his unnerving pale blue eyes. "The emphasis on smarts is new. I was led to believe that the average Doomer is bred for physical strength and aggression, not for intelligence."

The guy was sharp and didn't let himself get bogged down by minutiae. Like a laser beam, he kept his eye on the target.

The question was whether disclosing details about Navuh's new breeding program would be beneficial or detrimental to Lokan or the future of his people.

Adding smarts to the gene pool had been a good move. The modern world was run by geeks with computers and not by warriors with swords. The Brotherhood needed the infusion, and to achieve that, the program had to keep going.

But even if he told them about it, there was nothing the clan could do to stop it. The Brotherhood could collect genius geeks from anywhere in the world and bring them to the island to breed with Dormants.

"To compete in an evolving world, the Brotherhood needs its members to evolve as well. We need scientists and engineers more than we need muscled goons. We have enough of those."

Turner shook his head. "But the girls you collect are humans, not Dormants. How does it help you produce a smarter next generation?"

Lokan smiled. "That's what the boys are for. The clients. We used to lure in dangerous men. Warlords, arms dealers, drug lords, corrupt politicians, and they usually came with a goon squad of bodyguards. All fantastic gene donors given the old objectives of our breeding program. Now that the objective is brains, we lure in the computer geniuses, the startup mavericks, the heads of scientific research teams, and the like. We pair them with Dormants to produce our next generation of immortals, but in addition, we need to supply them with the kind of female companionship that will have them coming back for more. Hence the college girls."

"Fascinating," Kian said. "But what I want to know is how we can stop these abductions."

Lokan would have liked to help them, but the truth was that he didn't know how. Even if he were okay with eliminating Losham, which he definitely wasn't, Navuh would just replace his brother with someone else.

"You can't. The warriors work alone, befriending the young women and luring or thralling them into accompanying them on a weekend trip abroad. How are you going to prevent it? Check every girl's new boyfriend?"

Kian grimaced. "I need to think about it."

Reaching for his briefcase, Turner pulled out a large aerial photo. "Before we conclude our meeting, I want you to verify that we have the right island." He handed Lokan the photograph.

He recognized the shape immediately. "That's the one." He handed it back to Turner.

"Not so fast." Turner produced a sharpie from the briefcase. "Let's go over the terrain. Mark for me the area the Brotherhood compound occupies."

"It's underground." Lokan took the photo and drew a circle around the location of the subterranean compound.

"Are the harem and the Dormant enclosure in the same place as the other facilities?"

"They are not connected. The harem is here." He circled a small area north of the compound bordering the rock cliff. "The living quarters are underground, but they have several above-ground pavilions and a sizable fenced-off garden area." He drew another circle. "There is one more fence around it, and immortal warriors patrol the clean zone between the two. They have no access to the inner grounds. Only humans are allowed inside."

"What about the cliff?" Turner asked. "Is it fenced off too?"

"There is no need. Even professional climbers can't scale it without getting noticed. It's nearly vertical, covered with slimy moss, and about three hundred feet above sea level."

"I wonder why Navuh would leave it open. With how paranoid he is, I would think he would put a fence there too."

Lokan shrugged. "Perhaps he wants to give his concubines an illusion of freedom and an unobstructed view of the ocean. Besides, I assume that they are always guarded and never left alone when venturing outside. That area is not visible from outside the enclosure, only from the air, so I'm not familiar with its safety protocol."

Kian leaned over the photo. "So every time your father wants to visit his harem, he has to go above ground and then down again? That doesn't make sense. I'm sure he has a tunnel connecting his quarters to a secret entry into the harem."

"The thought has crossed my mind. But my father's personal quarters are guarded better than the US Treasury. They are just as inaccessible as the harem."

"Who cleans them?" Carol asked.

"His personal servants."

"Are they immortal or human?"

"Immortal."

"Damn. So, you can't compel them."

"What about the Dormants?" Turner asked. "Where are they held?"

"It's adjacent to the resort for obvious reasons." Lokan drew a circle around the area. "It's built the same way as the harem, but it is much larger and separated into two sections. On one side there are several individual bungalows for the assignations, and on the other side there is a play area for the children. The rest is underground."

34

KIAN

"*A*re you in a hurry? Or can we talk for a few minutes in my old office?" Kian asked Turner as they headed toward the elevators.

"What's on your mind?"

Kian chuckled. "Plenty. But what I want to talk about is what can be done about the San Francisco situation. I can't just ignore it and let the Doomers snatch up more girls."

"I agree. We need to go hunting."

"I like the sound of that," Anandur said.

As they exited the elevator, Andrew remained behind, holding the door open. "If you don't need me, I'd rather head home."

"You can go." Kian clapped his brother-in-law on his back. "Thank you for coming."

"Any time."

As the door slid shut, the four of them continued down the corridor to Kian's old office. The place was probably covered in dust, but Kian wanted to discuss the new information while the details were still fresh in his memory, and he knew Turner wouldn't want to leave his Tesla behind and carpool with them to the village. The guy loved his toy so much that he'd even had it retrofitted to meet the village's safety requirements.

Which hadn't been necessary since the bastard had discovered the location a long time ago, and Bridget, who sometimes rode with him, was a council member and privy to the information.

"I apologize for the dust," Kian said as they entered his office. "I should get Okidu to vacuum here from time to time."

Turner pulled out a chair and cleaned the seat with his hand. "This will do."

Kian followed suit and so did the brothers.

"Can you elaborate on your previous statement? How do you suggest we hunt for Doomers?"

Turner crossed his arms over his chest. "We will have to divert resources from the rescue missions and send Guardians to San Francisco. Remember how they hunted for your civilians in clubs and bars? Now that you have a large force, you can turn the tables on them."

"Hmm, I hadn't thought of that. To run the drug distribution and to lure girls to the island, they must have a large force in the area. If we catch one, we can discover where the rest are living and ambush them."

Turner smiled one of his rare smiles. "Precisely."

"I love it. Going on the offensive and giving them a taste of their own medicine would be immensely satisfying. What I don't like about it, however, is dividing the force and reducing the number of rescues."

Turner shrugged. "The SF mission qualifies as a rescue too. Only this time we would be preventing the abductions instead of freeing those who were already captured."

"True. But by splitting the force we will be weakening our defenses."

Turner arched his brows. "Up until not too long ago you had a total of seven Guardians, and you managed with that."

"I like the feeling of safety the large force provides. It gives me peace of mind."

"Could've fooled me." Anandur snorted. "You're just as stressed now as you were then. It's who you are."

Kian pinned him with a hard stare. "I wasn't aware that you'd gotten a therapist license."

The Guardian shrugged his massive shoulders. "I've known you for a long time. I don't need to be a shrink to get you."

Across the table, Brundar's lips curved in a shadow of a smile.

"Do you want to hunt for Doomers or not?" Ever the pragmatist, Turner ignored their banter.

"I do."

"Then we split the force and do it."

"Eventually, they are going to spread their operation to the Los Angeles area as well," Brundar said. "It's a much bigger market for drugs, and there are more colleges here. They've only gotten three girls so far and they are already attracting attention. They will want to spread out."

This was probably the most Kian had ever heard coming from Brundar's mouth at one time.

"You are right," Turner said. "When the time comes, we will address this problem as well. Right now, we need to focus on the Bay Area. We might be able to capture a big number of Doomers in one fell swoop."

"We don't have enough space in the catacombs," Anandur said. "Perhaps we should build new ones under the village."

Kian shook his head. "I thought about that when the original plans were made and I decided against it. The Doomers will stay in the keep, but I want to move our dead to the village where their loved ones can pay their respects."

Anandur nodded. "An excellent idea. But that still leaves the problem of available space for storing the Doomers in a temperature-controlled environment. The fuckers are troublesome even when almost dead."

"Perhaps you won't need to store them." Turner got up and dusted the back of his pants. "Maybe we can free the Doomers from Navuh's compulsion and bring them over. Now that we know what makes them the way they are, it will be easier to undo."

Kian looked up at him. "And how do you propose to do that?"

Turner lifted his briefcase. "Maybe when Parker grows up and his powers mature he will be able to compel immortals as well as humans."

"Not likely." Kian pushed to his feet. "Even Annani finds it difficult to do."

"You never know."

Anandur clapped Turner on the back. "A fellow optimist. I like it. Imagine Parker freeing all those Doomers from their compulsion. If we get enough of them, they might help us free the island. Who knows, perhaps in the distant future the wolf will dwell with the lamb, and the leopard will lie down with the kid, and the calf with the young lion."

"Quoting scriptures?" Turner asked.

Anandur shrugged. "I heard it somewhere and it got stuck in my memory."

Turner headed for the door. "I was thinking more along the lines of helping the Doomers live as free men on the island. Not coexisting with them. I'm not that optimistic."

It was an interesting thought, and it aligned with Lokan's vision.

Kian was never going to trust a bunch of Doomers with

the clan's safety, but he could see them fighting for the right to live free from Navuh's oppression. Maybe even under Lokan's banner.

35

ELLA

"*E*lla, sweetheart, it's time to get up." Julian sat on the bed and handed her a cup of coffee.

"Can I have five more minutes?" She pulled the comforter all the way under her chin.

It was so damn cold in the mornings, and Julian had left the window wide open.

"Can you close the window? I'm freezing." She shivered under the down blanket.

He frowned. "It's over seventy degrees in here. Are you feeling all right?" He leaned and touched his lips to her forehead. "I think you are running a low fever."

Excitement bubbled up in her tummy. "Maybe I'm transitioning?"

"It's possible."

He was infuriatingly calm in the face of such a monumental event.

"You're not excited?"

"I don't want to get my hopes up. You might have a cold. Any aches or pains? How is your throat?"

"Dry." She reached for the coffee. "Easily fixed."

A few sips later she felt much better. "Maybe you are right, and this is just a cold." She handed him the cup. "Can you get my bathrobe? I need to go to the bathroom, but I don't want to leave the warmth of the blanket."

"Sure."

When Julian came back with the bathrobe, she pulled it under the covers and shimmied into it, then tied the belt securely around her waist before swinging her legs over the side of the bed.

Standing up, though, proved problematic. As soon as Ella pushed off the mattress, her head started spinning and her knees buckled.

Julian was right there to catch her. "Let me carry you to the bathroom."

"I feel dizzy. Is it one of the signs?"

"I don't know. But just to be safe, once you get dressed, I'll take you to the clinic."

"I think I'll need help with that."

"I'm here for you, sweetheart."

He helped her into the bathroom, and after she was done with her morning routine, he carried her back and put her on the bed. "I'll get your clothes."

He brought her a pair of comfy leggings, a T-shirt and a sweatshirt, and then helped her get dressed.

"Maybe we should use the golf cart?" Ella suggested.

"Don't be silly." He swung her into his arms. "I love carrying you."

With a contented sigh, Ella wound her arms around his neck and rested her cheek against his chest. He was so strong, so solid, and he made her feel safe.

In the clinic, they were met by Bridget.

"How are you feeling?" The doctor motioned for Julian to follow her into one of the patient rooms.

"Dizzy and excited," Ella said.

Bridget smiled. "Let's check your vitals."

After that was done, Bridget noted the results on her tablet. "Except for the dizziness, your symptoms are very mild. Perhaps I should run a pregnancy test just to rule that out."

Ella's tongue stuck to the roof of her mouth that had suddenly gotten drier than the sandbox in the playground. "I can't be pregnant."

"Are you on the pill?"

Ella shook her head.

"Are you late?"

"No. I should be getting my period in a day or two."

"That might be another reason. Did you ever experience symptoms like this before the start of your period?"

"Not the dizziness. Sometimes I get sick around that time of the month, and I always have some cramps, but nothing a couple of Motrin's can't take care of."

"Pregnancy is not likely, but I would be remiss not to rule it out first. I'll get the kit."

As Bridget left, Ella let out a sigh. "I hope I'm not pregnant." Seeing the hurt look in Julian's eyes, she reached for his hand. "It's not that I don't want children with you, but I want to transition first."

"Of course." He took her hand and clasped it gently. "I want you to transition first too."

So that was what the look was about. Julian was worried, and frankly she was anxious as well.

"I'm glad your mom is here to take care of me. I like Merlin, but I feel more comfortable with a woman doctor. When is he coming back?"

"Ten days or so. The fertility convention ends this Friday, but since he is already in Europe, Merlin decided to take the opportunity to visit friends and family."

Ella closed her eyes and smiled. "By then I hope to be on

the other side of the transition."

"You will be." He sat on the hospital bed next to her. "You are young and healthy and everything is going to be all right."

"Roni was my age when he transitioned, but Sylvia told me that it wasn't easy for him. Several immortals bit him, but it didn't work until Kian did it."

"The guy was young, but not healthy. He suffered from pneumonia, lost a lot of weight that he couldn't afford to lose, and then it took him many weeks to recuperate."

Her eyes popped wide open. "I hope I don't have anything serious that will prevent my transition."

"You don't have pneumonia."

"Are you sure?"

He put his ear on her chest and listened. "I'm sure."

"You're just taking advantage of the situation to put your cheek on my boobies." She stroked his soft hair.

Chuckling, Julian kissed her nipple through the hospital johnny.

"Stop it." She pulled on his hair. "Your mom might walk in on us."

"I'll hear her." Ignoring the hair pulling, he reached over and kissed her other nipple.

"You are incorrigible."

He lifted his head and grinned. "And you are adorable."

MAGNUS

*W*henever Vivian got that faraway look in her eyes, Magnus knew that she was communicating with Ella. So, when she gasped and her hand flew to her chest, he knew something was up.

He waited as patiently as he could until she was done and her eyes refocused on him. "What happened? Is Ella all right?"

"She is in the clinic." Vivian pushed to her feet and motioned for him to follow. "This morning she woke up with a fever, and when she tried to stand up she got dizzy and collapsed, but Julian caught her before she hit the floor." Vivian hurried into the closet and pulled out a pair of jeans and a T-shirt. "He carried her to the clinic, and Bridget hooked her up to the monitors." She glanced at him. "You should get dressed. We are going."

He nodded and grabbed a pair of slacks off the hanger. "I need to wake Parker up and tell him to take Scarlet out." He shrugged his house robe off and pulled on his pants.

Vivian waved a dismissive hand. "Just let her out in the

back yard. It will take him forever to drag himself out of bed, and by the time he does she is going to pee on the carpet."

He chuckled. "As usual, you are right."

Magnus finished getting dressed, pushed his feet into a pair of loafers, and went to the living room to let the dog out. "Sorry, girl, but we have an emergency, and I can't take you out."

As if understanding what he was telling her, Scarlet lifted a pair of worried eyes to him.

"It's going to be okay." He slid the patio doors open. "Ella is a healthy young woman and she is going to be fine." He wasn't sure whether he was reassuring Scarlet or himself.

Next, he opened Parker's door and poked his head inside. "Parker, buddy, you need to wake up. Ella is in the clinic and your mother and I are going there. Scarlet is in the backyard and you need to let her in once she is done."

For a long moment, it seemed like Parker hadn't heard him, but just as Magnus was about to walk in and shake him awake, the kid sat bolt upright in bed. "What happened to Ella? Is she transitioning? I thought I was dreaming, but then I smelled your cologne, and I never dream about smells."

"We don't know yet. She might have come down with a cold or the flu."

"Can I come too?"

"Sure. But you need to get dressed and take care of Scarlet. You can come later. There is no reason to hurry. Those things take time."

"Okay." Parker rubbed his eyes. "Tell her that I'm on my way."

"I will."

As he walked back into the living room, Magnus was surprised that Vivian wasn't waiting for him by the door. She'd seemed in such a rush to get to Ella that he doubted she'd stopped to apply makeup.

But who knew? Women were strange creatures.

Magnus headed back to the bedroom to check for her, but she wasn't there. She wasn't in the bathroom either. Could she be still fussing with clothes?

He found her in the closet, sprawled on the floor.

"Viv!" He rushed to her side and lifted her wrist to check for a pulse.

When he found it, Magnus released a relieved breath. Vivian wasn't the fainting type, but the news must have been more of a shock to her than he'd realized.

He brushed a strand of hair away from her face. "Viv, sweetheart, can you hear me?" She might have hit her head and he'd read somewhere that it wasn't advisable to move a human until the extent of her or his injuries was ascertained.

Her eyes fluttered open and she gasped. "Oh my God. What happened?" She tried to sit up.

"Don't move. You might have hit your head."

She reached with her hand to check. "I don't think so. Did I faint?"

"It seems so. I found you on the floor."

"Help me up?"

Supporting her back, he lifted her gently to a sitting position. "How are you feeling? Are you dizzy?"

"Yes, very." Her eyes rolled back in her head and she slumped in his hold.

This wasn't shock. Could it be that Vivian was transitioning as well?

Scooping her in his arms, Magnus ran out and sprinted all the way to the clinic.

"Incoming patient!" he yelled as he entered.

Bridget rushed out of her office, or rather Merlin's, but Merlin wasn't there and she was filling in for him.

"What's wrong with Vivian?"

He was the wrong person to ask. "She fainted after

talking with Ella. I woke her up, but when she tried to sit up, she blacked out again."

"Let's see what's going on. Follow me." She strode down the hallway and opened a door. "Put her on the bed."

"Magnus?" Ella called from the adjacent patient room. "What's going on?"

"Your mom fainted. Bridget is checking her vitals."

"Oh my God! I'm coming."

"Don't!" Bridget commanded. "You have to wait for Julian to come back and unhook you from the monitors."

On the gurney, Vivian groaned. "What's happening to me?"

Bridget patted her arm. "You might be transitioning, my dear."

37

SYSSI

*S*yssi was heading out the door when her phone buzzed in her purse.

That was early for a call. She pulled it out and smiled as she saw Kian's handsome face on the screen. "You didn't forget to tell me that you loved me this morning."

"Can't I say it again?"

"Sure you can."

"I love you, and I have exciting news. Ella and Vivian are in the clinic, and Bridget believes that they are transitioning."

Syssi leaned against the doorjamb. "Both at the same time? What a wonderful coincidence."

"Not really. Well, it is wonderful, but since they both started working on it at the same time, it makes sense for them to enter the transformation at the same time too."

"Still, there is eighteen years of difference between them. Are they doing okay?"

"Ella has a slight fever and gets dizzy whenever she tries to get up, and Vivian blacked out twice, but she is awake now."

"It's so strange how each person reacts differently."

"Indeed. Have a great day at work, and just so I'm sure I didn't forget, I love you."

She chuckled. "I love you too. Don't work too hard."

"I'll try."

Syssi knew he wouldn't. Her man was a workaholic, or to put it in nicer terms, a leader fully dedicated to his people and the improvement of humanity at large. She just wished he could learn to delegate more and find capable help.

So far, his efforts on that front had been unsuccessful. She wasn't sure, though, whether the people he'd hired were not up to the task, or maybe Kian didn't know how to work with others. Probably a little of both.

Once Kian became a father, though, he would have to cut back. If he didn't, she was going to bring the baby into his office and force him to spend time with his child.

First, though, she had to find out whether there was a child.

She'd planned on stopping by Bridget's and collecting a pregnancy test, but the clinic was now buzzing with activity, and Syssi didn't want anyone aside from Bridget to know that she was taking the test.

The best thing would be to buy a kit at the pharmacy, but since she was carpooling to and from work with Amanda, that was a problem. She could call an Uber at lunchtime, but that seemed silly. After all, she had a car, and she should take it out for a ride once in a while.

Pulling out her phone, she texted Amanda. *I'm taking my own car today. I plan on doing some shopping after work.*

A moment later her phone pinged with a return text. *We can go shopping together. I can use a few new outfits.*

Syssi rolled her eyes. She'd forgotten that shopping was a trigger word for Amanda. But she knew how to wiggle out of it.

Great. Macy's is running a sale. We can stock up on cheap stuff. Smirking, she waited for the reply.

Ugh, I'm not setting a foot in that schmattes store. Have fun shopping alone.

Syssi felt a pang of guilt but quickly got over it. Not everything she wore had to come from high-end boutiques. And she really needed some comfortable everyday things. She hadn't planned on doing it today, but now she had no choice because Amanda was going to ask her what she'd bought.

38

CAROL

Carol was on her way to visit Ella and Vivian in the clinic, when her feet decided on a detour and led her to Kian's office.

She knocked on the door, and a moment later heard the gruff response.

"Come in."

Opening the way, she leaned in. "Do you have a couple of minutes?"

He grimaced. "Is it about going to the island?"

"Yes, but without Lokan. I have an interesting new idea."

"For that, I'll make time." He pushed his yellow pad aside.

Carol hadn't discussed the timing with Lokan, but her feet had followed her gut, and her gut said that it was time to tell Kian.

Pulling out a chair, she sat down and wondered where to start. She hadn't rehearsed the delivery of her plan, which was an amateurish move, but it was too late for that.

"Lokan has dirt on Gorchenco, and we can use that to make him get me onto the island."

"How?"

"He is a mobster and a returning client, so he won't get the careful scrutiny other visitors to the island get. He can bring me along as his plaything. The same excuse Lokan would have used. Then we pretend to have a fight, and he leaves me there."

Kian shook his head. "They'll put you to work in the brothel, which was your original idea, but that one is obsolete at this point, and there is no way for you to get from the brothel into the harem."

"They won't put me in the brothel if I have a medical condition that makes me undesirable. Lokan says that they have doctors who check the newcomers, but I'm sure Bridget can help me come up with a convincing disability."

Leaning back in his chair, Kian crossed his arms over his chest. "Let's assume that it works and that you are sent to housekeeping instead. How are you going to get into the harem?"

She shrugged. "I'll find a way to get assigned there. Or, if you allow Lokan to make some phone calls, supervised of course, he can pull strings from here and get me in."

That seemed to pique Kian's interest. "That's a possibility I didn't think of. And I assume that you can dream-share with him regardless of the location?"

"That's correct. He will have to switch to sleeping during the day, though. I doubt I would be allowed daytime naps, and there is a twelve-hour time difference to account for."

"How are we going to get you out?"

"I will fake my death. I hope Bridget can help me with that as well. When they take me out in a casket, Gorchenco will come back for me, claiming to have changed his mind. When they tell him that I'm dead, he will demand to take my body for burial back home. I don't see why they would refuse him. He is not only a good client but also their main arms supplier. They want to keep him happy."

Kian nodded. "I'm impressed. This could actually work, provided that Bridget can come up with a way for you to have a convincing disability and fake your own death. Naturally, the timing of your supposed death and Gorchenco's return to the island will have to be coordinated ahead of time."

Staring at Kian, Carol could hardly believe that he was considering her plan, especially since she'd come up with half of it on the spot. Having Gorchenco coming back for her and collecting her body was a spur of the moment idea.

"For it to work, we need to act fast. Lokan is due for his mandatory in-person reporting in twenty days. When he fails to show up and doesn't answer his phone, Navuh is going to assume that he either defected or is dead. In either case, he won't be able to make the necessary phone calls to his people."

Kian didn't look happy. "I don't like doing things under pressure. This is a complicated mission, and I don't want to rush into it without careful planning."

"It is what it is. The way I see it, we have ten days at most to get me to the island. For it to be believable, Gorchenco and I will have to spend a few days together, acting out the sugar daddy and young gold-digger charade. Then I need time to get into the harem, find out who Navuh is hiding there, befriend her so she opens up to me, and transmit the information via dream-sharing with Lokan. The more time I have, the better. If anything goes wrong, Lokan's ability to make phone calls and pull some strings might prove invaluable."

She didn't add that if the shit hit the fan, Lokan could come to get her. If and when that happened, Kian would realize it himself.

Kian nodded. "I'll run it by Turner and see what he thinks. The key is Gorchenco and whether the dirt Lokan has on him will be enough to convince him to cooperate with us to such an extent."

Carol smirked. "I think he will be willing to do almost anything."

"Oh, yeah? Do you know what Lokan has on him?"

"I don't have all the details. You should get the information from him directly."

He arched a brow, but thankfully didn't press her to reveal more. She'd promised Lokan not to tell Kian so he could use it to get something in exchange.

"I'm going to do it later today, and I'll bring Andrew along. I don't trust anything that comes out of Lokan's mouth unless I can verify it."

The insult to her mate hurt, even though Kian's opinion of Lokan was not entirely wrong.

"He didn't lie to you yet. Am I right? The island was where he told you it was."

"I'm still not sure about that. All I have is a satellite photo showing several thatched roofs. Turner is having someone verify it on the ground, or rather ocean."

"When will you have proof?"

"In a day or two."

Carol groaned. "Time is running out."

39

LOKAN

When Kian entered Lokan's cell with his bodyguards and Andrew, Lokan knew he was in for another interrogation.

Carol should get back from visiting Ella and Vivian soon, and Lokan was conflicted whether he wanted her to be there during the questioning or not. On the one hand, Kian was more reserved around her, but on the other hand, when she was there, Lokan had to put on a polite act as well.

Maybe it was better talking to Kian man to man without bothering to hide their inner aggression or their dislike of each other.

Lokan had a healthy respect for his cousin, but that didn't mean he liked the guy or would have enjoyed spending time with him if their circumstances were different. He had little patience for the holier-than-thou types, the do-gooders, the martyrs. They were all sanctimonious pricks who thought they were better than everyone else.

"To what do I owe the pleasure of your visit?" he asked, not bothering to hide the sarcasm from his expression or his tone.

Kian sat on one of the armchairs and motioned for the lie detector to take the other. The guy was about to join the bodyguards at the dining table, and he cast an apologetic glance at them before doing as Kian commanded.

"Carol came to see me this morning and reminded me of the dirt you have on Gorchenco. You promised to share it with me."

So, going to visit her transitioning friend had been an excuse to see Kian without telling him. They'd agreed that Lokan would be the one outlining the plan for Kian. What had prompted her to jump the gun?

Perhaps Carol had acted on impulse. She was eager to tell Kian her plan, and the truth was that time was running out.

"I assume Carol told you her idea of using the Russian to get her to the island?"

"She did, and I have to admit that it's not a bad one. I'll discuss it with Turner and see how we can tweak it."

Lokan's gut twisted. He hadn't expected Kian to agree so readily, and now that it seemed likely that Carol was going, he wanted to stop her. "Faking her own death might be impossible, and I doubt she can fake a disability that would disqualify her from working in the brothel. Unless these two conditions are met, she can't go."

Kian nodded. "She is going to talk to our clan doctor. We will know soon enough if either can be done."

"There is another problem. How is she going to get into the harem without my help?"

Kian raised a brow. "I thought you two had discussed it. She said you can call the person in charge of assigning people to the harem and ask him for a favor."

"That's news to me. Originally, I planned on doing it in person. I didn't consider a phone call."

Kian looked surprised. "I guess Carol filled in the blanks on her own. But can you do it over the phone?"

"What reason could I possibly give the guy without arousing suspicion?"

"You're doing a favor for Gorchenco. After all, you worked with him in the past and he is an important client as well as the Brotherhood's arms supplier. You want to keep him happy and feel that he owes you a favor. The story can be that he felt guilty about abandoning his lover on the island and asked you to find her a cushy job where she wasn't going to be bothered by other men."

"Not bad. This could work. How are we going to get her out, though?"

Kian shook his head. "I thought you were the mastermind behind this plan, but I see it was indeed Carol. Her idea was to have Gorchenco come back for her the same day she fakes her death. When he asks for her and is told that she died, he demands to take her body back home for a proper burial."

The woman was brilliant. How come he hadn't thought of that? Maybe because subconsciously he didn't want her to go.

"So, it all depends on the doctor now."

Kian nodded. "And on what you have on Gorchenco. With the amount of cooperation we expect to get from him, the dirt you have on him needs to be the size of a mountain."

Lokan chuckled. "Almost. But as we've discussed, I expect something in return for this information."

"Isn't the safety of your mate enough?"

Lokan pinned Kian with a level stare. "The safest thing for my mate is not to go on this mission, and if unavoidable, to have me accompany her. Gorchenco is an awkward work-around. I understand why you don't trust me, but you are endangering Carol by choosing a roundabout route."

Kian grimaced. "I know that. But there is no way I'm letting you go."

"Why? I don't know any more now than I knew before. I

don't know where you're hiding. You are not risking anything or anyone other than Carol, and we are both agreed that having me go with her is much safer than using Gorchenco."

"You know our faces, and that's plenty."

There was no reasoning with the guy, and the truth was that there was something to his claim. Lokan had seen the goddess. He knew what she looked like. But then Navuh had met her in person. It had been thousands of years ago, but the goddess probably still looked the same now as she did then.

"You're making a mistake, but since I can't convince you, here is what I want in exchange for the information on Gorchenco. I understand that you have a gym and a swimming pool down here. I want to be allowed to use them and any other recreational facilities you have here, with Guardian supervision of course."

Kian nodded. "I can do that. But I'll leave it up to Arwel which recreational facilities he feels comfortable taking you to."

It wasn't much, but that was all he could ask for. Getting out of the fucking cell would be a big improvement for sure. Besides, he might get the opportunity to steal a tool to somehow open the cuffs.

"That's acceptable."

"So what do you have on the Russian that's so big?"

"A nuclear submarine. He stole one, and if Putin ever finds out, Gorchenco is a dead man despite how chummy those two are."

The redhead Guardian whistled. "That's huge."

"How did he steal a submarine?" Kian asked. "And why?"

"I don't have the details, but it was done in cahoots with the crew. A fake accident of some sort. And the why is quite obvious. He wants to sell it for a shitload of money. That's how I know about it. Unfortunately, the Brotherhood is strapped for cash at the moment, and we couldn't afford it. It's a great weapon to have. I'm sure many would want to lay their hands on it, but only a handful can afford it. Also, there is the problem of operating it. Whoever buys it will have to hire the Russian crew as well."

"Do you know where it is?"

Lokan smirked. "I do. He took me to see it using a smaller submarine."

"What if he's moved it since?"

"Not likely. There aren't many places you can hide a submarine and also bring buyers to inspect it."

"What if he's sold it?"

"Then we are screwed, but I doubt that he did. The asking price is one hundred thirty billion dollars."

Kian's eyes widened. "Billion? Not million?"

"Billion. If the Iranians and Saudis turn him down, as a last resort he might offer it to the Chinese, but he is reluctant to approach them. They will reverse engineer it and build a fleet of them, and that's dangerous."

Kian snorted. "As if selling the sub to the Iranians or Saudis is not. Besides, the Chinese already have nuclear submarines."

"Not like this one."

40

SYSSI

*S*yssi's plan to get the pregnancy tests on her way back home wasn't going to work. By lunchtime, she could wait no longer. Surviving five more hours seemed impossible.

Dropping her phone in her purse, she walked into Amanda's office. "I'm going to Macy's. I should be back in an hour or so."

Amanda waved a dismissive hand. "Take as long as you want. We had two cancelations for today. Although I don't understand the rush. It's not like you're going to find anything exciting at freaking Macy's."

"I'm not looking for anything fancy. I need a few T-shirts and leggings for hanging around the house, but if I wait for after work, all the good stuff is going to get snatched up. It's a huge sale. Half off on all previously discounted items."

Mentioning the sale served two purposes. For starters, it guaranteed that Amanda would not offer to join her, and secondly, it would explain the anxious scent Syssi was no doubt emitting. Her sister-in-law would assume that it was about those items about to get snatched up by other shoppers.

Amanda's smile covered a thinly veiled disgust. "Have fun."

"I will."

Not likely.

Syssi was so nervous that she almost bumped into another car while pulling out. Casting the driver an apologetic glance, she left the university's parking lot at the most reasonable speed she could muster.

There was a pharmacy less than a five-minute drive away, but she opted to stop at the one near the mall. Fewer chances of anyone she knew seeing her checking out the contraband.

Armed with ten kits and two magazines to cover the stash, she stood in line and nervously waited her turn.

Scanning the items, the cashier smiled at her with an empathetic expression on her kind face. "Good luck."

"Thank you."

"Would you like a bag for your items?"

"Yes, please."

In her car, Syssi took out one of the kits and put it in her purse. Doing the test in Macy's ladies room was gross, but she just couldn't wait a moment longer.

The ten minutes it had taken her to drive to the mall, park the car, and walk into the department store's restrooms were the longest she'd ever experienced.

Thankfully, the family room was vacant, and she snuck into it, quickly closing the door behind her before anyone noticed that she didn't have a child with her.

Her hands shook as she tore the wrapping off, and as she sat on the toilet, nothing happened. She was too nervous to pee.

Taking a deep breath, Syssi imagined sitting on a sandy

beach and watching the incoming tide lapping gently at the shore.

A few moments later she finally managed to pee on the stick, then held it in front of her and waited. This was supposed to be the best kit on the market, with the most accurate and fastest results. The only negatives she'd read were women complaining about false positives, but the vast majority of reviewers were happy with its accuracy and speed.

When the faint pink line appeared next to the solid pink marker, Syssi got lightheaded, praying she wasn't one of the few who'd gotten a false positive.

Just to make sure, she pulled out another stick and forced a few more drops of urine out, then she waited again.

Another faint pink line appeared.

Oh, my God. I'm pregnant.

41

KIAN

"I'm calling Turner," Kian said as he and the brothers boarded the Lexus. "He's not going to believe it. In fact, I won't believe it until I have proof, and I mean photos of the fucking submarine."

"Why would he invent a story like that?" Anandur asked. "He knows we are going to verify it."

"That's why I need to call Turner. He can send someone to do it for us." He dialed the number.

"What's up, Kian?"

"A nuclear submarine."

"That would be down, not up."

Kian chuckled. "When you're right you're right. Anyway, that's the dirt Lokan has on Gorchenco. The guy stole a nuclear sub and is trying to sell it for the most impressive amount of one hundred and thirty billion dollars. I wondered why he would risk Putin's wrath, but for that amount he can buy a country. Isn't Venezuela for sale?"

"It's bankrupt, but I don't think a hundred and thirty billion would be enough to bail it."

"Joking aside, I need that verified. Lokan claims that

Gorchenco approached him about it, but it was too pricey for the Brotherhood, so he had to turn the offer down."

"What makes him think that the sub is still where he saw it last? Gorchenco might have moved it or sold it."

"I said the same thing, but Lokan is betting that it's still there, and he gave me the location. I need you to arrange for someone to take pictures of it, or better yet make a video, preferably showing an identifiable location marker. Naturally, it's submerged."

"How deep?"

"Lokan said that he was taken to see it in a smaller sub, so it must be too deep for divers. Can you get your hands on a private sub?"

"I know someone who has one. It's the newest toy of the super-rich. But it's not a quick in and out. It will take time to transport it to the location."

"That's a problem because we are running out of time."

"Time for what?"

"Carol came up with a plan that might actually work if Bridget finds a way for her to fake her own death. Her idea is for Gorchenco to take her to the island as his escort. After a day or two, they stage a fight, and he leaves her there. She fakes a disability that makes her unattractive for the brothel. Lokan makes a phone call to the guy in charge of supplying servants to the harem, asking him to get her assigned there. His excuse is that Gorchenco asked him to find her a job where she won't be hit on by other guys. Once in the harem, she investigates and communicates her findings with Lokan via dream-sharing. With that done, she fakes her own death, and when they take her out in a casket, Gorchenco comes back to collect her. When he is told that she is dead, he demands to take her body back home for burial."

"Carol came up with this on her own?"

"Surprising, I know. But since Lokan was missing half of the details, it couldn't have been him. It's all hers."

"Impressive, but it needs work."

"And it depends on us verifying that Gorchenco has the submarine, obtaining proof of it, finding a way to get in touch with him, and then getting him to cooperate."

"You mentioned a time constraint. How long do we have?"

"Lokan is due for his mandatory conference with Navuh in twenty days. After that, he won't be able to make calls and ask for things because he will be presumed dead, or a defector. Incorporating even a modest margin for error, that doesn't leave us much time at all."

"What else is new? I'll start working on it tonight. In a day or two, I should know if it's at all feasible. I'll also run it by Bridget and see if she has any ideas about the fake disability and death. There is no point in wasting time and resources on this until we know that it is all doable."

"Regardless of Carol's plan, we need proof of the submarine's existence to get Gorchenco off Ella's back."

"How can we prove that Gorchenco was the one who stole it? Even if we have physical proof of it, he can claim that he is not involved and that someone else did it."

"Good point. Maybe we can track the smaller submarine to him. You said that it's a rich boys' toy. Gorchenco either bought or borrowed it or maybe even rented it. There will be a record of that and where he took it. I think that, together with physical proof of the big sub, will be enough to tie him to its theft. It's not like we need to prove it in a court of law. Plausible suspicion will do."

"I'll get on it." Turner chuckled. "I can't believe the balls on that guy. And I also can't believe that I'm going to have to cooperate with the man who violated my daughter-in-law. I should kill him once this is done. Ella's gut feeling to spare his life was probably about him helping us infiltrate the island, and there is no need for him to keep on breathing after that."

"Unless that's not it at all. My wife keeps telling me that premonitions are tricky and can't be trusted because you can never know the when and where, and sometimes not even the what."

"Unfortunately, she is right. I'll go with my own gut feeling. If after this is done I still want to end Gorchenco, I will."

SYSSI

*T*oo excited to go back to work, nervous, elated, and a thousand other emotions coursing through her, Syssi called Amanda.

"How are things in the lab?"

"It's a slow day. Why? Are you finding good deals?"

Amanda must have detected the excitement in her voice.

"I'm done, but I want to go home and try on the stuff I bought." Hopefully, her sister-in-law would assume that this was what she was excited about. "Besides, I'm not in the mood to get back to the lab. If that's okay with you, I would like to take the afternoon off."

"You don't have to ask." Amanda chuckled. "Your hubby finances my lab. So, it's not like I'm your boss. It's more like the other way around."

"The clan finances your research, not Kian, and last I checked I wasn't a council member."

"Semantics. Anyway, enjoy your afternoon off."

"Thanks."

Syssi felt bad about lying to Amanda, but the first one to hear the news had to be Kian.

Except, what if the tests were false positives?

The prudent thing to do before running to Kian with the news would have been having Bridget do a proper test, but then he would not have been the first one to know.

As it was, Syssi felt guilty about not sharing her suspicions with him and not having him present when she did the test. It had been such a struggle between wanting to share everything with her mate and sparing him unnecessary anguish.

Kian was always so stressed out, and Syssi didn't want to be the source of more pressure. She was supposed to be the island of calm where he escaped the storm.

When she got home, Okidu rushed out of his room and bowed. "Good afternoon, mistress." He reached for her shopping bags. "You are home early today."

"Yes. I went shopping." She'd grabbed a few items without even trying them on, just so her shopping excuse wouldn't be a complete lie.

"Splendid. Let me put those away in the closet."

"Thank you."

Luckily, Okidu's programming wasn't sensitive enough to pick up on her excited mood.

A moment later he returned and bowed again. "May I serve you an early dinner, mistress?"

As if she could eat anything. "No, thank you. I'll wait for Kian to get home."

"Very well. I shall be back in time to serve it."

"Thanks."

Okidu and Onidu were in charge of cleaning the office building during the night and the underground complex during the day, which meant that Okidu was gone every day between two in the afternoon and six in the evening, and then again after eight.

Syssi appreciated the privacy it afforded her and Kian.

Even though Okidu wasn't really a person, he acted like one, and she couldn't help but be more reserved with him around.

In the bathroom, she put her purse on the vanity and took out the box with the two positive tests she'd wrapped in tissue paper. Pulling a fresh washcloth out of the closet, she spread it over the counter and put the two tests on top.

Perhaps she wouldn't say anything as Kian walked in this evening and just wait for him to use the bathroom.

She could fill up the jacuzzi with bubbles and wait for him there with a bottle of champagne and two glasses. Surely, a sip or two wouldn't harm the baby, but just to be safe, she pulled out her phone and did a quick internet search confirming that it was okay.

Watching the powerful water stream fill up the big tub reminded her of her and Kian's first time together. She'd used the jacuzzi in his penthouse, and when she'd gotten out, she'd found him waiting for her on the bed.

Remembering the Red Riding Hood story they had enacted, Syssi smiled. She'd been so scared and so excited at the same time.

That monumental night had been the beginning of them as a couple.

The difference was that this time she would be waiting for Kian. The similarity was that it would also be a prelude to a new beginning. In nine months, they would no longer be a couple. They would be a family.

It was a little scary.

Feeling guilty, Syssi put her hands on her belly and looked down. "Mommy is a little scared, but she wants you very much, and so does Daddy."

It was silly talking to what was at this point just a fertilized egg. But perhaps the soul of their unborn child was already hovering nearby, getting to know his or her parents, and it was important to let her know that she was wanted.

She.

Her baby was a girl.

The certainty of it settled over Syssi like a comfortable blanket. They were having a little girl and her spirit was already there.

Happy tears misting her eyes, Syssi spread her arms and hugged the air in front of her. So yeah, it was silly, but there was no one there to see her making a fool of herself.

"What's your name, little one?" she whispered.

Allegra. The name just popped into her mind.

"Allegra. I like it."

Shaking her head, Syssi kicked off her shoes.

She was imagining things. This didn't feel like one of her premonitions, and communicating with spirits was Nathalie's gift, not hers.

43

KIAN

*K*ian's greatest joy at the end of his workday was to walk through his front door and have Syssi rush up to meet him, wind her arms around his neck, and kiss him until they both ran out of breath.

This time, however, he was greeted by a lot of quiet. Did she stay late at work?

If she had, she would have called him.

Suddenly worried, he dropped his stuff on the kitchen counter and strode down the hallway to their bedroom.

The hum of jacuzzi jets brought a smile to his face. He remembered another time when his worry had been assuaged by that sound.

When he had first brought Syssi to his place, he'd been called away by some emergency in the office that he couldn't remember the details of, and when he had come back, he'd thought Syssi had left. Searching for her, he had been ready to turn the building upside down to find her. Then he'd heard the jacuzzi and figured out her whereabouts.

What had followed was forever etched in his mind. Every detail of their first time together was a cherished memory.

Should he reenact it? Wait naked in bed for Syssi to come out and then pounce on her like he had done that first time?

Or should he walk in and join her in the tub?

It was a hard decision, but in the end the tub won. He had so many exciting things to tell her, and the sex could wait for later.

Walking into the master bathroom, his eyes were immediately drawn to Syssi's breasts peeking out from the frothy bubbles.

"Now that's a sight for sore eyes." He took his clothes off in under two seconds, dumped them on the floor, and slid behind Syssi in the tub.

She turned to look at him over her shoulder. "Didn't you notice anything as you walked in?"

"Yes, I did." He cupped her breasts. "Two beautiful peaks bobbing in the water and waiting for my hands."

When Syssi seemed disappointed with his answer, Kian looked around and noticed the bottle of champagne and two glasses. Had he forgotten an anniversary?

Not the wedding one, that he remembered, but maybe the anniversary of their first time? It had been around this time of year, but he didn't remember the exact date. Or perhaps it was the anniversary of his proposal?

"The champagne means that we are celebrating something, but I need a hint as to what it is." He kissed her shoulder. "Not that I need a special occasion for that. Every day with you is a celebration, but am I forgetting an anniversary or something?"

She chuckled. "You didn't forget anything, but I'll give you a hint. Look at the vanity counter next to my sink."

Straightening up, he glanced at the counter, but all he saw was a washcloth with two white plastic sticks on top of it. He couldn't begin to guess what they were for.

"I need another hint."

Syssi let out an exasperated sigh. "You're spoiling my surprise." She pushed away from him and swung a leg over the tub.

"Where are you going?"

"Since you are clueless, I have to show you."

She padded to the vanity, took the two sticks and came back, but didn't enter the tub. Instead, she sat on the lip and lifted the two sticks, showing him the small windows that he hadn't noticed before.

"Do you see the solid pink lines?"

"Obviously."

"Do you see the faint pink lines next to them?"

"Yes."

"That's a positive result on both tests."

Pregnancy tests, that's what the sticks were. He was indeed clueless. He hadn't known what those looked like, but it was pretty self-explanatory. He should've guessed.

Wait, what?

"You are pregnant?"

Syssi nodded.

He stared at her in stunned shock, but just for a brief moment. As a grin spread over his face, he lifted her off the edge of the tub and crushed her against his chest, remembering too late that he shouldn't squash her.

"Thank the merciful Fates," he whispered against her neck. "We are going to have a baby."

Syssi lifted her head and smiled. "A girl. We are having a girl, and her name is Allegra."

Worry clouding his happiness, Kian frowned. "Did you have a premonition?"

Syssi hadn't had one in a long while, and he was very glad that she hadn't. The visions took a lot out of her, and he didn't like the way they drained her. He especially didn't want it to happen while she was carrying a child and couldn't afford the loss of energy.

"It wasn't a vision or even a premonition. Not the way I usually experience them, anyway. I just know that we are expecting a girl and that her name is Allegra."

There was nothing that could make him happier than having a little girl who looked like Syssi, and Allegra was a good name. It meant joyful.

"Are you happy?" Syssi asked.

"Are you kidding me? I'm ecstatic."

"So you are not disappointed that we are not having a boy?"

"No way. I don't want another version of me. I want another one of you."

"What if she looks like you and has your personality?"

He grimaced. "Then we are in for a lot of hard work."

Lifting up, Syssi kissed him gently. "You are too hard on yourself, my love. I couldn't be more happy or proud if our daughter turns out like you. She'll be smart, confident, assertive, loving, compassionate, and a great leader. Not to mention gorgeous."

"You forgot grumpy, demanding, uncompromising, and a general pain in the ass."

"As long as she gets all of the wonderful qualities that I mentioned before, I'm okay with that."

44

CAROL

*a*s Carol pushed a cart loaded with the dinner she'd prepared, she hoped the Beef Stroganoff would be the magic pill to mollify Lokan.

She'd jumped the gun by going to Kian without telling him, and then she'd somehow come up with the missing details on the spot, turning her idea from barely possible to doable. It had been almost eerie how the solutions had come to her as if someone had put them there.

That part he shouldn't be mad about, but men were strange creatures, very prideful, especially when it came to areas they were supposed to be experts on. Lokan's male ego might suffer a blow because a woman with no background in strategic planning had come up with solutions he hadn't thought of.

Hence, Beef Stroganoff to the rescue. From everything she'd made for him so far, this was his favorite dish.

Arwel rubbed his belly as she stopped the cart next to his cell. "I was afraid of getting fat on all that fabulous food you are feeding me, but I was saved."

Carol frowned. "What do you mean?"

Had Kian decided to end her time in the keep? He couldn't do that. Until she left for the island, Carol wanted to spend as much time as possible with Lokan. Even an angry Lokan was better than none.

"Your guy gave Kian useful information on Gorchenco, and in exchange, he asked for free access to the gym and the pool and the other recreational facilities we have here. Once Kian verifies the information, and provided that it is true, Lokan is going to be free to roam the underground. And since I have to go with him, I guess I will be hitting the exercise equipment as well."

That was a surprising development. "How are you going to ensure that he doesn't run away?"

Arwel shrugged. "Easy, I'll reprogram his cuffs the way I did for the catacombs visit. Besides, he is not going anywhere without me or one of the other Guardians. He doesn't have access to the elevators."

Leaning against the wall, Carol crossed her arms over her chest. "So you want to tell me that he could have been semi-free all this time and got caged in a cell for no reason?"

"There was a reason. A psychological one. Lokan needed to internalize that he was a prisoner and at our mercy. Turner knows what he's doing. His method is more effective than torture."

It seemed so.

She needed to have a talk with Turner. Heck, she needed to apprentice with the guy and learn as much as she could from him. Unfortunately, there was no way he would take her on. He was so damn secretive that it bordered on paranoid.

"How is Lokan's mood? Is he happy about Kian's concession?"

"I don't know. He's been sitting on the couch and sipping whiskey ever since Kian left."

That didn't sound good, but she'd dawdled long enough and the beef was getting cold. "Here's your dinner." She removed a container from the top of her cart. "Can you open the door for me?"

Instead of punching the numbers on the keypad, Arwel used his phone for a change. "I'm in a hurry to dig into this." He lifted the container and sniffed it.

"Thanks."

She rolled her cart the few feet separating the two cells and waited until the door swung all the way before pushing it inside the room.

Lokan was sitting on the couch with a bottle of whiskey in his hand, exactly the way Arwel had described.

She plastered a big smile on her face. "I made your favorite dish, Beef Stroganoff."

He looked up but didn't smile. "I wish you wouldn't waste your time on elaborate meals. I was waiting for you."

She ignored his comment and started setting up the table. "I heard the good news from Arwel. I just wish it had happened before we dragged the treadmill and the punching bag in here. Now that you can use the gym, we can take them out. The bedroom is too cramped."

With a sigh, Lokan pushed to his feet and sauntered over to the table. "Come here." He reached for her arm and pulled her against his chest. "Kiss me."

Her anxiety melting away, she happily obliged, giving him a heartfelt kiss that left him breathless. His mouth tasted of whiskey, but although she didn't like drinking the stuff, she loved the taste of it on his tongue.

"That's better." He cupped her ass, lifted her up, and started for the bedroom.

Makeup sex? Was this what he had in mind?

Not a good idea. They needed to talk first. Besides, she hadn't slaved in the kitchen only to have him eat it cold.

"Put me down, Lokan. I'm hungry."

"So am I." He kept walking.

"I meant for food." She pushed on his chest. "Come on. We can have sex later."

Reluctantly, he let her down.

As they sat at the table, Carol loaded both of their plates, arranging them so they looked appetizing and fancy despite being made of paper.

"You should have asked Kian to lift his ban on proper plates and utensils. I'm tired of serving gourmet meals on picnic plates."

He grimaced. "Soon you're not going to be serving meals at all. You are going to be hanging on the arm of a rich Russian mafioso."

"I'm sorry about going to Kian without discussing it with you first. I was on my way to the clinic, but my feet, or rather my subconscious, had other ideas. And once I started talking, the final details just poured out of me. I cooked up the rest of the plan on the spot." She rolled her eyes. "Believe me when I say that I was more surprised at myself than Kian was. I'm usually not such a quick thinker."

Lokan cut a piece of beef, lifted it, then put the fork down without eating it. "You've been thinking about this day and night for almost a week. Your subconscious processed all the information you were feeding it and then completed the work for you." He lifted the beef and put it in his mouth.

She nodded. "The total immersion method."

He lifted a brow.

"Supposedly, the best way to learn a new skill is total immersion. Which means 'going at it until you get it' sort of thing. Not that I've done it before, I lack the tenacity, but I've heard others talk about it."

Chuckling, Lokan nearly spat out the contents of his mouth. He chewed for a moment longer, swallowed, and then wiped his mouth with a napkin. "Are you kidding? You are one of the most tenacious people I know. Once you decided that you wanted to go to the island, you kept attacking it from all angles until you found a solution. And before that, you withstood torture and didn't reveal the clan's location. If that's not tenacity, I don't know what is."

"That's stubbornness."

"One and the same. Not that I'm happy about it. I don't want you to go."

"Because you are afraid for me?"

"That too. I don't want to be apart from you. Doesn't it bother you that you will not see me for weeks?"

Talk about drama.

"It's only going to be a few days or a week at the most. And considering what's at stake, I'm willing to sacrifice a lot more than my time with you. We have eternity in front of us. I think we can survive one week apart."

45

LOKAN

"*L*ogically, I agree with you. But my instincts don't. If we went in together, I could have protected you. But stuck here, I'm helpless."

Carol put her fork down. "I think we have a solid plan, and if you think about it, it's better than your original one. Have you ever brought a female to the island before?"

"I have not."

"So bringing me with you would have been out of character. Gorchenco, on the other hand, is a human who has lost his young wife recently and could be emotionally distraught. Bringing along a pretty plaything would not look suspicious. In fact, the entire scenario plays out perfectly because no one on the island knows Gorchenco well enough to expect or not expect him to behave in a certain way, and he is immune to thralling. Also, he is not disposable because the Brotherhood needs him."

Regrettably, Carol's assessment was correct. Her plan was better than his.

"Imagine how much smoother everything could have run if I were there too. You would have been much safer."

"Or not. Seeing me with Gorchenco would have had you foaming at the mouth. Immortals are very possessive of their mates."

He shrugged. "So everyone would have assumed that I have the hots for you, and that I'm angry because I can't take you away from the Russian since the Brotherhood needs him and can't afford to lose him as a supplier. You're a beautiful, seductive woman. It wouldn't have been much of a stretch."

Carol opened her mouth, no doubt to come out with a retort, but then shook her head. "Yeah, I would have felt better knowing that you were around to bail me out if needed. But it's not happening, and there is no point in dwelling on what-ifs."

"I think we should keep the pressure on Kian. Maybe he will change his mind. Besides, you still need to talk to the doctor, and Kian needs to talk to Gorchenco."

"Do you know how to get a hold of him?"

"I have his contact information on my phone, but your people took it away from me. If anyone tried to tamper with it, which I'm sure they did, it was wiped clean."

Carol smirked. "There are ways to retrieve that information even when it's erased. We have excellent hackers on staff."

"Let them try. We might be technologically backward compared to you, but we know where to buy the best services."

Carol frowned. "The plan also hinges on you calling your guy and asking him to arrange a job for me in the harem. How are you going to do that if you don't have the numbers memorized?"

"Kian will have to send someone to get my backup phone from my safe in Washington. Even if I remembered the numbers, the humans and lesser personnel on the island can only be reached from my phone, or the phones of my brothers. We can't allow them access to the outside world."

"Don't you think you should have mentioned that before?"

"It didn't cross my mind."

"Oh, really?" She narrowed her eyes at him. "Perhaps you didn't say anything because you wanted to drag things out until it was too late for me to go."

"And why would I do that?"

"Because you don't want me to do this without you."

"I don't, but I know you are going to do it anyway, and I want to give you the best possible chance of success. Delaying things would not have been conducive to that objective."

Letting out a breath, Carol slumped in her chair. "I'm sorry. The stress must be getting to me. Now that it seems like I'm going, I'm questioning my sanity for wanting to do it so much."

Lokan had been wondering about that. He was the one who had the most to gain from this. What was Carol's angle?

"Why do you?"

She eyed him for a long moment before answering. "I've been training for this for a very long time. This was what kept me going after I escaped the sadist. It was a way to prove myself. Suddenly everyone was looking at me with respect just because I had survived, and I didn't break, but I wanted more than that. I wanted to be the one who would go down in history as the woman who brought Navuh's evil regime to its end."

How the hell had she thought to do that?

Was his woman delusional?

Carol took a long sip of water before continuing. "The original idea was for me to somehow get myself to the island, get a high-ranking Doomer to fall for me, and start sowing the seeds of rebellion from within. We knew we couldn't win a war against the Brotherhood, and annihilating it was never on the table. The only way we could think that things would change was a revolution. But then one thing led to another, and we figured out that your father has the entire island population under compulsion, so no matter how good I was, my efforts would have been futile."

Her admission stunned him, mainly because it implied that she hadn't been plotting this insane scheme by herself, but that Kian had contemplated it as well. They were all fucking crazy. "So you are a spy after all?"

Smiling, she waved a dismissive hand. "I'm not. I was training to become a spy, and only for that particular mission."

"How did you plan on having a high ranking Brother fall for you?"

She tilted her head, giving him a questioning look as if it was self-explanatory. "The idea was to let myself get captured by traffickers and delivered to the island. I'm sure I don't need to spell out the rest for you."

His eyes widened. "You planned to work in the brothel?"

She shrugged.

"Do you have any idea how many males you would have had to service?"

She shrugged again. "I would have captured my sugar daddy in no time, and he would have bought all my time. I would have served only him."

Now her defense on behalf of prostitutes suddenly made sense. Carol really didn't see anything wrong with it. Hell, she'd volunteered to work in a brothel, which she must have known entailed servicing several males a day. And she was okay with that?

"Why are you looking at me like that?"

"Like what?"

"Like you are disgusted with me."

"I just find it hard to believe that you see no problem with working in a brothel and having sex with several males a night."

She shrugged for the third time, which he realized was more of a nervous tick than dismissal. "I have the stamina, and at the time, having an unlimited supply of immortal sex partners appealed to me. I didn't know that I was about to be gifted with a true-love mate, which would have voided that plan regardless of what we discovered later about Navuh's compulsory hold over his people. Now I cannot be with anyone but you."

"Do you regret it?"

CAROL

*C*arol crossed her arms over her chest. "Regret what?"

"Losing the appetite for multiple partners."

Fates, Lokan knew how to push her buttons.

She answered his question with one of her own. "Do you?"

"No, I don't. None of my previous partners can hold a candle to you. Even if it were possible, and even if you were unavailable to me, I would have had a hard time going back to human females. There is no comparison."

"You asked and you answered. I feel the same way."

He hesitated before dropping his next question, but he did it anyway. "Did you ever have multiple partners in one night?"

"Yes, but not at the same time. I'm not into orgies. The thing with human males was that sometimes the experience was so blah that I had to wash it off by trying to find someone better. Did you enjoy multiple partners?"

He smirked. "Yes, but at the same time, not one after the other. I was quite fond of threesomes, sometimes foursomes. Only with females, though."

She could picture Lokan pleasuring several women into oblivion. He was such a devil. But now he belonged to her, and there would be no more threesomes and foursomes for him. She wasn't the sharing type.

Lifting her chin, she looked down her nose at him. "Those fond memories will have to sustain you for the rest of your life because there will be no more of that for you."

Lokan laughed. "I like it that you are jealous, and you can rest easy. You are all the woman I'll ever need."

He pushed to his feet and rounded the table. "Come on. It's bedtime." He offered her a hand up.

Carol shook her head. Lokan was such a contradiction. One minute he could be seething with anger, suspecting her of the Fates knew what, and the next he was smiling like nothing had happened.

If only she could turn her emotions on and off like that, her life would be much easier. As it was, she needed a few minutes to switch gears and get into a sexy mood.

"I have an idea. We've only dream-shared once, and we need to practice it. How about we take a shower and then cuddle in bed until we fall asleep, and then you can visit me in my dream, and we can have dream sex?"

He lifted a finger. "On one condition."

"Shoot."

"I choose the scenery, and anything I want goes."

Carol wasn't born yesterday. "No threesomes."

"I wouldn't dream of that." He smirked at his own double entendre.

"Give me a hint."

"It would be a role reversal scene. You will be my captive and I will be your jailer."

She liked the sound of that. "And what are you going to do to me?"

"You'll have to find out."

"Ooh, the suspense. I'll be too excited to fall asleep."

"We will see about that."

As it turned out, Lokan had a number of tricks under his belt.

First, he treated her to a scalp massage in the shower, then he massaged her in bed, very carefully avoiding any sensual touches, and when he'd got every muscle in her body to relax and loosen up, he climbed in bed behind her and covered them both with the blanket.

Carol was asleep before he finished saying goodnight.

The dream started almost immediately, and at first she thought it was a continuation of what they had been doing before.

She was lying on her stomach in a plush bed, and Lokan was massaging her thighs. The difference was that this massage was definitely sensual, and she was tied up.

Well, sort of.

Her wrists were wrapped in silk scarves which were tied to the front posts of the bed, and Carol suspected that the same was happening with her ankles.

All she had to do to get free was stretch her arm and loosen the tension on the scarves. This was symbolic, a game she was comfortable playing. Anything more serious would have been a trigger for her, and Lokan was smart enough to realize that.

She could love him for that alone.

Most men didn't think about such details, even those who really cared about their partners. It was just lack of awareness, to put it nicely, or stupidity, to put it more bluntly.

But Lokan didn't suffer from either.

With a sigh, she rested her cheek on the small pillow below her face and wiggled her bottom on the larger one under her hips.

Lokan's hands dipped lower, his thumbs brushing against

her lower lips. Her legs spread wide, she was at his mercy, but it felt good. She trusted him, which was a revelation after all the worry she'd put herself through.

"Are you enjoying yourself, baby doll?"

"Yes."

He pressed his thumb against her moist opening and then pushed it inside.

Carol moaned. This was good.

Then his second thumb came to play, scooping some of her juices on its upward trek and then pressing against her tight rosette.

She tensed. Despite her colorful past, this was the one thing she'd never done. Not because she thought there was anything wrong with it, but because she just hadn't thought she would enjoy it.

There was a limit to how much control she was willing to give a man over her, or rather the illusion of control because at no point had she ever given it over for real.

"Relax," Lokan whispered behind her. "I'm not going to hurt you."

"I know."

Still, she found it impossible to loosen up, and clenched her bottom protectively.

Surprising her, Lokan withdrew his thumb, replacing it with his soft lips.

He was kissing her there?

Even for an experienced courtesan, it was scandalously wicked.

Then again, none of this was real. They were dream-sharing, which provided a perfect opportunity to try something new, something kinky.

She was starting to relax, her bottom finally unclenching, when Lokan did the unthinkable and licked her there.

"What are you doing?"

He chuckled and blew air on her rear entrance. "Are you a virgin here, my angel?"

"Yes, and I'm not eager for a change of status."

His thumb returned to gently massage her rosette, sending heat waves throughout her body.

"Aren't you curious?" He applied a little pressure.

It was intense but pleasurable in a different way from anything that she'd experienced before.

Leaning over her, he whispered in her ear, "Admit it. You want to try it out." He licked inside her earlobe. "With me."

"Go slow."

"I will."

JULIAN

"I'm worried about my mom." Ella swung her legs over the side of the bed. "I want to go sit with her."

"She is fine." Julian put a hand on her shoulder. "Magnus is there, and you still get dizzy whenever you get up."

She smiled. "But you are here to help me. Come on, it's boring to lie in bed all day long. Besides, Bridget said it was okay for me to move around as long as I used something for support."

Ella wasn't the kind of patient who listened to her doctors and did what she was told without arguing about it. First, she'd demanded to get unhooked from the monitors because she wanted to use the bathroom without having to go through the procedure of detaching and reattaching the wires. And then she'd used that to argue that if it was okay for her to go to the bathroom, it should be okay for her to go visit her mother next door.

Next, she was going to ask to go for a walk outside, and then to go home.

The truth was that she was doing great. Low fever and some mild discomfort was the extent of her symptoms. That and the dizziness. Vivian, on the other hand, was running a very high fever and slipping in and out of consciousness.

"Am I that something?" Julian asked.

"Yes. Now help me up."

He wrapped an arm around her middle and straightened up, pulling her against his chest. "Can I steal a kiss before we go?"

Ella grinned. "Always."

He kissed her gently, his hands sneaking under the hospital johnny and cupping her exposed bottom.

As the scent of her arousal flared, Julian closed his eyes and inhaled, checking for the slight change that would indicate she was turning immortal, but so far it had remained the same.

Other than that, the only way to determine whether Ella had transitioned was to inflict a small injury and watch how fast her body healed it. But it was too early for that, and Bridget wanted to wait another day.

"The door is open," Ella murmured against his lips.

He gave her bottom another squeeze before letting go. "I knew no one was out in the corridor."

Holding her up as she slipped her feet into her flip-flops, he kissed the top of her head. "I should get you a wheelchair."

She shuddered. "No way. I'd rather walk.

Stubborn, prideful girl.

With his arm propping her up, they walked over to the next room.

"How is Mom doing?" Ella asked.

Magnus got up and motioned for her to take the chair. "She woke up twice during the night. Bridget says that there is nothing to worry about and that she is progressing well. But I don't know what she bases that on. I can't see any changes."

Julian helped Ella to the chair. "Vivian's blood pressure is fine, and her heart is not showing any signs of distress. Those are all good signs. And the fact that she wakes up from time to time is an excellent sign too. Turner was out cold for a very long time. Everyone aside from my mother was losing hope for him, but the dude is a fighter. He made it through."

"Of course he did." Bridget walked in. "I wouldn't have it any other way. How are you feeling this morning, Ella?"

"Good. I'm just worried about my mother. I hate seeing her passed out like that."

"Her body is using every bit of energy available to it for the transition. But she still has a little bit left over to wake up now and then. I'm not worried about her." Bridget put her tablet into her coat pocket. "What I'm worried about is the new developments in San Francisco, splitting the Guardian force and canceling half of the scheduled rescue missions."

"What's going on?" Ella asked.

Magnus and Julian had gotten the update yesterday, but Julian hadn't told Ella about it. She had enough to worry about without getting upsetting news. But now that his mother had started, there was no point in keeping the rest from her.

"It seems that Doomers are kidnapping college girls from the UCSF campus. Five are missing so far, and we are afraid that they will spread their operation to other campuses as well. Kian and Turner decided to go hunting for Doomers, which means relocating half the force to San Francisco."

"Last I heard three were missing," Magnus said.

"Turner updated the number this morning."

"Why college girls?" Ella asked.

"Apparently, the island's clients demand educated, English-speaking company."

Ella grimaced. "I didn't realize that pervs want to talk. I was under the impression that they were interested in other things."

Bridget sighed. "According to Lokan, Navuh's new breeding plan is all about improving the intelligence of future Doomers. They are bringing in smart guys to improve the stock, and apparently those men are interested in stimulating conversation as much as they are interested in physical stimulation."

"How are they luring them in?" Ella asked. "From what I understand, only the super-rich or super-influential can afford a Pleasure Island sex vacation."

"We don't know, but that's one of the things the Guardians are going to investigate. I suspect that they run fake sweepstakes or that they approach the men in person with a promise of a free sex vacation to an island paradise in exchange for some work done. I don't think anyone is naive enough to think that they are getting something for nothing."

Julian rubbed his hand over his jaw. "I'm just thinking out loud here, but if we find the bait they are using to lure the men in, we might find the Doomers. Follow the breadcrumbs, so to speak."

Magnus nodded. "That's a possibility. What I love about this idea is that we are going to hunt for them for a change." He glanced at Vivian. "Not me personally, though. My place is here with my mate."

SYSSI

*a*s Syssi and Kian walked out the door hand in hand, Syssi lifted her face and took a deep breath, luxuriating in the crisp morning air.

It was a beautiful day. Not too cold and not too hot, the sun was warm on her skin, and the birds were chirping so excitedly that Syssi felt like they were cheering for her and Kian, congratulating them on their happy news.

"I'm glad Bridget is in the clinic on a Saturday," Kian said. "And that Vivian and Ella are there too, so we can pretend that we came to visit them."

"That's what we are doing."

He glanced down at her. "I thought you wanted Bridget to verify the pregnancy."

"I do. But I also want to visit Vivian and Ella so it's not like we are pretending to do it. Besides, once Bridget confirms it, I don't mind sharing the happy news. I just didn't want anyone to know before you did."

He lifted her hand to his lips and kissed the back of it. "Thank you. You've made me the happiest man on the planet."

Kian hadn't stopped smiling since she'd told him the news, and Syssi wondered how long it would last. The only other time she'd seen him so happy was on their wedding day.

In the clinic, Kian knocked on Bridget's office door.

"Come in."

"Good morning, Bridget. How are your patients doing?" He pulled out a chair for Syssi and sat on the other one.

"As expected, Ella is doing great, refusing to be attached to the monitoring equipment. She is in her mother's room right now. Vivian is unconscious, but she wakes up from time to time, which is a very good sign. I'm not worried about her."

"That is excellent news," Syssi said. "We want to visit them, if that's okay."

"I'm sure it is, but I'll have to ask." Bridget started pushing to her feet.

Kian lifted a hand to stop her. "Before you do that, there is something else we need you to do." He turned to Syssi. "Go ahead, tell her."

Instead, Syssi pulled out her phone, scrolled to a close-up photo of the two positive tests, and showed it to the doctor. "I need you to confirm."

For a long moment, Bridget just stared at the screen. "You're pregnant." A big smile spreading over her face, she rounded her desk, walked up to Syssi, and put her arms around her. "Congratulations." She let go and hugged Kian. "I'm so happy for you two."

"I still need you to run a proper test," Syssi said. "In my heart I know that I'm carrying a child, but I want to remove this last shred of doubt."

"Then come with me and let's see how far along you are."

Syssi looked at Kian. "Do you want to come?"

He seemed conflicted. "Only if you are comfortable with me being there."

"Of course I am." She smirked. "Think of it as prep for the actual birth."

Her big guy paled.

Bridget patted his shoulder. "You can sit behind the exam table, and I'll drape a sheet over Syssi's lower half. That way you can participate without having to watch what I'm doing."

"Don't worry about me. I'll be fine."

Syssi and Bridget exchanged knowing looks.

"Of course." The doctor opened the door leading to the patients' rooms, peeked her head out, and then motioned for them to follow. "The coast is clear." She led them past three closed doors and opened the fourth.

Despite his verbal bravado, Kian sat on a chair next to Syssi's head while Bridget performed her internal exam hidden behind a blue sheet.

"You're about three weeks pregnant," the doctor said as she pulled the gloves off and tossed them in the trash.

Unbelievable. They had started taking Merlin's potion only about six weeks ago. Could it have worked that fast? Or was it a coincidence?

"Are you sure?" Kian asked.

Bridget nodded. "Give or take a couple of days. Do you want me to take a blood sample too?"

"Why, is there any doubt?" Syssi asked.

"No, no doubt. You are definitely pregnant."

"Then I don't see a need."

"Again, congratulations, you two," Bridget said. "Merlin is going to be ecstatic. Do you want to call him with the good news or should I?"

"I'll call him," Syssi said. "The least I can do is personally thank him for this most amazing gift."

"Very well. I'll go check with Ella and Magnus if they are okay to receive guests."

After Bridget had left, Syssi put her pants back on and turned to her husband, who looked a little shell-shocked. "What's the matter, Kian?"

"It's official. We are having a baby."

She sat on his lap and wrapped her arms around his neck. "Are you scared?"

He nodded.

"Why?"

"I had a daughter once. A long time ago. I watched her get old and die."

Syssi had forgotten about that. Kian had been married before to a human girl, and they'd had a daughter, but he'd never gotten to even hold his baby in his arms. Because his human wife started suspecting him of witchcraft, Kian had been forced to fake his own death and then watch another man raise his child.

"I'm so sorry, my love. This must bring back painful memories."

He shook his head. "I'm blessed beyond measure for having been granted another chance." He put his hand on her belly. "I'm going to be the best father possible to this little one. I promise."

"You're going to spoil her rotten." Syssi kissed his forehead. "Not that I have anything against it. I'm probably going to do the same. It's just that I can imagine you with her, holding her and kissing her until she pushes you away and tells you that she wants to start dating boys already, but she can't do it because you're carrying her everywhere."

He laughed. "She is not dating until she is thirty, so I have plenty of time to worry about that."

49

ELLA

"I brought you some treats." Carol entered Ella's room with a large box of chocolates and a carton of premium coffee-flavored ice cream.

"Yummy. I'm sick of the sandwiches from the café. Wonder offered to cook real food for us, but I didn't want her to bother. The poor girl is overworked as it is."

Carol put her loot on the side table and sat on Ella's bed. "You should have told me. I'm going to bring you stuff from my frozen stash. Julian can take it home and heat it up for you. In fact, I'm going to give him most of it so he has something to eat too. By the way, where is he?"

"I sent him home to grab a shower and get some sleep. He wanted to roll a gurney in here, but I told him that it was a bad idea. The room is small as it is, and people keep popping in to ask how I'm doing."

Carol smiled. "So, how are you doing? Any change from yesterday?"

"I wish. Bridget says there is no point in doing the test so soon because it seems like my body is not in any rush to transition. It's so frustrating. My mother might be ready for the test before me."

"Really? Why?"

"Because her body is working hard on it and mine is not. I was hoping to gain an inch or two, but Bridget measured me this morning and there wasn't even a millimeter of growth. So, I guess I'm stuck with my five feet and four inches."

Carol chuckled. "That's two inches more than I have. Count yourself lucky."

"I thought you were taller."

Carol lifted her foot. "I always wear heeled shoes. Even my flip-flops have a two-inch platform." She fluffed her hair. "And my curls add another inch."

The woman was full of tricks.

"So yeah, no added height for me, but maybe my special talent will get a boost. I want to be able to communicate telepathically with other people and not just my mother."

"I'll keep my fingers crossed for you. When I can." Carol winked.

As Ella's vivid imagination came up with several scenarios for the kind of things Carol's fingers could be busy with, she felt herself blush.

Carol laughed. "I meant when I'm not cooking."

"Right. By the way, did you hear the news about Syssi and Kian?"

"What news?"

"Syssi is pregnant."

"Oh, wow, that's big. When Merlin returns from the convention, he's going to have a long line of ladies waiting for him."

Ella nodded. "Magnus said that after my mom recuperates, they are going to join the program too."

Carol tilted her head. "How do you feel about it?"

"Awesome. I love babies, but I don't want to have one myself yet. Besides, I think a new baby will bring us all closer together as a family."

"I wonder what talent he or she will have. You and your mom and Parker all have unique and strong abilities. And your father was a human. With Magnus as a father, that baby could be a powerhouse."

Ella frowned as it occurred to her that given her mother's limited ability it was indeed a bit strange that she and Parker had such strong talents. "What if my father was a Dormant? Maybe the talents came from him. My mom's telepathy only started when she got pregnant with me."

"Did your father have any siblings?"

"One sister. But we were never close. She is in pharmaceutical sales and travels extensively."

"Did he mention anything peculiar about her?"

Ella tried to remember if he had, but nothing came up. "I need to ask my mom. Maybe he told her something. All I know is that his sister's name is Eleanor and I have a vague memory of her being tall. It might be worth checking her out, except, she is even older than my mom. I think she is like thirty-nine."

Carol shrugged. "Andrew was forty when he transitioned, and Turner even older than that. It may not be too late."

"Yeah. Imagine if Eleanor can do what Parker does. That would make her a sales superstar. She could compel people to buy from her."

"I heard that pharmaceutical reps make a lot of money. If she can compel, she should be a millionaire by now."

"Now you've made me really curious. I can ask Roni to do some hacking and find out stuff about her. It's a shame she thinks us dead, though. It's not as if I can pick up the phone and call her."

"If she is a Dormant, that might be possible. She might join the clan."

Ella shook her head. "It's all speculation. I loved my dad, but he was most likely just an ordinary human, and so is his sister."

"He couldn't have been ordinary to father two extraordinary kids like you and Parker." Carol patted her arm. "How is your brother doing? Is he freaking out over you and his mom transitioning at the same time?"

"Not over me, he knows I'm fine, but he worries about our mom. The dude had to do so much growing up in a short time that I feel sorry for him. Imagine a twelve-year-old having to release his mother and sister from a powerful immortal's compulsion. And he did it remotely using video chat."

Carol arched a brow. "I thought Lokan removed the compulsion when you asked him to."

"He removed the one concerning Julian. But when we got rescued, my mother and I were still compelled to sing his praises if asked. All that would come out of my mouth was that Logan was a wonderful fiancé and I was madly in love with him."

"Why didn't you ask him to remove that too?"

"Because by then he was pumped full of narcotics. He compelled us to say nice things about him in preparation for the airport security inspection, but then Turner showed up, and things moved very quickly. My mother and I were whisked away, and Lokan was shot in the leg and then put to sleep. If not for Parker, we would have been stuck parroting those stupid phrases until Kian was done interrogating Lokan days later and forced him to release us."

"So Parker did it via video chat while you were still in Washington?"

"That's right. First, he tried to do it over the phone, but it didn't work. Then he or someone else came up with the idea of a video, and that worked."

"How?"

"He just told us to say nasty things about Lokan. He didn't actually remove Lokan's compulsion, he overrode it with his own."

Carol's eyes widened. "Fascinating. I have to tell Lokan about it. Does he know about Parker?"

"Not that I know of. Maybe it's better that he doesn't?"

Carol waved a dismissive hand. "It's not like he can do anything about it. Parker is safe."

50

CAROL

*C*arol left Ella's room feeling much better about her planned mission than she had going in.

Parker's ability to compel remotely opened up possibilities she and Lokan hadn't been aware of. If Parker could do it, so could Lokan, which meant an additional measure of safety for her. He didn't need to be on the island to compel the humans working there to help her. He could do that over the phone.

Carol couldn't wait to tell him about it, but first she needed to check with Bridget whether faking her own death was at all possible. If not, the entire plan would go down the drain and the ability to compel over the phone wasn't going to change that.

Knocking on Bridget's office door, she waited for an invitation to come in, but it seemed like the doctor wasn't there.

She might have gone to the bathroom.

Plopping down on a chair in the waiting room, Carol pulled out her phone and checked the clan's virtual bulletin board. There were a couple of new jokes posted by Anandur, a new recipe from Callie, and several want ads, including the one Ella had posted a while ago searching for an illustrator.

The biggest surprise was Eva's post of the first chapter of the book she'd written. As far as Carol knew, she hadn't finished it yet. Was she going to post chapters as she went? That could be cool.

She started reading the story when Bridget walked in with a cup of coffee from the vending machine.

"Are you waiting for me, Carol?"

"Yes." She pushed to her feet. "I need to discuss something with you. I hope you have a few minutes for me."

Bridget nodded. "Come on in." She opened the door to her office and waved Carol to a chair. "Take a seat." She closed the door. "I know why you are here. Turner told me what you are planning to do."

That was a relief. She wouldn't have to explain everything again. "Is it doable?"

Bridget pulled out a chair and sat facing Carol. "It might be. I will need to test it first. But to be frank, I think this is an ill-conceived plan. At least as it stands now."

"I think it will work."

"To what end? Even if everything goes without a glitch, which it never does, and even if you find that Navuh is hiding Areana in his harem, how are you going to get her out of there?"

"First, we need to verify that she is indeed there."

"That's where you are wrong. Unless you have the means to extract her, all the effort you are putting into this is futile. You are endangering yourself for nothing more than your own vanity and a need to prove something."

Ouch. Talk about being direct, and not entirely wrong.

"But what's the point of planning an extraction if she is not there?"

The doctor lifted a brow. "By the same token, what's the point of you going to the island if she's not there?"

Damn. Bridget was right. "Then I guess we need to plan an extraction. I'm sure Turner can come up with something."

"He might. But unless he does, you shouldn't go. Turner shares my opinion."

Naturally.

"Assuming Turner finds a way to get Areana off the island, do you know how I can fake my death?"

Bridget nodded. "An insulin pump. It's a programmable device that diabetics can choose instead of injections. It releases insulin in a steady flow throughout the day and night and extra doses at mealtimes. No one is going to question your need for it, and it's going to disqualify you from working in the brothel as well."

"How big is it?"

"About the size of a cell phone. It has a thin plastic tube that is inserted under the skin."

"What if the island doctors remove it and give me shots instead?

"It's a risk, but I don't think they are going to bother. Especially since you'll arrive under very different circumstances than the other women."

"Is it really going to deliver insulin?"

"You'll have control over it. You can stop the supply, and if you can't for whatever reason, your body is going to take care of the excess. That's not something you need to worry about."

"Okay, so that takes care of my supposed disability. How does it help me fake my death?"

"If you were a real human diabetic, a pump malfunction, where it stopped delivering insulin, could be potentially deadly. It's called acute diabetic ketoacidosis. I'll give you a link to an article that explains what it is. Anyway, my idea is to rig the pump with a dose of toxin that you'll be able to release when you are ready. It will mimic the ketoacidosis, so when you supposedly die, this will be assumed to be the cause. A poisoning is not going to kill you, but you'll appear dead while your body fights the toxin."

"What if they check me and find that I'm not really dead? The heartbeat slows down to almost nothing in stasis, but it doesn't stop completely."

"True, and your brain will show some activity too. They might try to revive you, but it's not going to work, and they will assume that you are in a coma. We need to ask Lokan for more details about their medical facilities and what kind of care they offer the humans on the island. I have a feeling it's just the basics."

"Probably."

"When Gorchenco comes back and asks for you, they should have no qualms about handing you over to him whether you are dead or in a coma."

"Am I going to come back on my own, or will I have to be revived?"

"That depends on the dosage and how long you are going to be in stasis. Depending on the injury, the body repairs the damage in a matter of minutes or hours, but if it fails to do so in two days, a revival is needed. It's easy to do, though. Even Gorchenco can pour pure water over you."

"That's all that's needed?"

Bridget nodded. "Just don't tell anyone. Someone might get a crazy idea and go to the catacombs to try to revive Doomers. Especially after the happy endings a couple of ladies have had with them."

Carol chuckled. "I think they will change their minds once they see their wilted carcasses. It's not a pretty sight."

"You never know. Anyway, we will need to test the toxin

on you in a controlled environment where I can resuscitate you if something goes wrong."

"You mean that I'll have to die twice?"

That was some scary shit, but it was better to test it than go in blind and die for real.

Bridget nodded. "It's crucial."

"Right. When do you want to do it?"

"Only after all the other pieces of the puzzle are in place."

"Makes sense."

"In the meantime, I'm going to buy several insulin pumps and bring them to William to fiddle with. We need to check if they can be rigged to secretly deliver a deadly dose of toxin on command."

51

CAROL

*C*arol walked out of Bridget's office in a daze. Sitting on a bench outside the clinic, she dropped her head back and let the sunshine warm her face.

What the hell was she doing?

Why was she taking such an incredible risk?

Was she an adrenaline junkie?

What would she gain by doing this?

She'd always been an attention seeker, which had been one of the reasons she'd become a courtesan. Carol liked doing things others wouldn't or couldn't and then boasting about them, getting a rise out of people.

It wasn't a positive quality, but it wasn't bad either. She wasn't harming anyone except maybe herself, but since she was an immortal, the risks had never been all that terrible.

At least she was interesting.

But this time the stakes were infinitely higher, and it occurred to her that she should be rewarded for such a monumental mission with more than just praise and admiration.

If she got Areana out of Navuh's harem, could she bargain for Lokan's freedom?

Carol wanted a life with him that was not confined to the keep's underground. They didn't necessarily need to live in the village, but they could go somewhere that was outside the Brotherhood's sphere of influence as well as that of the clan.

Perhaps a town in some small country in South America? Or maybe a remote village in Tibet? As long as they were together, free to live their lives, she didn't care where they settled down.

The time for bargaining, however, was now and not after the fact.

She needed to talk to Kian about the test Bridget had suggested. But even before that she had to tell him about Lokan's phone and his ability to compel humans on the island into helping her by using a video chat application. And while she was at it, she could also start bargaining.

The problem was that Kian didn't work from his office on weekends, and she would have to trouble him at home, which he wouldn't appreciate. But time was not on their side, and she couldn't wait for Monday.

Pulling out her phone, she typed up a text. *Congratulations on the happy news. I hate to bother you, but after talking with Bridget, there are a few things I need to discuss with you. Can you meet me at the café?* She pressed send.

His answer came a couple of moments later. *Come over to the house. Syssi is making cappuccinos.*

Carol smiled. Syssi was her exact opposite and one of the nicest people she knew. She deserved all the happiness coming her way.

Their house was less than a five-minute easy stroll from the clinic, and the door was open when she got there.

"Come on in," Syssi shouted over the thumping noise that her cappuccino contraption was making.

Carol walked up to her and gave her a one-armed hug. "I'm so happy for you."

"Thank you." Smiling, Syssi shook her head. "Did someone already post the news on the clan's virtual board?"

"I don't think so. I came here after visiting Ella. She didn't tell me it was supposed to be a secret."

"It's not. I was just surprised that you knew so soon. Kian is outside." She motioned to the living room sliding door. "I'll be there in a minute with the cappuccinos."

"Thank you."

Carol found Kian reclining on a lounger and smoking a cigarillo.

"Good morning. Take a seat." He motioned at a rocker chair.

"Good morning." She eyed the small cigar. "You shouldn't smoke around Syssi. She is an immortal, but the baby isn't. Not yet."

"I'm well aware of that. What did you want to talk to me about?"

"Several things. The most pressing one is Lokan's phone. Did William try to get into it?"

Kian grimaced. "Yes, and all the information was infected."

"Can you retrieve what was lost?"

"William and Roni tried. It's gone."

So Lokan had been right about that. He would be glad to know.

"He needs his phone to make the call to the island. First of all, because he doesn't remember the number, and secondly, because humans and the lesser personnel of the island can only be reached by using the special issue phone. Luckily, Lokan has a backup in a safe in his Washington apartment.

Someone will have to get it for him. I have the address and the combination for the safe."

"What about the keys to his place?"

"Whoever took his things when he was captured should have them. I assume his laptop suffered a similar fate to the phone?"

"It did." Kian stubbed out the remainder of his cigarillo in the ashtray. "I can't help thinking that Lokan is setting up a trap. Touching his safe might trigger an alarm."

Carol shrugged. "We need that phone. Whoever goes to retrieve it will have to be very careful."

"I'll ask Turner to send human professionals. He knows all the best operators. In fact, he can probably find someone in Washington to do it and save us the time of sending people from here. But that means that they would have to break into Lokan's place. There won't be time to send them the keys."

"Here are the cappuccinos." Syssi stepped out with a tray. "Can I join you, or is it hush-hush spy stuff?"

"I have no secrets from you." Kian got up and took the tray from her.

Carol could have sworn that she'd smelled a little bit of guilt accompanying that statement. Was Kian hiding something from the love of his life?

If he was, it must be something of vital importance. Her curiosity was piqued, but she was probably never going to find out.

Kian put the tray down on the table, pulled Syssi to sit with him on the lounger, and wrapped his arm around her before turning his attention back to Carol. "Anything else you wanted to talk to me about?"

"Yes. When I talked with Ella this morning, she told me about Parker removing Lokan's compulsion using a video chat, and it gave me an idea. If Parker can do it, I'm sure

Lokan can do it too, which means that he can compel his people from here using his phone. It will provide me with an additional layer of security. If anything goes wrong, he can pull strings from here."

"We need to test it."

"Of course. Once he gets his phone back, we can have him instruct someone on the island to do something atypical and see if the guy does it."

Kian narrowed his eyes at her. "Did Lokan suggest this?"

"I haven't spoken to him about it yet, and I doubt he knows it's even possible."

Letting out a breath, Kian raked his fingers through his hair. "I don't trust him."

This was getting annoying, and with an attitude like that, Kian was not likely to be open to bargaining.

"Yeah, you keep saying that over and over again. But he hasn't done anything to justify your mistrust."

"Not yet."

"What does he have to do to prove himself to you?"

Kian pinned her with a hard stare. "Let's put it this way. If he helps you to complete your mission, and if we get Areana out, and she proves to be his mother, I will be more inclined to trust him. But we will need to check how he feels about her, and what he will be willing to do to keep her safe."

That was progress.

"If all those conditions are met, would you let him go?"

"I'll consider it. But I won't welcome him into the clan, if that's what you are asking for."

"No, I didn't expect you would. But if Lokan and I chose to settle somewhere else, would you be okay with that?"

"If all of my conditions were met, and no new damning information came out, I would consider letting him go."

Syssi shook her head. "I don't want to lose you, Carol.

You are like the heart of the village, the hub everyone hovers around."

Carol chuckled. "The café is the central hub that the village life revolves around, not me, and it's doing perfectly well with Wonder at the helm."

52

KIAN

"Would you like a canapé, master?" Oridu bowed, holding the tray up for Kian to choose one of the artfully prepared sandwiches.

"Thank you." Kian took one and headed outside, where Syssi, Amanda, and Alena were fawning over Phoenix while Annani was chatting with Nathalie.

The little ball of energy was talking up a storm, sounding like someone five times her age. Andrew would have his hands full with this one.

He wondered what Allegra was going to be like. Was she going to be shy and reserved like Syssi or bossy and demanding like him?

Or maybe she was going to be calculating like Andrew, or dramatic like Amanda, or serene like Alena, or entrepreneurial like Sari? Or Fates forbid a daredevil like her grandmother. He wouldn't have a moment's peace.

Over the last week, Annani had taken full advantage of her temporary residence, inviting people over for lunches and dinners and afternoon teas. Today's lunch, however, was only for the family, which provided a perfect setting for his and Syssi's announcement.

Glancing around the backyard, Kian searched for Andrew and Dalhu, finding them standing under a tree and laughing over something on Andrew's phone.

He walked over. "Did Anandur post new jokes?"

Andrew shook his head. "It's a meme that has gone viral. Here." He handed Kian the phone.

Kian didn't find it all that funny, but that was probably because his head was someplace else. He smiled and handed Andrew his phone back.

With everyone accounted for, it was a good time to make the announcement.

It would have been better to do it after lunch, but rumors spread lightning-fast through the village, and he didn't want his family to find out about it on the clan's virtual bulletin board, or read a congratulating text from someone who had visited Ella that morning.

Walking over to Syssi, Kian offered her a hand up, and then leaned to whisper in her ear. "Now?"

She nodded. "You do it."

No surprise there. Syssi didn't like being the center of attention and found it much more comfortable to have him as her champion, a role he embraced wholeheartedly.

"If I may have everyone's attention for a moment, Syssi and I have an announcement to make."

Amanda turned around with a big grin spreading over her face and clapped her hands, which Phoenix mimicked right away, clapping her chubby little hands with glee.

Her hand over her heart, a beatific smile spread over Alena's gentle features.

Annani glided over and hugged Syssi. "I am so happy."

Kian shook his head. "We didn't make the announcement yet."

His mother wiped a tear from the corner of her eye. "Get on with it already so I can hug you too."

"In about thirty-seven weeks, Syssi and I are going to become parents." He bent down to make it easier for his mother to embrace him.

"I could not be happier." She glanced at Amanda. "Maybe if I got some great news from you too, Mindi…"

"Not likely." Amanda put her arms around Syssi and Kian. "I'm satisfied with being the cool aunt. I hope you are having a girl."

Syssi nodded. "I have a feeling that I am."

"Then it's a girl for sure. Your feelings are as good as a promissory note."

Next it was Andrew's turn. "In case you're wrong, and it's a boy, I would like you to consider Jacob as his name."

"Of course." Syssi teared up and hugged her brother.

It was good that they were having a girl because Kian didn't like the idea of naming a child of his after someone who had died tragically. He'd lost a brother too, but as much as he'd loved Lilen, he would not name his son after him.

Alena gave them each a gentle hug and a kiss on the cheek. "When the time comes, you need to travel to the sanctuary. That's the safest place to deliver your baby."

Syssi nodded, but he knew she wouldn't want to leave him behind, and there was no way he could take such a long vacation, especially since his mother would insist that they stay a few weeks after the delivery.

Except, he might be able to work from there. Most of what kept him busy was done in the office, and if he couldn't avoid meetings, he could fly in for the day and come back at night.

Yeah. That was a good plan. This baby was going to get every advantage and safety measure possible. He shouldn't let his work jeopardize even one hair on her precious head.

Next was Dalhu, who shook their hands and congratulated them, and lastly Nathalie, who'd been wiping tears from her eyes from the moment he'd made the announcement.

"I'm so happy that I can't contain it. You give us hope for the future." She embraced and kissed Syssi, then hesitantly gave Kian a quick hug.

"Let's have a toast," Andrew said, waving one of the Odus over. "Do you have champagne in the house? "

The Odu bowed. "Of course, master. Should I bring it out with wine flutes for everyone?"

"Yes, please."

Once that was done and everyone was holding a flute, Andrew raised his. "To Syssi and Kian. May the next thirty-seven weeks pass easily and uneventfully, and may they welcome their healthy child with joy and love in their hearts."

When everyone was done cheering, Andrew continued. "May this child be the first among many more to come. I want that playground to get so overrun with kids that we will have to double its size."

Everyone drank to that too.

"To the future of the clan." Annani lifted her flute. "May all my children and their children and their children's children find true-love mates, and may their unions be fruitful."

53

ANNANI

*A*s Annani looked at the long table loaded with platters of food, surrounded by her family, her heart swelled with love and gratitude. Still, like every other happy moment in her life, this one was tinged with sorrow as well. Her happiness could never be complete without all her children and her beloved husband gathered around her.

Sari could have been there, but Lilen and Khiann…well, there was no way to bring back the dead.

Not in the flesh, anyway.

Nathalie could converse with spirits, but she could not call them to her. They had to find her.

Secretly, Annani had hoped that her loved ones would find the conduit Nathalie provided and communicate through her, but they had either passed beyond the veil or had forgotten her.

After many months of hoping to hear from Nathalie that either Lilen or Khiann had communicated with her, Annani had to accept that it was not going to happen.

The disappointment had been devastating, but as always,

Annani had hidden her anguish behind a cheerful mask and kept on going because there was no other choice.

Life went on.

Instead of dwelling on what could not be, she should focus on her blessings. In thirty-seven weeks, a new grandchild was going to brighten her days, and if the Fates were willing, she would soon get her sister back.

Lifting her goblet, Annani leaned back in her chair. "Kian, how are things progressing with the plan to save Areana?"

"We are still working on the details, but it seems that we have at least the part about getting Carol onto the island nailed down. What we don't have is a way to get Areana out, but Turner is working on it."

"How are you going to get Carol in?" Andrew asked.

Kian glanced around the table, his eyes stopping on Nathalie, the only one who he believed was out of the loop. Except, Annani was sure that she knew more than Kian would have liked because there were no secrets between mates. If Kian had not explicitly forbidden it, Andrew had most likely shared the news with her.

"Please keep everything I'm going to tell you to yourselves. I don't think we have spies in our midst, but as always, I'd rather be careful."

"Of course." Nathalie nodded.

"We are going to use the Russian mobster who had held Ella captive. Lokan has damning information on Gorchenco that should be enough to get him to cooperate with us. He's been a client of the island for many years, so he'll have no problem booking another vacation, but this time he will arrive with his new girlfriend, Carol. They will pretend to have a lovers' quarrel, and he is going to leave her on the island. Lokan is going to use his connections to get her working in the harem, and she is going to dream-share with him her findings. If Areana is there, we will communicate with Carol via Lokan and give her instructions on how to proceed. Regrettably, we don't have that part figured out yet."

Andrew rubbed his hand over the back of his head. "Did you figure out how Carol is going to fake her death yet?"

Annani gasped. "What is he talking about?"

"The only way Carol can get out of the harem is by faking her death. Gorchenco will come back for her, and demand to take her body for burial back home. Bridget is working on rigging an insulin pump with a deadly dose of toxin. To humans, that is. We know it can't kill Carol, but it can put her in stasis, which they will assume is either death or coma. In both cases we believe that they will have no problem handing her over to Gorchenco. He is an important arms supplier to the Brotherhood, and they will want to keep him happy."

Amanda crossed her arms over her chest. "You are making an awful lot of assumptions."

Kian raked his fingers through his hair. "You don't need to tell me that. The good news is that in case something goes wrong, Lokan might be able to bail Carol out. Just as Parker removed Lokan's compulsion from his mother and sister via a video chat, Lokan can compel humans on the island, specifically the pilots. They can help get her out."

Annani did not understand the difficulty. "You can just fly a helicopter in, hover over the harem and drop a ladder. Now that we know where the island is, it should not be difficult."

Kian chuckled. "I wish it were that easy. First of all, they have anti-aircraft missiles and can shoot the helicopter down before it even gets near the target. Secondly, the island is blanketed in dense tree cover, so hovering low enough to drop a ladder is not possible. Third, Areana is not a trained commando, and even they have trouble climbing a ladder into a hovering helicopter. And fourth, her guards are going to follow her and drag her down. She is a goddess, and stronger than a human female, but I'm sure she has many human guards surrounding her at all times. She can't outrun and overpower them all."

Annani lifted her chin. "I do not have military training, so I would not know those things. Do you have any other ideas?"

"Not yet. My own military training is obsolete, but as far as modern rescue missions go, Turner is the best there is. I trust him to come up with a plan."

Annani nodded. "I hope so. What about Carol faking her own death, is it safe?"

"Bridget is going to test it first, making sure that she can resuscitate her. I would appreciate it if you could give Carol your blessing."

"Of course. It is the least I can do for her. What about Vivian and Ella? I hear that Ella is doing well, but should I give Vivian a blessing?"

"Vivian is also doing well. Bridget assures me that she is stable and going to transition just fine. But if anything changes, your blessing would be appreciated."

The only one at the table who knew what they were really talking about was Alena, who looked down at her hands while stifling a smile. The rest regarded Annani and Kian with curious glances.

"You never cease to surprise me, Kian," Amanda said. "You are supposed to be a devout heretic, not someone who believes in blessings."

"The psychological effect of a blessing can help the healing," Syssi said.

Amanda waved a hand. "Not to someone that is unconscious. If they don't know they are getting a blessing, it's not going to help them."

Annani knew Syssi well enough to read the stubborn expression on her otherwise gentle face. She was not going to acquiesce. Her daughter-in-law only seemed timid to those who did not know her well.

"You of all people should know that there are forces at play we don't understand," Syssi said. "People might feel the positive energy even when they are unconscious. Besides, there is no harm in it, and it gives their loved ones hope."

54

LOKAN

*W*hile Carol was gone, Lokan had been running on the treadmill, sweating mentally more than physically, but about two hours later he still had no solutions.

What the hell could he do to convince Kian that he could trust him? At least as far as Carol's safety and well-being were concerned?

For a brief moment, he'd even considered giving him Losham. He knew where his brother lived, and he also knew how exposed Losham was at his residence. Secure in his anonymity, his brother relied on a fancy alarm system for his safety, and other than his assistant, he didn't keep warriors on the premises.

On the one hand, it was smart because they couldn't betray his location, but on the other hand, it wasn't prudent because he was vulnerable to an attack.

If the roles were reversed, Losham would have had no qualms about selling Lokan out, and frankly, Lokan would have sold Losham if he'd thought it would help his cause. But all it would prove was that he lacked loyalty and couldn't be trusted.

Was he going to spend the rest of his immortal life in this underground complex? Even with Carol by his side, it was a depressing prospect.

His only hope was that once Areana was rescued and her parentage of him confirmed, Annani would pressure Kian into releasing him.

If he failed to show up on the island in nineteen days, his father would start a search for him, and once it became clear that he was missing, Navuh was going to assume that he'd either deserted or died. In either case, that would be the end of Lokan's Brotherhood membership card, and Kian would have nothing further to fear from him, and he would also have no reason to keep him locked up.

Except, with Kian it wasn't about logic, it was about hatred and mistrust that ran way too deep for reason to prevail.

When Lokan's stomach growled, signaling that it was lunchtime and that Carol would be back soon, he stepped off the treadmill and walked over to the punching bag, giving it a short but intense beating before heading into the bathroom.

After the shower, he walked into the closet and got dressed.

Having exercise equipment to burn off stress was great, but it created another problem. He was running out of clean clothes. Such a mundane and unimportant thing, but it had to be addressed. The thing was, with all that was going on, asking Carol to do his laundry didn't feel right. Perhaps he could ask Arwel?

The Guardian seemed like a down to earth kind of guy, and Lokan was sure he didn't have anyone doing laundry for him.

He was about to pick up the phone and call Arwel when the door started whizzing, and a moment later Carol walked in holding a couple of food containers.

"You smell nice." She put them down on the counter and walked up to him. "Did you miss me?" She wrapped her arms around his neck.

"Terribly." He kissed her long and hard.

As his stomach growled again, she pushed at his chest. "My poor baby is hungry. Let me feed you."

No one had ever called him poor or baby, but coming from Carol it felt nice.

"What do you have in there?" he asked as she popped the containers into the microwave.

"I keep a stock of frozen meals at home. I knew that I wouldn't have time to prepare lunch, so I grabbed two. I gave the rest to Julian. They've been eating sandwiches from the vending machines."

He frowned. Every time Carol left to visit Ella or to talk to Kian, she made it seem like a long trip. Could it be that it was a smokescreen and that everyone lived in this same structure just above ground?

"Do they have vending machines at the other location as well?" he probed.

She nodded. "The same guy stocks both, so they have the same kind. I think most of the clan survives on those. Not many people cook at home."

Since he hadn't smelled any deceit or anxiety while she explained, it must have been true.

Standing behind Carol, Lokan enveloped her in his arms. "With how rich you guys are, I would have thought that you could afford meals delivered to you."

"First of all, we are not all rich. The basic share in the clan profits isn't big. Those that work for the clan get paid an additional salary, and depending on what they do, they can make a lot more. Like the Guardians. They are paid very well."

"When you are not supplying Arwel with your tasty meals, he eats sandwiches from the vending machine."

"That's his choice. He can afford to splurge on deliveries if he wants to."

The microwave beeped, and Carol pulled out the two containers. "I should have made a salad to go with these." She took the boxes to the table and removed the lids. "Something fresh would have been nice."

"Having you here with me is nicer." He sat down and dug into the spaghetti dish.

"I talked with the doctor today," Carol said. "She has an idea for how I'm going to fake a disability and later my death using the same device. An insulin pump. Do you know what it is?"

He shook his head.

"Some humans have a problem metabolizing sugars, and they need insulin shots throughout the day. The pump replaces the shots and delivers the insulin as needed. It is programmable, so more insulin is supplied after meals and less during sleep. Anyway, she can hide a toxin inside the pump, and when I activate it, the result will mimic death from lack of insulin, so it would look like the pump malfunctioned. And since it's an ugly device and it's attached to the body, it will also disqualify me from working in the brothel."

"Isn't it dangerous? What if your body can't repair the damage?"

"That's why she is going to test it on me first. If something goes wrong, she can revive me."

A heavy weight settled in the pit of Lokan's stomach. "You will have to die twice?"

She nodded. "Maybe more than that if Bridget needs to test different doses."

"I don't like it."

Carol put her fork down. "Well, tough. I don't like it either. But that's the plan."

"Damn."

She waved a dismissive hand. "Eat. You can worry about it after your stomach is full. Besides, I have good news too."

Lifting spaghetti to his mouth, he arched a brow. "I could use some good news."

"Remember how you compelled Vivian and Ella to say only nice things about you?"

He nodded.

"You've never removed that compulsion."

"I forgot about it." He smirked. "Is Ella still saying that I'm a wonderful fiancé and that she is madly in love with me? That should annoy the hell out of Julian."

"No. The compulsion was removed by Ella's younger brother, who can compel humans same as you."

Lokan nearly choked on a mouthful of spaghetti. "I'll be damned. The kid can compel?"

She nodded. "Not only that, he did it via a video chat, which means that you can do the same. You can video call one of your pilots and compel him to do whatever you need him to do."

Lokan dropped his fork and leaned back in his chair. "Unbelievable. But I'm not sure I can do that. What if the kid's power is different than mine?"

"Once Kian gets your spare phone from Washington, you can test it."

"Right. As if he is going to allow that."

"I've already talked to him, and he is all for it. Your ability to remote compel people on the island means added safety for me. Naturally, he is going to have his tech people follow the call and monitor it."

"That's fine." He let out a breath. "That's a significant weight off my chest. It makes me feel not as powerless."

She smiled. "There is more. I did a little bargaining with Kian. If everything goes according to plan and I come back safely, and Areana is freed and proven to be your mother, he is willing to consider letting you go, or rather us. I asked him if he was willing to let us settle somewhere on our own, and he said he will consider it."

It wasn't a promise or a pledge, but it was better than nothing.

Carol frowned. "You don't look happy."

"He didn't promise to do it, he promised to consider it. There is a big difference."

"I believe he will deliver. There is no reason for him not to."

"He doesn't like me."

"It's not personal. Kian hates Doomers, and you can't blame him for it. Nevertheless, he accepted Dalhu and Robert into the clan. Not that he is going to accept you as well, but that's because he fears that you are too powerful to trust. He is going to let you go, though, and that's a promise from me to you. I will not accept anything less as payment for delivering Areana to her sister."

55

KIAN

On the way home, Kian's phone buzzed with a message from Turner. *We have confirmation of the sub's location including an underwater video.*

"What is it?" Syssi asked.

"Turner's people found the Russian's submarine and made an underwater video of it, confirming Lokan's information."

She waved a hand. "You see, he is trustworthy."

"I wouldn't go that far. This serves his agenda."

Syssi threaded her arm through his. "Maybe we can use the submarine to get close to the island."

"I doubt it. It depends how deep the water around the island is. A sub this size probably can't get close enough to do us any good. Besides, it needs people to operate it."

"I'm sure Turner can find retired sailors. Maybe even Russian speaking ones."

Kian chuckled. "You're probably right. I need to call him."

"Go ahead." She pulled out her arm. "I don't mind. In fact, I love hearing all about this spy stuff. I just wish I didn't know the spy in person. I worry about Carol. She is taking so many risks, and I can't help wondering what her motivation is. Is she a thrill seeker?"

"She obviously is, but in this case she has another strong motive. She bargained for Lokan's freedom."

Syssi waved a dismissive hand. "That's an add-on. She probably asked herself the same question, wondering what's in it for her, and realized that she has a valuable bargaining chip she could use to free her mate. In her shoes, I would've done the same."

Kian smirked. "Would you have embarked on a dangerous mission to free me?"

Syssi nodded. "I would have been scared shitless, but yes, I would have done everything in my power to free or save you. But that would be the only reason I would ever walk voluntarily into danger. And, of course, the same goes for our child."

He couldn't help but push her further. "What about Andrew? Would you have done it for him?"

There was no hesitation. "Yes. And before you keep asking about every person I care for, the answer is also yes. I would have done it for my parents and for your sisters and mother as well."

He leaned and kissed the top of her head. "My mate is courageous."

She rolled her eyes. "Right."

"You are. Courage is not the absence of fear. It's doing what's right despite it."

As Kian pulled out his phone, they were only a few steps away from their house, and he motioned for Syssi to go ahead.

She patted his arm. "I'm going to make us cappuccinos."

Nodding, he selected Turner's contact number.

"I was expecting your call, and yes, I have the footage. Do you want me to send it to you?"

"Sure. What about Lokan's phone? Any progress there?"

"His place is being watched by a human detective agency. My guy said that they weren't top-notch. It's just basic surveillance from the rooftop across the street. Since he found no bugs in the elevator or the hallway, it seems that whoever is watching Lokan's apartment is interested only in monitoring his presence there."

"Interesting. I wonder if it's his father's doing or one of the crooked politicians he deals with."

"Could be either. Whoever is doing it does not want to spend a lot of money. The detective agency they hired deals mainly with cheating spouses."

"Could it be an ex-girlfriend?"

"I doubt Lokan ever engaged with anyone for longer than one night."

"True. He is too smart to have done otherwise. So, what's the plan? We need that phone."

"My guy is going to do it tomorrow morning using a house cleaning crew as a cover."

"I want him or one of his people to fly over and deliver the phone in person. I don't trust it to a delivery service. If the thing gets lost, the entire operation goes down the drain."

"I'll see to it."

"The sooner we have it, the sooner you can contact Gorchenco and set up a meeting. Do you know where he is now?"

Turner chuckled. "I have several probabilities but nothing definite. He hasn't changed his habits since Ella's so-called death, and he is still an elusive bastard. I'm not going to wait for the phone, though. I have an idea of how to convey a message. Sandoval's appraiser must have been the snitch that told Gorchenco about the ring being back on the market. I'm going to put the fear of God in that Russian and get him to contact Gorchenco for us. If that doesn't work, I'll wait for the phone to get here and for Lokan to give me the bastard's phone number."

"What about the extraction plan, did you make any progress?"

Turner sighed. "What I'm working on is sneaking a communication device in, something Areana could use after Carol leaves. We don't have enough information or time to plan a rescue mission of that caliber. We still might, but first I want to make sure that Carol's efforts are not wasted."

"I've given the drone idea some more thought. They can detect unauthorized communications."

"What I'm looking into is a low powered signal that should escape detection. All I need is a two-mile range to reach a boat we'll have nearby."

"How are you going to get it into Areana's hands? Despite Gorchenco's status, he and Carol will be thoroughly searched."

"A tiny drone the size of a hornet that will fly into the harem's enclosure when Carol is still there so she can look for it."

"We talked about that. A drone this small doesn't have the necessary range."

"True. But I came up with an idea how to solve that problem and I have my guy working on it. We will attach the small drone to a military-grade one that will fly high above the island and drop the little one. Falling doesn't require an expenditure of power. It would only use it to reach the target."

"What are the chances of it working?"

"It looks good."

Kian raked his fingers through his hair. "Syssi had a crazy

idea. What if we bring Gorchenco's submarine near the island? Can that give us some advantage?"

Turner didn't laugh, and for a long moment the line went silent. "Let me think about it. She might be onto something."

"I'll be damned."

ELLA

*M*agnus poked his head into Ella's patient room. "Your mother is awake and she wants to see you."

"Awesome." Ella flung the blanket off and swung her legs over the side of the bed. "I hope she stays with us for more than a few minutes this time."

"Bridget thinks she's done. She's been awake for fifteen minutes, drank some water, and talked with me. It looks good."

In a practiced move, Julian wrapped his arm around Ella's middle and helped her up. "Are you dizzy?"

"Not at all. I think you can let go."

He removed his hold but kept his hands hovering near her waist where he could catch her if she wavered.

Forgoing the flip-flops, Ella took a small step and then another one. "I'm good. No dizziness."

"Take it slow, sweetheart." Like a mother goose, Julian stayed close, his hands at the ready to assist if needed.

Ella huffed out a breath. "I'm not going to jog. It's just a few feet."

She made it without falling, but seeing her mother sitting up in bed with Parker holding her hand made her light-headed with happiness and brought tears to her eyes. "Oh, Mom, I'm so glad you're all better." She closed the rest of the distance and sat on the other side of her mother's bed. "Bridget kept saying that everything was fine and that we shouldn't worry, but I still did."

Vivian reached out with a feeble hand and cupped Ella's cheek. "I'm sorry that I gave you a scare."

Putting her hand over her mother's, Ella leaned into the touch. "It's not your fault. I'm just happy that it's over."

"What about you, any changes?"

"Nope. I'm still five foot and four inches, and my cup size is still C. I was hoping to gain at least one more inch either in height or protrusion." She pushed out her chest.

"Maybe you will." Bridget entered the room. "The transition process continues for about six months. You might still grow a little."

Leaning against the wall, Julian crossed his arms over his chest. "I'm glad that nothing has changed. I love you just the way you are."

"You're so sweet." Ella blew him a kiss.

"Ready to get tested?" Bridget asked.

Ella's gut twisted in a knot. What if her dizziness and fever were caused by a virus, and she hadn't transitioned? Her hearing hadn't improved, nor her eyesight, and neither had her sense of smell.

Unless she was a defective immortal, she was still human.

"I am ready," Vivian said.

"I'm not, but I will anyway." Ella looked at her mother. "No changes, including my senses. Nothing has improved."

Vivian frowned. "Now that you mention it, mine didn't improve either."

Parker looked worried. "Mine started improving right

away, but I think they are still getting better. Maybe it will just take longer for you?"

"It's a possibility," Bridget said. "Every person is different, and every transition I've witnessed so far has been different too. Let's do the test and get that out of the way."

"Can we do it at the same time?" Ella asked. "Julian can do mine." As much as she trusted Bridget, Ella felt safer with Julian.

"Of course."

"I'll prepare the trays." Julian pushed away from the wall and walked out.

"While you were out, I was thinking," Ella said. "What if Dad was a Dormant too? Do you know if Aunt Eleanor ever did any weird stuff?"

Vivian frowned. "Your father didn't talk much about her, but he called her an odd bird. So maybe. What makes you think your father was a Dormant, though?"

"Because of Parker's and my superpowers. You didn't develop your telepathic ability until you became pregnant with me."

"That's true, but what are the odds of two Dormants finding each other?"

"The affinity brings them together. If it exists between immortals and Dormants, why shouldn't it exist between Dormants?"

"I did feel an immediate attraction to your father, but that was normal. He was a very handsome boy." Vivian cupped Parker's cheek. "Like you."

Parker rolled his eyes. "Was he a walking twig too? I look like the teenage Groot from the *Guardians of the Galaxy*."

"Don't worry about it. You'll fill out."

The conversation must have made Magnus uncomfortable because he kept smoothing his hand over his goatee, and

Ella had noticed that he only did that when something troubled him or when he was preoccupied.

"Anyway." Ella decided to redirect the conversation back to her aunt. "I think it's worth checking Eleanor out. We can't do it ourselves because she thinks we are dead, but maybe one of the Guardians can track her down. She shouldn't be too hard to find."

"Everyone ready?" Julian came back with the two trays and handed one to Bridget.

"Let's do it." Ella offered him her hand.

He squirted a little liquid on it and then wiped it away with gauze.

"I'll wait over there." Parker jumped off the bed and traded places with Magnus, who walked over to stand next to Vivian.

"On a count of three," Bridget said after cleaning Vivian's palm. "One, two, three."

Julian made a tiny cut, but it stung like hell and Ella couldn't help the hiss that escaped her lips.

"I'm so sorry, sweetheart." He blew air on the cut, which helped a little.

They all waited with bated breath, watching the blood well over the incision and then stop.

Another moment passed before Julian cleaned the blood away with another piece of gauze, and Bridget did the same with Vivian.

"It's closing," Julian murmured. "Look."

His eyesight was much better than hers because it took another second before she saw what he was talking about.

"Wow, it's like watching the cut in reverse. It's closing up on itself."

"Congratulations, Vivian and Ella." Bridget grinned. "Welcome to immortality."

KIAN

*K*ian pulled Syssi into his arms. "Turner is coming over. I hope you don't mind."

"Why would I?"

"It's Sunday, and I'm not supposed to be working, but this can't wait. We need to act fast."

Stretching on her toes, she kissed his lips. "You should know better than to worry about me begrudging an important meeting like this. Can I listen in, though?"

"Of course. You can also participate. Turner didn't dismiss your submarine idea when I mentioned it. Perhaps you can come up with other interesting suggestions."

She blushed. "Frankly, I just threw it out there. I never expected you or him to take it seriously."

"That's why you should never be shy about voicing your opinions. You never know, right?"

As he kissed the top of her nose, his phone buzzed in his pocket. Expecting it to be Turner, he was surprised to see Bridget's face on the screen.

"Good morning, Bridget."

"Good morning indeed. I thought you would like to know

that Vivian and Ella have both successfully transitioned. We just completed the tests."

"That calls for a celebration."

"I think so too. Should I call Amanda?"

He chuckled. "By all means. She'll have a party ready by this evening."

Syssi nudged his arm. "Ask Bridget if they are going home or staying in the clinic. I want to come over and congratulate them in person."

Kian switched to speakerphone even though it wasn't necessary.

"They are going home," Bridget said. "Give them some time to process the good news with their family."

Syssi nodded. "I forgot how I felt waking up. I wasn't ready to see anyone. I'll text them."

"Good idea," Bridget said.

Kian wrapped his arm around Syssi's middle, pulling her against his side as he issued an invitation to Bridget. "Turner is coming over and we are going to talk about the new missions. Do you want to join us?"

"No, thank you. I'm going home to take advantage of what's left of my weekend."

"Enjoy."

"Thanks."

Pulling away, Syssi headed for the kitchen. "I'm going to prepare snacks. Are you going to talk with Turner outside on the patio?"

Remembering that he couldn't smoke next to his pregnant wife, Kian grimaced. "It's your choice."

Syssi looked at him from behind the counter and smiled. "Go ahead and light up because I'm not going to be joining you. I expect Amanda to call me in a minute asking for my help to organize the party for Vivian and Ella."

"A premonition?"

"Past experience."

Syssi pointed at the house phone that started ringing. "Can I time it, or what?" She picked up the receiver. "Hello, Amanda."

Shaking his head, Kian walked out into the backyard, sat on a lounger, and pulled out a cigarillo from the box that he'd left on the side table.

Less than five minutes later, Syssi answered the door for Turner and sent him with the tray outside.

"Compliments of your lovely wife." Turner put the tray down and reached for a strawberry from the fruit bowl.

"Did you call Sandoval?"

Turner shook his head. "No need. We are going to have Lokan's phone around three o'clock in the afternoon. As per your request, the guy is flying it in and my secretary is meeting him at the airport to collect it. We need a secure location away from the keep to test Lokan's ability to compel his pilots via video chat. You also need to bring William along to monitor the connection."

"I already talked to him. He's waiting for me to tell him when."

"Good." Turner popped another strawberry into his mouth.

Syssi waved from behind the screen. "I'm going to Amanda's. Call me if you need me."

"Have fun."

"I will. Amanda is turning her house into a war room. She invited I don't know how many people to assign tasks to."

"Tell her not to plan it for this evening if she wants me and Andrew to attend. We have a meeting with Lokan scheduled for later today."

"How long is it going to take?"

"Too long to make it back to a party. Besides, Vivian and Ella need time to recuperate."

"I'll see what I can do." She blew him an air kiss. "Goodbye, Turner." She waved again.

"Goodbye, Syssi."

Kian took another drag from his cigarillo. "Did your guy encounter any trouble from the detectives watching Lokan's apartment?"

"Nope. He showed up with a bunch of maids, put two of them to wash the windows and block the view from across the street, and did his thing. He left them behind to keep on cleaning while he snuck out of the building. They are probably still there."

"I'm curious. Did he find anything other than the phone inside the safe?"

"Lots of cash, but he didn't touch anything other than the phone."

"I'm still worried about it being a trap. This could be a perfect setup for tracking Lokan. He might not be even aware of it. Navuh is all about control, and I find it hard to believe that he is not monitoring his sons' whereabouts."

Turner shrugged. "William took apart the phone and the laptop Lokan had with him and found nothing other than the signal. But that's enough to locate Lokan by, and that's why he did it off-site. Which we are doing with this phone as well. Did you choose a location?"

Kian nodded. "I'll have Lokan knocked out and brought to the cabin. William is going to join us there with his equipment van."

Turner glanced at his watch. "How long is the drive there?"

"About an hour and forty-five minutes."

"Don't you have a closer location?"

"Nothing as secluded."

"Then I guess it will have to do."

"Any progress with the extraction plan?"

"I'm still working on it."

"Care to share?"

"Not yet. There are several conditions that I need to check first, and I need to incorporate a backup plan for getting Carol out in case something goes wrong. We can't place all the cards in Gorchenco and Lokan's hands. When I have all the information, I'll let you know."

LOKAN

G etting out of the cell had been glorious, especially the swim in the Olympic pool. Arwel had verified that Lokan's cuffs were waterproof up to a depth of twenty-five feet, which was more than enough.

The only downside had been the Guardians watching him and Carol, which precluded sexy fun in the water.

They'd made up for it later in the privacy of their shower.

Wrapping a towel around her beautiful body, Carol eyed the full clothes hamper. "I should do laundry. Do you even have anything clean to wear?"

He was glad she offered and he didn't have to ask. "I'm down to my last clean pair of underwear."

"That's not good. You should have told me." She pulled the hamper out of the cabinet and took it out to the bedroom. "Any of it need dry cleaning?"

"Most of it. All my slacks and dress shirts."

"I'll separate them. And I'll also order you some training clothes and swimming trunks. Now that you have access to the gym, you'll need them."

Having a woman buy things for him felt uncomfortable.

If anyone should be buying anything for the other it was him for her, and not the other way around, but he was a fucking prisoner and utterly dependent on Carol.

"Arwel has access to my wallet. I'll ask him to reimburse you."

She narrowed her eyes at him. "I can afford to buy you clothes. You don't need to pay me back."

"I don't want you spending your money on me."

"Why? Because you think you don't deserve it, or because the chauvinist in you can't tolerate being dependent on a woman?"

Rubbing his hand over the back of his head, he took a moment to think about it. Was he being chauvinistic?

"Frankly, I think it has more to do with being accustomed to wealth, and not being accustomed to having things bought for me."

Her expression softening, Carol sauntered up to him and wrapped her arms around his neck. "Then get used to it. You are my mate, and I want to take care of you. I know it's a novel concept for you, and after a millennium of being on your own, getting accustomed to having a partner looking after you is not easy. But you are no longer alone, and you are never going to be again. I've got your back."

Carol's words struck Lokan with the force of a tsunami, causing an emotional overflow he didn't know how to deal with. So, he did the only thing he could think of and kissed her, pouring all of that maelstrom of energy into it.

When they came up for air, Carol touched a trembling finger to her lips. "Wow, Lokan, if I didn't know better, I would have thought that you loved me." She smiled. "I always thought that the way to a man's heart was through his stomach, but apparently it's offering to do his laundry and buy him training clothes."

He was glad that she'd made light of it because he wasn't

ready to admit that he loved her. At the moment, his feelings were too raw, too volatile to coalesce into coherency. He needed time to process them.

When the phone rang, he was grateful for the distraction.

"Yes, Arwel."

"Get ready. I'm coming in half an hour to knock you out and take you to a remote location to test your phone."

"What do you mean by knocking me out?"

The Guardian chuckled. "Don't worry. I'm not going to do it with my fists, only with a syringe."

"Ask him if I can come along," Carol said.

"I heard. Let me check with Kian." Arwel ended the call.

"That was fast."

Was it possible that he was still in Washington? Was that how they'd gotten his phone so quickly? Until now, he'd been sure that they had flown him to the West Coast.

He decided to do some fishing. "I didn't expect them to have the phone at least until Monday. They must have had someone fly over with it."

"Turner has his ways." Carol walked into the closet and dropped the towel on the floor, distracting him again.

She'd neither confirmed nor denied his statement, but it seemed that his original assessment was correct. His brother believed that the clan's headquarters were in Los Angeles, and this sprawling underground facility was probably part of the complex.

But knowing his general location wasn't all that important. At least not at the moment.

What Lokan needed to figure out was how to prevent Kian from forcing him to unlock the phone and hand it over. There was a lot of information on the device, including his Washington contacts, as well as those of his brothers and other key personnel. Kian could do a lot of damage with what he could find there.

Lokan would have to bargain with him and appeal to his sense of honor. The question was whether any of it would work.

All dressed, Carol stepped out of the closet and grabbed the hamper. "I'm going to rush upstairs and load the washer." She headed for the door, which was now left open. "The dry cleaning will have to wait for some other time. Do you want me to launder one pair of slacks and a dress shirt, though? Just to tide you over until I can get the rest to the dry cleaners."

"That's a good idea." He reached for the hamper. "Let me carry this for you at least part of the way."

He wasn't allowed to get anywhere near the elevators without a Guardian escorting him, but he could walk with her up to the end of the corridor.

Arwel met them outside and lifted his hand. "Kian said no."

"Why?" Carol put her hands on her hips, readying for a fight.

"Safety concerns."

"Oh, really. Can you get me my phone? I'm going to give him a piece of my mind."

Shaking his head, Arwel pulled out Carol's phone from his back pocket and handed it to her. "Stay over there." He motioned for Lokan to stand next to the wall.

Carol selected the contact and put the phone to her ear, then tapped her foot while waiting for him to reply.

Arwel leaned against the wall next to Lokan. "This should be good."

It still amazed him how brazen clan members were with their regent. And yet, he knew they respected Kian. It was an interesting model of leadership he would have liked to learn more about. If he ever got free, and if he ever got to implement his plans, it could be beneficial.

Yeah, like that was ever going to happen.

"I want to go with Lokan," Carol said as soon as Kian answered.

Kian's exasperated sigh was loud enough for Lokan to hear even though he was several feet away. "It's a safety concern. Lokan's father is most likely tracking his whereabouts using his phone. That's why we are taking him to a remote location with a bunch of Guardians to secure the perimeter. If we are attacked, I don't want to worry about you getting hurt."

It was possible that Navuh was keeping tabs on him, but Lokan doubted it. Knowing where his sons were at any given point in time was not important to Navuh, and he wouldn't be wasting his time on that. But he was likely to do so when Lokan didn't show up to report.

"Oh, really? So, I can go on a super dangerous mission in enemy territory, basically on my own, but I can't accompany Lokan and a bunch of Guardians to a place that is under our control and will most likely not get attacked? Come on, Kian, it doesn't make sense. Besides, if you give me a gun, I can outshoot most of the Guardians and you know it."

Damn, he was so proud of his mate. His little angel was a badass, and she was fighting for him.

Kian sighed again. "You make a valid argument."

"So can I come?"

"Yes."

"Thank you."

As Carol disconnected the call, Arwel clapped, and Lokan joined him. And as she tossed the device to the Guardian, Lokan reached for her and pulled her into his arms.

"You're awesome." Ignoring Arwel's chuckles, he kissed her long and hard.

59

KIAN

*K*ian's Lexus led a procession of five vehicles up the narrow mountain road, with William's van sandwiched between two cars full of Guardians, and Turner's car bringing up the rear.

They were spread out, those following behind checking for a tail the entire time, including from above, but it seemed like no one was following the phone.

Just to mix things up, Kian had taken it from Turner at the foot of the mountain, so if it was transmitting, the signal was now coming from a different car. The phone was turned off, but according to William that didn't mean that it couldn't be tracked.

When they reached the dirt road leading up to the cabin, two of the cars stayed behind to guard the perimeter, and the rest continued up the hill, with William's heavy van groaning with the effort. The guy had loaded his moving lab with equipment to rival a spy plane.

As Kian, Andrew, and the brothers entered the cabin, Arwel's car arrived, and Anandur went back out to help him carry the unconscious Lokan.

"He doesn't weigh much." Anandur walked in with the guy draped over his shoulder. "I thought he would be heavier, but apparently he's just full of air." He chuckled at his own pun.

Carol slapped his back. "He is not. He's just not as beefed up as you are. Lokan has an athletic build."

Arwel shook his head. "Be wary of the mother hen. This one comes with claws."

Two more Guardians entered behind them. Walking in last, Turner closed the door.

As Anandur laid Lokan on the couch, Carol hurried to put a pillow under his head. "Do you have bottled water in here? He is going to be thirsty when he wakes up."

Brundar walked over to the fridge, pulled out a six-pack of bottles, and brought it to the coffee table.

Earlier, Kian had had the foresight to send Okidu to clean up and resupply the place.

"Thank you." Carol sat next to Lokan and tore one out of the pack.

Lokan groaned, turned on his side, draped an arm over Carol's thighs, and sighed contentedly.

Although Kian had harbored doubts before about the two being mates, that small gesture was the last push he needed to convince him that they were. Lokan was still out, but he instinctively sought comfort from Carol.

An old immortal like him, who had spent a millennium alone, would not have reacted like that to just any female.

Carol stroked Lokan's hair and leaned to kiss his forehead. "Are you awake?"

Instead of answering, he tightened his arm around her and buried his nose in her shirt.

"You need to wake up, Lokan. Kian is waiting for you."

It took another five minutes and half a bottle of water until Lokan finally sat up and pressed the heels of his palms to his temples. "My head hurts like a son of a bitch."

Carol patted his arm. "I'll make you coffee, and you'll feel better."

Next to Kian, Arwel murmured, "Imagine having to listen to this all day long."

"Would you rather they argued?" Kian asked.

"They do that too."

"Every couple does that from time to time."

Arwel shrugged. "I guess."

When Carol came back with coffee for everyone, Kian pulled Lokan's phone out of his pocket and put it on the table out of Lokan's reach. "Before you take the device, I want to warn you. The cuffs on your wrists and ankles contain explosives in addition to the neurotoxin. You say one word that you are not supposed to, and I'll press the remote. Did you ever have to regrow a limb, Lokan?"

Given his grimace, he had. "Hurts like hell and takes months." He glanced at Carol who sat on the couch next to him. "You have nothing to worry about. Carol is my number one priority, and I'll do anything to ensure her safety."

"Truth," Andrew said.

Well, that was good to know.

Kian nodded. "So this is how it's going to go. Your first call is going to be to a florist. You are going to order flowers and have them delivered to your penthouse. While you do that, my guy is going to track the call." He pulled a piece of paper out of his pocket and put it on the table. "I wrote down the number for a Washington florist for you."

Lokan reached for both the phone and the paper. "Is the phone charged?"

"Yes."

He still didn't open it. "I want to make a bargain."

Kian arched a brow. "Now?"

263

"Before I unlock the phone, I want to make sure that you are not going to force me to hand it over unlocked or give you the passcode. I vow to help Carol in any way I can on the island and compel whoever I need to compel, but I'm not ready to give you more."

"And if I don't promise that, will you refuse to help?"

Lokan nodded. "Without me calling the guy in charge of staffing the harem, Carol cannot go, and frankly, I don't want her to. With me by her side, or at least in the background, the risks she is taking would have been halved. But you refuse to let me go."

Andrew didn't react, but Kian was sure Lokan was bluffing. "It would mean giving up on finding whether your mother is still alive and if she happens to be Areana, not to mention getting her out of there."

Lokan nodded. "To ensure my mate's safety, I'm willing to keep living with that question unanswered."

"Truth," Andrew confirmed.

"Are you also willing to live with the knowledge that your mother might be suffering at the hands of your father?"

"I'm quite sure she is not suffering. My father is not a sadist." He cast a quick glance at Carol. "She might not be happy, but I'm sure she lives in the lap of luxury. The one thing I do know about the harem is that the goods delivered there are the best money can buy."

Listening to the exchange, Carol's expression changed from touched to annoyed. "What about me? It's my choice to risk my life to save Areana, and I want to do that. Heck, I'm willing to die at least twice for that."

Kian cringed. "Going into stasis is not dying, Carol."

She shrugged. "It will feel the same to me."

He couldn't argue with that. "I see that I have no choice but to grant your request, Lokan." He leaned forward, putting his elbows on his thighs. "But think about it. Giving that information over may be your best chance to prove your loyalty to the clan."

Looking him straight in the eyes, Lokan nodded. "I'll take it under consideration. In the meantime, however, I need your word that you will not force me to do so."

Kian nodded. "You have my word."

Lokan let out a relieved breath. "Thank you. In appreciation, I'll give you something that you'll find very valuable. It's a piece of information that I was saving as a bargaining chip, but I want you to have it."

He opened the phone and typed in a long code while shielding the screen with his forearm. Stupid he was not.

"I recorded Gorchenco trying to sell me the submarine. That together with the physical proof you got should be enough to end his career on this earth if he refuses to cooperate with us."

Turner, who until this moment hadn't taken part in the conversation, let out an impressed whistle. "It will certainly fortify our bargaining position."

60

CAROL

*C*arol listened with half an ear as Lokan made the call to the florist.

Thinking about what he'd said and what he was willing to sacrifice to keep her safe, she couldn't help but feel guilty for wanting to go anyway.

It was ironic how a day or two ago she'd questioned his feelings for her, and now she was doubting her feelings for him. He was willing to sacrifice his dreams for her, but she wasn't willing to do the same for him.

Except, that wasn't entirely true. Perhaps it had been true to start with, but now she was also doing it for the two of them. This was the only way to earn Lokan's freedom, and the only way they could have a normal life together.

Perhaps they could live in this cabin?

Ingrid's professional touch was evident in the decor, but it still felt homey, and Carol loved having nothing but nature all around. She was a city girl, but she was ready for a change.

Was Lokan, though?

What would a wheeler and dealer like him do in a secluded cabin in the woods? After making love for a couple of weeks, he would start to get bored, and after a month, he would go crazy.

The problem was that the same fate awaited him in the keep's underground.

Kian's phone ringing snapped Carol's attention away from her daydreaming.

"Yes, William."

"You can go ahead with the next call."

"Thanks." Kian looked relieved. "Have you video chatted with people on the island before?" he asked Lokan.

"Just once. My servant didn't understand what I wanted her to pack for me, so I had her go into my closet and told her exactly what to take."

Kian frowned. "Can you think of an excuse to use with one of the pilots?"

Frowning, Lokan rubbed his hand over the back of his head. "I guess I could ask him to get something from my house and mail it to me when he lands in one of the neighboring islands. The problem with that is that he would do it without any compulsion, so that's not a good way to prove it."

"Good point." Kian looked at Carol. "Any suggestions?"

She shrugged. "Get him to mail you something that is not supposed to leave the island."

Lokan's eyes widened. "I know exactly the thing. My father's portrait. I have one hanging in my quarters, and it's certainly not supposed to leave the island. I can have him wrap it up and sneak it out."

"Go ahead." Kian waved a hand.

"What time is it?"

"Seven in the evening."

"Good. It means seven in the morning on the island."

Lokan turned sideways so only his face was visible on the screen and made the call.

"Arjun. I need you to do something for me."

"Yes, sir."

"I need you to go to my quarters, get the small portrait of my father that is hanging behind my desk, wrap it up, and take it with you on your next flight, then mail it from the airport to my Washington address."

"Very well, sir. I shall go do it right now."

"I'll call you in half an hour to verify that you have it in your possession."

"Very well, sir."

"And, Arjun…"

"Yes, sir?"

"Don't forget to bring wrapping paper with you. It's important that no one sees you take the portrait out. It's not allowed, but seeing my father's face gives me so much inspiration that I decided I need it here with me."

"I understand, sir."

Lokan disconnected the call. "Now we have to wait for half an hour."

"Do you think it was the compulsion, or would he have obeyed regardless?"

"I wasn't sure he knew Navuh's portraits were not allowed to leave the island. That's why I told him that, but in case he gets caught, I also gave a plausible excuse for my actions."

Kian nodded. "While we wait, you can send me the recording with Gorchenco's sales pitch."

"Not to your phone," Turner said. "Have William come in and record it on a safe piece of equipment. He needs to check that there is nothing piggybacking on it."

"I'll do that."

As Kian called William and explained what he needed, Turner handed Lokan a sheet of paper and a pen.

"Write for me Gorchenco's private number. I'm going to call him tonight and introduce myself."

"As who?" Lokan asked.

"As an operative of a secret branch in the secret service."

"That's good," Lokan said as he wrote down the number. "If I thought that you guys were from the government, he might too."

Turner shrugged. "What else is he going to think? Does he have any clue that his favorite vacation spot is run by immortals?"

"He certainly does not."

"How do you ensure that the brothel service providers don't talk about their fanged customers?" Turner asked.

"There are hidden cameras and microphones in every room, and the penalty for talking is execution. They keep quiet."

Carol shuddered. She hadn't known that.

"What if they get drunk or high?" she asked.

"The consumption of alcohol and recreational drugs is highly regulated and monitored. They can't partake in excess. Besides, it's not a problem with most of the customers because we can thrall the memory away. Some are immune, though, and that's why there is such a harsh penalty for revealing our secret."

When William entered with a bulky device under his arm, Lokan greeted him with a cold smile. "So you are the guy who devised these devilish cuffs." He lifted a hand.

William shrugged. "You should thank me. Without them, you would have spent your time chained to the wall instead of romancing Carol."

61

LOKAN

*W*hen Lokan woke up again, he was curled around Carol in their bed in his underground bedroom.

It took him a few moments to remember how he'd gotten there. Apparently, narcotics messed with his memory, and he wondered whether they had the same effect on other immortals too or was he unusually sensitive to them.

The headache was another side effect of the drug Arwel had used to knock him out.

He remembered William the tech guy coming in with a device and recording Gorchenco's sales pitch. Later, Lokan had called Arjun, verifying that the pilot had Navuh's portrait in his possession. Then after some talk about the mission Kian had wrapped things up and Arwel had given Lokan the narcotics shot.

"How are you feeling?" Carol shifted in his arms. "You've been asleep for a long time."

"I think I'm allergic to whatever Arwel shot me with. It affects my memory and gives me headaches."

"You can't be. Your body is a fine-tuned machine that

takes care of allergens. It's just a new experience for you, so you are a bit sensitive to it."

He pulled her closer against his body. "I hope that was the last time."

"Sorry to disappoint you, but when Kian lets you go, he will do the same thing so you can't find this place."

"For that I'm willing to suffer through it again." He stroked her back. "It seems like everything is ready, and it doesn't make me happy."

"Not everything. I don't know if Turner contacted Gorchenco tonight, and if the extortion worked. And when that's done, I still need to test Bridget's toxin."

As cold fingers of dread wrapped around Lokan's heart, he tightened his arms around Carol. "It's not too late to abort the entire thing. Don't let the momentum carry you. You can still back out and no one is going to judge you for it."

"I can't. If for no other reason than for the chance of setting you free and giving us a shot at a normal life." She chuckled. "Or as normal as two lone immortals can have it. We will be isolated from our people. Especially you. I can still count on mine to help out if needed."

Fear was an emotion Lokan hadn't felt since he was a boy. With no one to care for, and no one caring for him, it was easy to be fearless. But now that he'd gotten a taste of what it meant to have a life partner, someone who would always have his back, always care for him, fight for him, perhaps even love him, Lokan was terrified of losing her.

He buried his nose in Carol's hair. "I don't want to think about the future. Right now all I want to do is make love to you."

She chuckled. "I thought you had a headache."

"It's not that bad. And holding you in my arms is the best cure."

She lifted up and propped herself on her elbow. "Where does it hurt?"

He pointed at his temples.

"I'll kiss the hurt away." She touched her soft lips to one temple and then the other.

It was a sweet gesture, something a mother would do for a child. He'd seen some of the Dormants in the enclosure do that, kissing the hurts of their children away. But he had been no one's child. The one tasked with taking care of him had four children of her own, and he'd been a burden. Or maybe that was just how he'd felt. She'd never been harsh with him, had never raised her voice or her hand at him, but she hadn't loved him either.

Did Carol love him?

She cared for him, that much he was sure of, but love? That was a big word and an even bigger step. They hadn't known each other long enough, and half of that time he'd spent suspecting her.

"Did it help?"

"Yes." He bent down and took her sweet lips in a gentle, chaste kiss. "I need to brush my teeth, but I'll be right back."

"I want to freshen up too." She followed him into the bathroom.

They ended up taking another shower together, and since the urgency had been sated earlier in the day, Lokan luxuriated in exploring every inch of Carol's body with long, gentle caresses, soaping and massaging and rinsing and then repeating the process again.

She didn't rush him to do more, letting him memorize her. Because that was what he was doing. Consciously, Lokan was thinking about the days of separation he would have to endure, but subconsciously he was terrified that she might never come back.

Would his father kill Carol if he discovered that she was an immortal?

Probably not. Navuh was many things, but wasteful wasn't one of them. He would give her to the soldiers, which was terrible but at least she would live, so he could come for her. Kian was not going to stop him if that happened. He was sure of that. His cousin would launch an attack on the island to free Carol.

That was the most significant difference between the clan and the Brotherhood, between Annani and Navuh. Annani cared for each one of her people and treated them as individuals, precious and cherished, as family, and so did Kian.

To Navuh, they were all cogs in his machine and a means to an end.

CAROL

*L*okan was in a strange mood.

Up until now, Carol had experienced him as mostly playful and flirtatious, sometimes suspicious, often contemplative, and on occasion frustrated and angry, but never desperate or clingy.

He was too proud to voice his fears, but Carol could see it in his eyes and feel it in the way he was touching her. It was as if he was trying to memorize every inch of her body, her face, looking into her eyes and kissing her so softly, so tenderly, it made her feel like crying.

Carol had had men lust after her, obsess over her, and Robert had even thought that he'd been in love with her, but none of them had ever touched her and looked at her like Lokan was doing now.

"You are not going to lose me," she whispered as his hands coasted down her rib cage, dipping into her waist and smoothing over the flare of her hips.

He looked surprised that she'd read him so easily "I know. Logically, that is." He cupped her ass and pulled her closer. "But my gut and my heart are in cahoots against my brain.

My instincts scream for me to hold on tight and never let you go out of my sight, while my brain calls me an emotional fool. The dissonance creates a storm."

Wrapping her arms around his neck, she pulled him down for a kiss. "That's the mated male in you. It will get easier with time. The Guardians' mates must go through the same emotional turmoil every time their partners go out on a mission, but they deal with it because they have to. Can you imagine Anandur telling Kian that he can't go out and fight because his mate can't handle it? Or Brundar?"

"The blond? He is mated as well?"

"Yes, he is." She touched a finger to his elongated fang, then stretched on her toes to lick around it.

Lokan groaned and pushed her against the tiled wall. "I want to pleasure you."

Slowly bending down to his knees, he kissed her breasts, her belly, the top of her mound.

"My Aphrodite." He cupped her breasts. "I wish I was a talented sculptor. I would have erected a temple in your honor."

Carol chuckled, happy that Lokan was back to his playful, flirtatious self.

"You think I'm joking?" He tweaked her nipples, then cupped them again. "I'm serious. When I'm king of the island, I'll make you its official goddess."

Carol let her head drop back against the tiles and laughed.

But as Lokan lifted her leg over his shoulder and teased the top of her sex with his tongue, the laughter died on her lips, replaced by a throaty moan.

Then he delved between her puffy folds, and the leg holding her up buckled, but he caught her, twisted over to the bench, and set her down.

"Spread your legs for me," he said as he applied light pressure on her inner thighs.

Carol obeyed readily, and Lokan rewarded her with more delicious tongue teasing, giving the top of her sex all the attention it craved and pushing a finger inside her. Then another.

There was nothing hurried in the way he pleasured her. Alternating between soft kisses and delicate licks, his fingers gently followed the rhythm of her undulating hips.

With all her vast experience, Carol had never had a lover so attuned to her, so focused on her pleasure, and it felt odd to her to just receive and not reciprocate. But she felt that Lokan needed this, and she needed to let him have his way this time.

Pleasuring her with his lips and his tongue and his long fingers, he brought her to one orgasm after another, and then lifted her in his strong arms and entered her in one powerful thrust.

Carol climaxed again, and as he pounded into her like a man possessed, pushing her against the wet tiles and growling like an animal, she felt the coil inside her tighten until it could tighten no more. It sprung loose as Lokan sank his fangs in her neck.

Floating on the wings of euphoria, she felt him come inside her and had the insane thought that maybe this time they had created a new life. Letting her imagination carry her away, she pictured a little boy with Lokan's dark eyes and her blond curls.

63

LOKAN

*L*okan dived off the edge, propelling himself up in the air before reversing direction and cutting into the water with his steepled hands. He was on the other side of the pool in seconds, flipped around, and continued in butterfly style, just because it showcased his back and arm muscles, making Carol drool.

Besides, he had shitloads of nervous energy to burn.

They were waiting to hear from Turner, and if his phone call with Gorchenco went well, the next step was the toxin test, which was terrifying.

The boost in adrenaline propelling him faster, Lokan reached the other side of the pool and flipped around, continuing in freestyle.

Sitting by the side of the pool, Carol dangled her legs in the water and watched him with an amused smile on her face.

They were both putting on an act.

He didn't need Arwel's empathic ability to sense Carol's stress and fear. Lokan had never been in stasis, but those who had had reported that it felt like death. Warriors were prepared for that to happen, and Lokan had been too, but Carol wasn't a warrior. She was a civilian with dreams of becoming a spy.

His mate was courageous, but she wasn't stupidly so. Carol was well aware of the huge risk she was taking, which was oddly reassuring. He would have been even more worried if her attitude were nonchalant.

When Arwel's phone buzzed with a message, Carol's head snapped in his direction. Lokan swam to where she was sitting and clasped her hand.

"It's a go," Arwel said. "Turner is flying to New York to meet with Gorchenco and iron out the details."

Carol sucked in a breath. "I'd better get dressed."

"Is there a chance your doctor can perform the test here? I want to be with you."

"We have a clinic here, but I don't know if it has all the equipment she needs. Besides, I can't ask her to come here. She is extremely busy."

"Ella and Vivian have already transitioned. Your doctor can't have too many patients to take care of, and you don't have humans who get sick or injured."

"That's not the only thing Bridget does. But I'll ask her."

Arwel shook his head. "Don't. Kian mentioned something about Annani wanting to give you her blessing. You can't ask the goddess to come here as well."

"Right." She looked at him with apologetic eyes. "It seems that you will have to wait for me with your fingers crossed."

Lokan rested his head on her lap. "I'll go insane waiting and not knowing what's going on with you."

Stroking his hair, she bent down and kissed the top of his head. "I'll tell you what we will do. Arwel is going to stay with you, and I'll ask someone to call him with updates. That way you will know what is happening every step of the way."

He lifted his head and looked into her eyes. "What if the unthinkable happens?"

"It won't. I'm an immortal, Lokan. What are the only ways to kill one of us?"

He shook his head.

"Say it. What are the three ways to kill an immortal?"

"Four."

"Okay. Let's have them."

Reluctantly, he lifted a finger. "One, decapitation." He lifted a second one. "Two, cutting out the heart. Three, massive injuries that overwhelm our bodies' self-repair mechanism, which can happen in an explosion or a fire or a big-ass bullet to the head or the heart. Four, nuclear wind."

She waved a hand. "You see? There is no mention of poisons or toxins."

"What if that was never tried and poison is method number five?"

Carol arched a brow. "I'm sure it has been tried, and more than once. But I can ask the doctor. And in any case, Bridget has an antidote."

"Did she tell you that?"

"No, but I'm sure she does. I'll ask her as soon as I get there and let you know. How about that?"

"Don't forget."

"I won't."

64

CAROL

*F*ear coursing through her veins, Carol drove to the village in a daze, missing turns and having to backtrack to continue in the right direction.

Having Lokan with her would have made this so much easier. He could've held her hand. Perhaps she could ask Ella to be with her. The girl had just transitioned, but she should be fine. Ella was a fighter, and she wasn't the type who would faint at the sight of a needle.

In the short time they had known each other, Ella had become Carol's best friend. Perhaps the violation they had both suffered and survived had made them kindred spirits, or perhaps it was the warrior souls that they both possessed under their small, feminine forms, and their refusal to be labeled as victims.

Or maybe it was all of those combined. The bottom line was that Carol had never had a bestie before and now she did.

After placing the call, she tapped her fingers on the steering wheel, waiting for Ella's voice to come through the car's loudspeakers.

"Hi, Carol. What's up?"

"I'm on my way to the village, and I wondered if you are busy."

"I'm never too busy to meet up for coffee and juicy gossip. When are you going to get here?"

"Twenty minutes or so. Coffee and gossip sound lovely, but that's not what I'm calling about." Carol closed her eyes for a split second. "I'm heading to the clinic to meet Bridget, and I need you to hold my hand when I die."

Ella sucked in a breath. "Oh my God, Carol, is this some kind of a joke? Because it's not funny!"

"I'm sorry. With all that's going on, I thought that I told you about the experiment. I'm not really going to die, but I'm going to enter stasis, which feels like dying, and I'm scared shitless even though Bridget is going to monitor me every step of the way and then revive me. That's why I need my bestie to hold my hand."

"Of course, I'll be there for you. But what the hell are you talking about, and why do you need to enter stasis?"

Could it be that she hadn't told Ella any of it?

Apparently, falling for a guy messed with a woman's head, because Carol couldn't remember who she'd told about the mission. It was either that or stress.

"This is supposed to be kept quiet, but I'm sure Julian knows, so it's okay if you want to talk with him about it, or with Bridget or Turner." She took a deep breath and then slowly released it. "So here is the story in a nutshell. We have reason to believe that Annani's half-sister Areana is alive and held captive in Navuh's harem. We also believe that Areana is Lokan's mother."

"Oh, wow, that's huge."

"Precisely. So, we came up with a plan for me to go to the island and get assigned a servant job in the harem. I can then dream-share with Lokan and tell him what I've found. But the only way to get out of there is to fake my own death. Bridget suggested an insulin pump that will be rigged with a toxin that is deadly to humans, but she wants to test it first in a controlled setting."

"Obviously, there is much more to this story, but I should get dressed and head to the clinic to meet you. You can tell me the rest after you are revived."

"Thank you. You are the best. See you in a few."

Puffing out a breath, Carol felt like at least half of her anxiety had been lifted. The prospect of dying was much less scary with a loved one holding her hand. But since Lokan couldn't be with her, Ella was the next best one.

When Carol arrived at the clinic, she found Ella in the waiting room, as well as Kian.

She arched a brow. "Are you here to hold my hand as well?"

Usually, she wouldn't have dared to tease Kian, but as someone who was about to experience death, Carol figured that she was allowed some leeway.

Looking uncomfortable, he raked his fingers through his hair. "I'm here for moral support in any shape or form. If you need me to hold your hand, I'll gladly do it."

That was so sweet of him that Carol felt like kissing his cheek. So she did. "I appreciate the offer, but I already asked Ella to do that. What you can do for me is to keep Arwel informed at every stage of the process, so he can keep Lokan in the loop. Naturally, this is very stressful for him."

"I can imagine. I'll keep a steady stream of updates."

"Thank you. I appreciate it."

The door opened and Bridget stepped out. "Good afternoon, Carol. I understand that you invited Ella to be with you during the procedure?"

Carol nodded.

"Do you mind if Kian joins us as well?"

As if she could refuse him even if she wanted to. But Bridget was just following protocol, and it was the patient's decision who she allowed to witness the procedure.

"I want him here. Kian is going to keep Lokan informed."

Bridget nodded. "Very well. Do you want something to calm you down before we proceed? I can hear your heart racing from here."

Carol was tempted, but that would be a mistake. She wouldn't have anything to calm her nerves on the island, and it was better to find out if she was capable of pulling the trigger, so to speak, while freaking out.

"No, thank you. This test is more than just about the effect of the toxin. I need to find out if I have the guts to inject myself while knowing it will feel like death."

"I agree." Bridget waved a hand toward the patient room Ella was in just the day before. "Let's do it."

After Carol changed into a hospital johnny, Bridget had her pee on a freaking stick to make sure she wasn't pregnant, and then she took a blood sample without saying what it was for.

Carol hoped the doctor didn't think she was still using drugs, but she could understand why Bridget felt the need to double check.

When the doctor returned from her lab, she hooked Carol to the monitoring equipment, attached the rigged insulin pump to her belly, and explained how to trigger the toxin delivery.

"Any questions?"

"Is it going to hurt?"

Bridget smiled. "I wouldn't do that to you. You'll feel lightheaded, then dizzy, and then you will pass out. Any other questions?"

"How long is it going to take until I lose consciousness?"

"No more than five minutes. Anything else?"

Carol remembered that she'd promised Lokan to ask some questions, but she was so nervous that they hovered at the edge of her consciousness and she couldn't get a grip on them. "There was something else."

"Take your time. We are not in a hurry. I plan on leaving you in stasis for several hours and monitoring you throughout."

"Oh, right. Now I remember. Do you have an antidote?"

"I do, but it won't be necessary. Our bodies can handle the toxin."

"Are you sure?"

"Yes. But just in case, the antidote is insurance."

Was there anything else? Carol couldn't remember.

"I want to text Arwel." Since her hands were shaking, she handed Ella her phone. "Can you type it for me?"

"Sure."

"I'm ready to go, and I'm doing fine. Ella is here with me to hold my hand, and Kian is also here for moral support. He is going to keep the updates going via texts. Wish me luck."

"That's it?" Ella asked.

When Carol nodded, Ella sent the text, put the phone on the bedside table, and took Carol's hand.

"I'll try not to squeeze too hard." Her lips were trembling almost as bad as her hands, but Carol managed to force a smile.

Kian frowned. "Maybe I should hold your hand. Ella's bones are not strong enough yet."

Carol shook her head. "No offense, Kian, but Ella is my best friend. The positive energy flowing from her to me is precious. I'll be mindful of the fragility." She offered Ella another weak smile.

Kian patted her shoulder. "Just to ease your fears, Annani is on standby to offer her blessing, and I can attest to its effectiveness. When Syssi didn't do well during her transition, my mother's blessing helped her through."

"I appreciate it. Thank you. I'm good to go."

Taking a deep breath, Carol closed her eyes, counted back from three, and pressed the trigger.

As she waited for the toxin to do its thing, she wondered what or who she would miss most about this life if she died for real. Flipping through her mental album of loved ones' faces, she kept coming back to just one.

Lokan's.

She loved him.

Damn. Hopefully she would live to tell him that.

LOKAN

he wait was intolerable. As Carol had promised, she'd texted Arwel before proceeding with the test and told him that from that point on Kian would be the one keeping them updated.

When Kian's first text arrived several minutes later, Arwel read it out loud. "Carol administered the toxin, and she looked comfortable as she passed out. It hasn't been painful. She is hooked to monitoring equipment and Bridget is watching it like a hawk. Tell Lokan that everything looks good so far."

Lokan was starting to change his mind about Kian. He was a pretty decent guy. First of all, he was a man of his word. Secondly, it seemed he had a good heart under his gruff exterior, as evidenced by that last comment. He empathized with Lokan and his concern for Carol, and given that Kian didn't trust or like him, it was unexpected.

About twenty minutes later, Arwel's phone buzzed with another message. "Carol's vitals have slowed down to stasis level, and Bridget says that everything is fine and Carol is in no danger. She is going to keep her in stasis for three hours to see whether her body revives on its own or requires intervention. So, unless something changes, don't expect texts from me until three hours from now."

Arwel pocketed his phone and pushed to his feet. "Well, I guess I should go."

Lokan didn't want to be left alone. "Can you stay? You can tell me about the Brothers who joined your clan. I'm curious about them."

Arwel sat back down. "What do you want to know?"

"Both of them helped Carol, Robert by saving her from Sharim and Dalhu by avenging her. I would like to thank them in person. Do you think Kian would allow them to come here?"

Arwel shrugged. "Dalhu and Robert are trusted clan members now, so I don't see why Kian would have a problem with that, but I don't think they would want to come."

"What makes you think that?"

"Dalhu doesn't want to be reminded of his past. He has a loving mate and an occupation that is his passion. His life with the clan is full of light and hope. He wishes to put his warrior days behind him and not think about the lives he took."

That didn't sound like the same guy who'd taken Sharim's head off with a sword.

"And yet he joined you in a battle against his Brothers and fought by your side. According to you, Dalhu wishes to stay away from bloodshed."

Arwel smiled. "I guess he gets the itch from time to time. Besides, he had a personal vendetta against that bastard. From what I heard, Dalhu had befriended one of the girls in the brothel, and when he found out that she was tortured by the sadist, he dreamed of the day he could end him."

"He got his wish."

"Yeah, and then some. You should have seen that sword

fight. They were both magnificent, but Dalhu is a big guy, incredibly strong, and it was personal for him. He won even though he was less skilled."

"Did he join any other battles?"

"Yeah, one more. As I said, he gets twitchy from time to time and needs some action. What bugs me, though, is that other than some weight-lifting, he doesn't train at all, and he still is a formidable fighter. He's a natural."

"Interesting fellow. He must feel conflicted."

"Not really. He is usually quite serene, and I would've known if it was just a façade. His art fulfills him."

"Good for him. I wish I knew what could do it for me. If Kian doesn't release me, I might take up sculpting."

Arwel chuckled. "Do you have any talent?"

"I don't know. I never tried. But I'm inspired to sculpt Carol. A thousand years from now humans will discover her statues and think that she was a goddess."

"You are a man in love."

Was he?

"What is love?"

Thinking he was joking, Arwel chuckled.

"I'm serious. I've never loved anyone, and no one has ever loved me. How does it feel?"

The Guardian shrugged. "I've never been in love either, but I love my mother and I have a very close relationship with some of the Guardians. We are like brothers." He chuckled again. "It's funny that you guys call yourself a Brotherhood but don't act like it."

By now Lokan should have been used to the jabs at the Brotherhood coming from Carol and Arwel and other clan members, but it still annoyed him. "You call yourself a clan, a family, do you like everyone in your clan?"

"No, not everyone. But many."

"Same here. The organization can be different, the leadership might be different, but people are the same. Good and bad and everything in between."

Arwel sighed. "I might appear judgmental to you, but it's not on a personal level. I judge the Brotherhood based on its deeds, and those are damning no matter what you say or how you try to twist things around to make yourself look good. And by you I mean the Brotherhood, not you personally."

Lokan couldn't argue with that logic. He decided to change topics. "What can you tell me about Robert?"

"He's a quiet fellow. Kian has him working in acquisitions. I've heard that he is dedicated and methodical."

"So, he has left his soldiering days behind as well?"

"Not only that. He left his old name behind as well. I don't think even Carol knows what he was called before."

"Do you like him?"

"I've hardly ever spoken to him. He keeps to himself."

"But you can feel him the same way you feel Dalhu and me and everyone else?"

"Not everyone, but yes. Robert gets nervous around people, so all I get from him is anxiety."

"What about his mate? What is she like?"

"His exact opposite. Sharon is a firecracker. I think it's common for mates to have complementary characters."

"Interesting. I think that Carol and I are more alike than different."

CAROL

"Wake up, Carol. It's all over. You can open your eyes."

Someone squeezed her hand. "If you don't wake up right now, I'm going to pee on this freaking chair."

Opening her eyes required concentrated effort, as did processing the two different voices. Her head felt as if it was stuffed with cotton balls.

"That's good. A little more." Someone rubbed her arm with a wet washcloth.

As the fog lifted a little, Carol identified the speakers. The authoritative voice belonged to Bridget, and the one who needed to pee so badly was Ella.

Forcing her fingers to loosen their hold on Ella's hand nearly made her pass out again.

"Thank God," Ella breathed. "I'll be right back."

By the sound of her flip-flops slapping the floor, Ella ran out of the room. Carol's field of vision was limited to the blue sheet draped over her.

"The experiment went very well," Bridget said. "You were in stasis for three and a half hours when your vitals started coming back on line. Would you like me to raise the head of the bed?"

Carol nodded.

"I'll get you some water to drink."

A moment later, Bridget touched a straw to her lips, and Carol took a tentative sip, then another, and another. The more she drank, the better she felt.

"Was there anything in this water?" she asked when she emptied the cup. "It felt like I was drinking from the fountain of life."

"Water is the fountain of life." Bridget poured her another one. "It's clean spring water. For some reason, this is what works best after stasis."

"You said I was reviving on my own."

Bridget nodded.

"Then I will need a larger dose for the island. Three and a half hours are not long enough. I need to be out for at least twelve."

Now that she'd been through it, Carol was no longer scared to try it again. It had felt like falling asleep. The waking up was not fun, but it wasn't terrible either.

"Do you want to give it another go?" Bridget asked.

"Not now, but perhaps in a few days when I'm back to normal. Right now I feel like my bones are made from Play-Doh."

"You're awake." Kian entered the room. "How are you feeling?"

"Ready to go dancing. Did you text Arwel?"

"I'm going to do it right now. Any message that you want me to convey?"

"Yes, please. Tell him that I'm awake and that I'm coming home as soon as I find someone to take me. I don't think I will be okay to drive anytime soon."

"I'll take you," Ella said, walking in.

Tears pooled in Carol's eyes as she thought about her friend sitting next to her and holding her hand for hours. "Thank you for not letting go of me."

Ella leaned and kissed her cheek. "Never."

"My mother wants to visit Lokan again, so we can take you," Kian said. "There is plenty of room in the limo."

Great. Just what she needed in her weakened state. A limousine ride with the goddess. But that wasn't the worst of it. Carol had imagined Lokan rushing up to her and lifting her in his arms, and then she was going to tell him that she loved him. Now it would have to wait for later.

But it wasn't as if she could refuse.

"Do I have time to go to my house and change clothes?"

Kian nodded. "Meet us in the parking garage in an hour."

As Kian left the room, Bridget shook her head. "I would have preferred for you to stay a little longer. But I understand your need to get back to your mate after a difficult experience like that." She started removing the various tubes and needles attached to Carol, including the innocent-looking insulin pump.

"Are you expecting any complications?"

"You are going to be dizzy and weak, and I suggest that you get in bed and rest until tomorrow."

"Not a bad idea, doctor. My mate can pamper me for a change."

Bridget arched a brow. "You should order takeout."

"Yeah, you're right. I had to teach the pampered prince how to operate the coffeemaker, and I don't think he knows what a washer and dryer even look like. He had servants doing everything for him."

As Carol swung her legs over the side of the bed, Ella gave her a hand and wrapped an arm around her middle. "Try to get up on your own. If you can't, I'll pull you to me."

"Wait," Bridget said. "I'll bring a wheelchair. I don't want you walking more than a few steps to the bathroom."

Surprisingly, Carol didn't feel the urge to pee. Were her internal organs still numb? Or was she dehydrated?

Almost an hour later, Ella wheeled Carol to the parking garage, where Brundar and Anandur were already waiting with Okidu by the limousine.

"I heard that the test went well," Anandur said. "How are you feeling?"

She grimaced. "Like the walking dead. Poor Ella had to help me in the shower and to get dressed, and then she had to wheel me here."

"Julian offered to take you, but I wanted to finish what I started. Besides, it's a chance to see the goddess again. Regrettably, we didn't get an invitation to one of her lunches or dinners yet. I hope she'll get to us before she leaves."

Just then the elevator pinged before opening, and Kian stepped out together with Annani.

Gliding over as if she was walking on air, Annani smiled warmly at Carol. "I am so glad that everything went well and that you are all right."

"Greetings, Clan Mother," Ella said and bowed her head.

Anandur and Brundar did the same, and then Anandur bent down and lifted Carol off the chair. "Let me get you inside."

She patted his shoulder. "I could've done it myself. I'm not that weak."

Not letting go of her, he slid into the back seat and then deposited her next to him. "I know you don't like the role of a damsel in distress, but it gives me pleasure to assist you."

Hopefully, Anandur wasn't planning on carrying her all the way to Lokan. Even though he was her cousin and happily mated to another, it would have been awkward.

"Perhaps you should load the wheelchair in the trunk. It's a long walk from the parking garage to the dungeon."

LOKAN

"*W*ear something nice," Arwel said. "The goddess is coming to see you. Carol is hitching a ride with her and Kian."

Normally, Lokan would have been enthused about a visit from Annani, but right now the only person he wanted to see was Carol.

He needed to hold her in his arms and confirm that she was okay. The hours of waiting had been made tolerable by Arwel's company and Kian's updates, but they were still the hardest he'd ever experienced, and he'd been through enough shit throughout his life to fill ten books the size of *War and Peace*.

He'd been to hell and back more times than he cared to remember, and yet nothing had affected him as much as the prospect of losing Carol had.

And the thing was, she'd never even been in real danger.

The doctor had an antidote.

"I think I figured out what love is," he murmured.

Arwel arched a brow. "I'm all ears."

"It's when you can't imagine yourself going on without

her, when being apart from her feels like a big piece of you is missing, and when you are willing to give up everything you ever held dear to be with her and you don't even feel guilty about it."

"It sounds like an obsession to me."

"It is."

"Then I hope I'm not going to meet my mate anytime soon. I have enough trouble dealing with life as it is."

Lokan shook his head. "All of that will change when you meet her. You'll feel grateful, and you'll thank your Fates for the blessing they bestowed upon you. You know why?"

"I can't imagine."

"Because being with her will make you feel better than you've ever thought possible."

Arwel snorted. "I can't believe that I'm getting a lecture about love from a Doomer. Go get dressed, Lokan. They should be here shortly, and I know that you like to look fancy for the goddess."

Lokan looked down at his rumpled shirt and slacks. Carol had offered to iron them for him, but he'd refused to let her waste her time on that, when all he'd wanted her to do was have fun and not think about the upcoming test.

"I don't have anything better. Besides, I don't think Annani cares what I wear, and I know for a fact that Carol doesn't." He walked over to the bar and pulled out another bottle of beer.

His fifth that day.

"Do you want a beer?" he asked the Guardian.

"No, thank you." Arwel went back to reading on his phone.

Several minutes later, Arwel's phone buzzed with a message.

"They are coming down. You know the drill."

Yeah, he did. He was supposed to sit on the couch with his hands on his knees and not make any sudden moves.

Except, when the door opened and Anandur wheeled in Carol, Lokan cast Kian a pleading look.

"It's okay, you can get up and go to her."

Carol started pushing up from the wheelchair, but he was there to lift her in his arms before her bottom left the seat. "You told me that you were okay."

She had dark circles under her eyes, and her skin had a gray hue instead of her regular peach one.

"I am fine." She wrapped her arms around his neck and buried her nose in his chest. "Fates, you smell good. I missed you."

Behind them, the goddess chuckled, the sound more reminiscent of chimes than anything a human would have uttered.

"Love, it is the greatest force in the universe."

Lokan bowed with Carol in his arms. "Greetings, Clan Mother."

"Oh, do not bow. I would have suggested that you take Carol to the bedroom so she could rest, but I know she would not want to miss out on the conversation. Am I correct, Carol?"

"Yes, Clan Mother."

The goddess waved a glowing hand in a dismissive gesture. "Please call me Annani. We are friends now after our shared ride."

"May I sit with Carol in my lap?" Lokan asked.

"Of course. It warms my heart to see you two so much in love."

Carol lifted her head and smiled at him. "I love you," she mouthed, and then quickly rested her cheek on his chest as if afraid of his response.

Rubbing her back, he kissed the top of her head. "I love

you too," he said out loud, not caring who heard him. "When I feared for your life, I realized that I would not want to go on without you. That you are everything to me. And then I realized that's what love is."

She lifted her face and looked at him with such an unguarded expression of adoration that it took his breath away. "When I thought I was dying, I thought about all the people I cared about, seeing their faces flash from one to the next as if I was watching a slideshow. But I kept coming back to yours, and I realized that you were the one I was going to miss the most. My biggest regret was not telling you that I loved you before pressing the trigger and injecting the toxin. I promised myself that I was going to tell you as soon as I came back."

Someone started clapping, and then others joined in, but Lokan's eyes were riveted to Carol, and he couldn't care less who was clapping for them and who was not.

"Come on, Kian. Bring your hands together," he heard the goddess chide her son. "Love needs to be applauded, celebrated, and cherished. It is the strongest force in the universe."

CAROL

$\mathcal{I}$t hadn't been Carol's intention to profess her love for Lokan in front of a bunch of people. If not for how happy it made Annani, she would have felt embarrassed.

And it wasn't only the big smile on the goddess's face. Her glow had intensified so much that it was almost blinding.

"You glow brighter when you are happy, Clan Mother," she said. "I didn't know that."

Annani sat on an armchair and crossed her legs. "Extreme emotions affect the intensity of the glow." She grinned. "That is why I never allow myself to get depressed. I always fear that my glow is going to get snuffed out for good. It happened to my sister. Well, almost. The one time I've seen her emit any light at all was when she talked about your father, Lokan."

His eyes widened. "She loved him?"

"I would not use as strong a word as love, but he awakened her femininity, which had lain dormant ever since Areana had lost her true-love mate. She mourned her beloved for seven decades, ignoring all the suitors that came calling until they gave up on her." The goddess leaned forward as if to tell them a secret. "They were all gods, but the one to awaken her spirit was just an immortal, albeit a very powerful one."

"Did Navuh love Areana?" Carol asked.

"He was certainly taken with her." Annani sighed. "But he was a different man back then. There was decency in him. I do not know what made him change. Perhaps it was losing his father, or perhaps it was misplaced guilt for what his father had done, or maybe he just inherited Mortdh's insanity and it has taken many years to manifest."

"Is there a point to this story, Mother?" Kian asked.

She waved a dismissive hand. "I am just reminiscing, that is all. I came here to hear from Lokan what he thinks about the plan to rescue Areana."

Lokan's arms tightened around Carol. "I think it might work, but I don't want my mate to risk her life for it. Not even to save my mother. I know it is selfish of me, but I just found her, and I don't want to lose her. My life is worthless without her."

Annani nodded. "I understand perfectly. When my Khiann decided to embark on a trading expedition, I did not want him to go either. We were newly mated, and I loved him with intense passion. But loving him also meant accepting him the way he was and respecting his wishes and his choices. He would have felt stifled by palace life, and in time he would have grown to resent me for keeping him by my side. I had to let him go, and there has not been a day since that I have not regretted it. But I keep reminding myself that if he had stayed with me, both of us would have perished with the rest of the gods. So, in a way, by going away he saved me."

A tear slid down Annani's face, and she wiped it off with the back of her hand. "After all these years, I still get emotional." She took a fortifying breath. "What I am trying to say is, that we cannot shield our loved ones from every danger, and we cannot smother them with our love either. There is this silly saying that if you love someone you need to let them go. I think it should say that if you love someone you need to give them space to breathe."

Carol nodded. "The Fates have been working long and hard to bring us to this point. I don't know what their end game is, but I know that going to the island is my destiny. Everything is pointing in that direction." She turned to Lokan and cupped his cheek. "And I also know that the Fates are not cruel enough to bring us together and then tear us apart. We are meant to be together, and we will be. I promise you that."

To be continued...

COMING UP NEXT
THE CHILDREN OF THE GODS BOOK 31
DARK PRINCE'S AGENDA

Dear reader,

Thank you for reading the ***Children of the Gods***.

As an independent author, I rely on your support to spread the word. So if you enjoyed the story, please share your experience with others, and if it isn't too much trouble, I would greatly appreciate a brief review on Amazon.

Kind words will get good Karma sent your way -:)

<u>Click here to leave a review</u>

Love & happy reading,

Isabell

RECOMMENDED READING BEFORE
BOOK 31 IN THE DARK PRINCE TRILOGY
1: ANNANI & KHIANN'S STORY
GODDESS'S CHOICE
2: AREANA & NAVUH'S STORY
GODDESS'S HOPE

DON'T MISS OUT ON
THE PERFECT MATCH SERIES
PERFECT MATCH 1: VAMPIRE'S CONSORT
PERFECT MATCH 2: KING'S CHOSEN
PERFECT MATCH 3: CAPTAIN'S CONQUEST

THE CHILDREN OF THE GODS SERIES

THE CHILDREN OF THE GODS ORIGINS

1: Goddess's Choice

When gods and immortals still ruled the ancient world, one young goddess risked everything for love.

2: Goddess's Hope

Hungry for power and infatuated with the beautiful Areana, Navuh plots his father's demise. After all, by getting rid of the insane god he would be doing the world a favor. Except, when gods and immortals conspire against each other, humanity pays the price.

But things are not what they seem, and prophecies should not to be trusted...

THE CHILDREN OF THE GODS

1: Dark Stranger The Dream

Syssi's paranormal foresight lands her a job at Dr. Amanda Dokani's neuroscience lab, but it fails to predict the thrilling yet terrifying turn her life will take. Syssi has no clue that her boss is an immortal who'll drag her into a secret, millennia-old battle over humanity's future. Nor does she realize that the professor's imposing brother is the mysterious stranger who's been starring in her dreams.

Since the dawn of human civilization, two warring factions of immortals—the descendants of the gods of old—have been secretly shaping its destiny. Leading the clandestine battle from his luxurious Los Angeles high-rise, Kian is surrounded by his clan, yet alone. Descending from a single goddess, clan members are forbidden to each other. And as the only other immortals are their hated enemies, Kian and his kin have been long resigned to a lonely existence of fleeting trysts with human partners. That is, until his sister makes a game-changing discovery—a mortal seeress who she believes is a dormant carrier of their genes. Ever the realist, Kian is skeptical and refuses Amanda's plea to attempt Syssi's activation. But when his enemies learn of the Dormant's existence, he's forced to rush her to the safety of his keep. Inexorably drawn to Syssi, Kian wrestles with his conscience as he is tempted to explore her budding interest in the darker shades of sensuality.

2: DARK STRANGER REVEALED

While sheltered in the clan's stronghold, Syssi is unaware that Kian and Amanda are not human, and neither are the supposedly religious fanatics that are after her. She feels a powerful connection to Kian, and as he introduces her to a world of pleasure she never dared imagine, his dominant sexuality is a revelation. Considering that she's completely out of her element, Syssi feels comfortable and safe letting go with him. That is, until she begins to suspect that all is not as it seems. Piecing the puzzle together, she draws a scary, yet wrong conclusion...

3: DARK STRANGER IMMORTAL

When Kian confesses his true nature, Syssi is not as much shocked by the revelation as she is wounded by what she perceives as his callous plans for her.

If she doesn't turn, he'll be forced to erase her memories and let her go. His family's safety demands secrecy – no one in the mortal world is allowed to know that immortals exist.

Resigned to the cruel reality that even if she stays on to never again leave the keep, she'll get old while Kian won't, Syssi is determined to enjoy what little time she has with him, one day at a time.

Can Kian let go of the mortal woman he loves? Will Syssi turn? And if she does, will she survive the dangerous transition?

4: DARK ENEMY TAKEN

Dalhu can't believe his luck when he stumbles upon the beautiful immortal professor. Presented with a once in a lifetime opportunity to grab an immortal female for himself, he kidnaps her and runs. If he ever gets caught, either by her people or his, his life is forfeit. But for a chance of a loving mate and a family of his own, Dalhu is prepared to do everything in his power to win Amanda's heart, and that includes leaving the Doom brotherhood and his old life behind.

Amanda soon discovers that there is more to the handsome Doomer than his dark past and a hulking, sexy body. But succumbing to her enemy's seduction, or worse, developing feelings for a ruthless killer is out of the question. No man is worth life on the run, not even the one and only immortal male she could claim as her own...

Her clan and her research must come first...

5: DARK ENEMY CAPTIVE

When the rescue team returns with Amanda and the chained Dalhu to the keep, Amanda is not as thrilled to be back as she thought she'd be. Between Kian's contempt for her and Dalhu's imprisonment, Amanda's budding relationship with Dalhu seems doomed. Things start to look up when Annani offers her help, and together with Syssi they resolve to find a way for Amanda to be with Dalhu. But will she still want him when she realizes that he is responsible for her nephew's murder? Could she? Will she take the easy way out and choose Andrew instead?

6: DARK ENEMY REDEEMED

Amanda suspects that something fishy is going on onboard the Anna. But when her investigation of the peculiar all-female Russian crew fails to uncover anything other than more speculation, she decides it's time to stop playing detective and face her real problem —a man she shouldn't want but can't live without.

6.5: MY DARK AMAZON

When Michael and Kri fight off a gang of humans, Michael gets stabbed. The injury to his immortal body recovers fast, but the one to his ego takes longer, putting a strain on his relationship with Kri.

7: DARK WARRIOR MINE

When Andrew is forced to retire from active duty, he believes that all he has to look forward to is a boring desk job. His glory days in special ops are over. But as it turns out, his thrill ride has just begun. Andrew discovers not only that immortals exist and have been manipulating global affairs since antiquity, but that he and his sister are rare possessors of the immortal genes.

Problem is, Andrew might be too old to attempt the activation process. His sister, who is fourteen years his junior, barely made it through the transition, so the odds of him coming out of it alive, let alone immortal, are slim.

But fate may force his hand.

Helping a friend find his long-lost daughter, Andrew finds a woman who's worth taking the risk for. Nathalie might be a Dormant, but the only way to find out for sure requires fangs and venom.

8: DARK WARRIOR'S PROMISE

Andrew and Nathalie's love flourishes, but the secrets they keep from each other taint their relationship with doubts and suspicions. In the meantime, Sebastian and his men are getting bolder, and the storm that's brewing will shift the balance of power in the millennia-old conflict between Annani's clan and its enemies.

9: DARK WARRIOR'S DESTINY

The new ghost in Nathalie's head remembers who he was in life, providing Andrew and her with indisputable proof that he is real and not a figment of her imagination.

Convinced that she is a Dormant, Andrew decides to go forward with his transition immediately after the rescue mission at the Doomers' HQ.

Fearing for his life, Nathalie pleads with him to reconsider. She'd rather spend the rest of her mortal days with Andrew than risk what they have for the fickle promise of immortality.

While the clan gets ready for battle, Carol gets help from an unlikely ally. Sebastian's second-in-command can no longer ignore the torment she suffers at the hands of his commander and offers to help her, but only if she agrees to his terms.

10: DARK WARRIOR'S LEGACY

Andrew's acclimation to his post-transition body isn't easy. His senses are sharper, he's bigger, stronger, and hungrier. Nathalie fears that the changes in the man she loves are more than physical. Measuring up to this new version of him is going to be a challenge.

Carol and Robert are disillusioned with each other. They are not destined mates, and love is not on the horizon. When Robert's three months are up, he might be left with nothing to show for his sacrifice.

Lana contacts Anandur with disturbing news; the yacht and its human cargo are in Mexico. Kian must find a way to apprehend Alex and rescue the women on board without causing an international incident.

11: Dark Guardian Found

What would you do if you stopped aging?

Eva runs. The ex-DEA agent doesn't know what caused her strange mutation, only that if discovered, she'll be dissected like a lab rat. What Eva doesn't know, though, is that she's a descendant of the gods, and that she is not alone. The man who rocked her world in one life-changing encounter over thirty years ago is an immortal as well.

To keep his people's existence secret, Bhathian was forced to turn his back on the only woman who ever captured his heart, but he's never forgotten and never stopped looking for her.

12: Dark Guardian Craved

Cautious after a lifetime of disappointments, Eva is mistrustful of Bhathian's professed feelings of love. She accepts him as a lover and a confidant but not as a life partner.

Jackson suspects that Tessa is his true love mate, but unless she overcomes her fears, he might never find out.

Carol gets an offer she can't refuse—a chance to prove that there is more to her than meets the eye. Robert believes she's about to commit a deadly mistake, but when he tries to dissuade her, she tells him to leave.

13: Dark Guardian's Mate

Prepare for the heart-warming culmination of Eva and Bhathian's story!

14: Dark Angel's Obsession

The cold and stoic warrior is an enigma even to those closest to him. His secrets are about to unravel...

15: Dark Angel's Seduction

Brundar is fighting a losing battle. Calypso is slowly chipping away his icy armor from the outside, while his need for her is melting it from the inside.

He can't allow it to happen. Calypso is a human with none of the Dormant indicators. There is no way he can keep her for more than a few weeks.

16: Dark Angel's Surrender

Get ready for the heart pounding conclusion to Brundar and Calypso's story.

Callie still couldn't wrap her head around it, nor could she summon even a smidgen of sorrow or regret. After all, she had some memories with him that weren't horrible. She should've felt something. But there was nothing, not even shock. Not even horror at what had transpired over the last couple of hours.

Maybe it was a typical response for survivors--feeling euphoric for the simple reason that they were alive. Especially when that survival was nothing short of miraculous.

Brundar's cold hand closed around hers, reminding her that they weren't out of the woods yet. Her injuries were superficial, and the most she had to worry about was some scarring. But, despite his and Anandur's reassurances, Brundar might never walk again.

If he ended up crippled because of her, she would never forgive herself for getting him involved in her crap.

"Are you okay, sweetling? Are you in pain?" Brundar asked.

Her injuries were nothing compared to his, and yet he was concerned about her. God, she loved this man. The thing was, if she told him that, he would run off, or crawl away as was the case.

Hey, maybe this was the perfect opportunity to spring it on him.

17: Dark Operative: A Shadow of Death

As a brilliant strategist and the only human entrusted with the secret of immortals' existence, Turner is both an asset and a liability to the clan. His request to attempt transition into immortality as an alternative to cancer treatments cannot be denied without risking the clan's exposure. On the other hand, approving it means risking his premature death. In both scenarios, the clan will lose a valuable ally.

When the decision is left to the clan's physician, Turner makes plans to manipulate her by taking advantage of her interest in him.

Will Bridget fall for the cold, calculated operative? Or will Turner fall into his own trap?

18: DARK OPERATIVE: A GLIMMER OF HOPE

As Turner and Bridget's relationship deepens, living together seems like the right move, but to make it work both need to make concessions.

Bridget is realistic and keeps her expectations low. Turner could never be the truelove mate she yearns for, but he is as good as she's going to get. Other than his emotional limitations, he's perfect in every way.

Turner's hard shell is starting to show cracks. He wants immortality, he wants to be part of the clan, and he wants Bridget, but he doesn't want to cause her pain.

His options are either abandon his quest for immortality and give Bridget his few remaining decades, or abandon Bridget by going for the transition and most likely dying. His rational mind dictates that he chooses the former, but his gut pulls him toward the latter. Which one is he going to trust?

19: DARK OPERATIVE: THE DAWN OF LOVE

Get ready for the exciting finale of Bridget and Turner's story!

20: DARK SURVIVOR AWAKENED

This was a strange new world she had awakened to.

Her memory loss must have been catastrophic because almost nothing was familiar. The language was foreign to her, with only a few words bearing some similarity to the language she thought in. Still, a full moon cycle had passed since her awakening, and little by little she was gaining basic understanding of it--only a few words and phrases, but she was learning more each day.

A week or so ago, a little girl on the street had tugged on her mother's sleeve and pointed at her. "Look, Mama, Wonder Woman!"

The mother smiled apologetically, saying something in the language these people spoke, then scurried away with the child looking behind her shoulder and grinning.

When it happened again with another child on the same day, it was settled.

Wonder Woman must have been the name of someone important in this strange world she had awoken to, and since both times it had been said with a smile it must have been a good one.

Wonder had a nice ring to it.

She just wished she knew what it meant.

21: Dark Survivor Echoes of Love

Wonder's journey continues in *Dark Survivor Echoes of Love*.

22: Dark Survivor Reunited

The exciting finale of Wonder and Anandur's story.

23: Dark Widow's Secret

Vivian and her daughter share a powerful telepathic connection, so when Ella can't be reached by conventional or psychic means, her mother fears the worst.

Help arrives from an unexpected source when Vivian gets a call from the young doctor she met at a psychic convention. Turns out Julian belongs to a private organization specializing in retrieving missing girls.

As Julian's clan mobilizes its considerable resources to rescue the daughter, Magnus is charged with keeping the gorgeous young mother safe.

Worry for Ella and the secrets Vivian and Magnus keep from each other should be enough to prevent the sparks of attraction from kindling a blaze of desire. Except, these pesky sparks have a mind of their own.

24: Dark Widow's Curse

A simple rescue operation turns into mission impossible when the Russian mafia gets involved. Bad things are supposed to come in threes, but in Vivian's case, it seems like there is no limit to bad luck. Her family and everyone who gets close to her is affected by her curse.

Will Magnus and his people prove her wrong?

25: Dark Widow's Blessing

The thrilling finale of the Dark Widow trilogy!

26: Dark Dream's Temptation

Julian has known Ella is the one for him from the moment he saw her picture, but when he finally frees her from captivity, she seems indifferent to him. Could he have been mistaken?

Ella's rescue should've ended that chapter in her life, but it seems like the road back to normalcy has just begun and it's full of obstacles. Between the pitying looks she gets and her mother's attempts to get her into therapy, Ella feels like she's typecast as a victim, when nothing could be further from the truth. She's a tough survivor, and she's going to prove it.

Strangely, the only one who seems to understand is Logan, who keeps popping up in her dreams. But then, he's a figment of her imagination—or is he?

27: Dark Dream's Unraveling

While trying to figure out a way around Logan's silencing compulsion, Ella concocts an ambitious plan. What if instead of trying to keep him out of her dreams, she could pretend to like him and lure him into a trap?

Catching Navuh's son would be a major boon for the clan, as well as for Ella. She will have her revenge, turning the tables on another scumbag out to get her.

28: Dark Dream's Trap

The trap is set, but who is the hunter and who is the prey? Find out in this heart-pounding conclusion to the *Dark Dream* trilogy.

29: Dark Prince's Enigma

As the son of the most dangerous male on the planet, Lokan lives by three rules:

Don't trust a soul.

Don't show emotions.

And don't get attached.

Will one extraordinary woman make him break all three?

30: Dark Prince's Dilemma

Will Kian decide that the benefits of trusting Lokan outweigh the risks?

Will Lokan betray his father and brothers for the greater good of his people?

Are Carol and Lokan true-love mates, or is one of them playing the other?

So many questions, the path ahead is anything but clear.

31: Dark Prince's Agenda

While Turner and Kian work out the details of Areana's rescue plan, Carol and Lokan's tumultuous relationship hits another snag. Is it a sign of things to come?

32 : Dark Queen's Quest

A former beauty queen, a retired undercover agent, and a successful model, Mey is not the typical damsel in distress. But when her sister drops off the radar and then someone starts following her around, she panics.

Following a vague clue that Kalugal might be in New York, Kian sends a team headed by Yamanu to search for him.

As Mey and Yamanu's paths cross, he offers her his help and protection, but will that be all?

33: Dark Queen's Knight

As the only member of his clan with a godlike power over human minds, Yamanu has been shielding his people for centuries, but that power comes at a steep price. When Mey enters his life, he's faced with the most difficult choice.

The safety of his clan or a future with his fated mate.

34: Dark Queen's Army

As Mey anxiously waits for her transition to begin and for Yamanu to test whether his godlike powers are gone, the clan sets out to solve two mysteries:

Where is Jin, and is she there voluntarily?

Where is Kalugal, and what is he up to?

35: Dark Spy Conscripted

Jin possesses a unique paranormal ability. Just by touching someone, she can insert a mental hook into their psyche and tie a string of her consciousness to it, creating a tether. That doesn't make her a spy, though, not unless her talent is discovered by those seeking to exploit it.

36: Dark Spy's Mission

Jin's first spying mission is supposed to be easy. Walk into the club, touch Kalugal to tether her consciousness to him, and walk out.

Except, they should have known better.

37: Dark Spy's Resolution

The best-laid plans often go awry...

38: Dark Overlord New Horizon

Jacki has two talents that set her apart from the rest of the human race.

She has unpredictable glimpses of other people's futures, and she is immune to mind manipulation.

Unfortunately, both talents are pretty useless for finding a job other than the one she had in the government's paranormal division.

It seemed like a sweet deal, until she found out that the director planned on producing super babies by compelling the recruits into pairing up. When an opportunity to escape the program presented itself, she took it, only to find out that humans are not at the top of the food chain.

Immortals are real, and at the very top of the hierarchy is Kalugal, the most powerful, arrogant, and sexiest male she has ever met.

With one look, he sets her blood on fire, but Jacki is not a fool. A man like him will never think of her as anything more than a tasty snack, while she will never settle for anything less than his heart.

39: Dark Overlord's Wife

Jacki is still clinging to her all-or-nothing policy, but Kalugal is chipping away at her resistance. Perhaps it's time to ease up on her convictions. A little less than all is still much better than nothing, and a couple of decades with a demigod is probably worth more than a lifetime with a mere mortal.

40: Dark Overlord's Clan

As Jacki and Kalugal prepare to celebrate their union, Kian takes every precaution to safeguard his people. Except, Kalugal and his men are not his only potential adversaries, and compulsion is not the only power he should fear.

41: Dark Choices The Quandary

When Rufsur and Edna meet, the attraction is as unexpected as it is undeniable. Except, she's the clan's judge and councilwoman, and he's Kalugal's second-in-command. Will loyalty and duty to their people keep them apart?

42: Dark Choices Paradigm Shift

Edna and Rufsur are miserable without each other, and their two-week separation seems like an eternity. Long-distance relationships are difficult, but for immortal couples they are impossible. Unless one of them is willing to leave everything behind for the other, things are just going to get worse. Except, the cost of compromise is far greater than giving up their comfortable lives and hard-earned positions. The future of their people is on the line.

43: Dark Choices The Accord

The winds of change blowing over the village demand hard choices. For better or worse, Kian's decisions will alter the trajectory of the clan's future, and he is not ready to take the plunge. But as Edna and Rufsur's plight gains widespread support, his resistance slowly begins to erode.

44: Dark Secrets Resurgence

On a sabbatical from his Stanford teaching position, Professor

David Levinson finally has time to write the sci-fi novel he's been thinking about for years.

The phenomena of past life memories and near-death experiences are too controversial to include in his formal psychiatric research, while fiction is the perfect outlet for his esoteric ideas.

Hoping that a change of pace will provide the inspiration he needs, David accepts a friend's invitation to an old Scottish castle.

45: Dark Secrets Unveiled

When Professor David Levinson accepts a friend's invitation to an old Scottish castle, what he finds there is more fantastical than his most outlandish theories. The castle is home to a clan of immortals, their leader is a stunning demigoddess, and even more shockingly, it might be precisely where he belongs.

Except, the clan founder is hiding a secret that might cast a dark shadow on David's relationship with her daughter.

Nevertheless, when offered a chance at immortality, he agrees to undergo the dangerous induction process.

Will David survive his transition into immortality? And if he does, will his relationship with Sari survive the unveiling of her mother's secret?

46: Dark Secrets Absolved

Absolution.

David had given and received it.

The few short hours since he'd emerged from the coma had felt incredible. He'd finally been free of the guilt and pain, and for the first time since Jonah's death, he had felt truly happy and optimistic about the future.

He'd survived the transition into immortality, had been accepted into the clan, and was about to marry the best woman on the face of the planet, his true love mate, his salvation, his everything.

What could have possibly gone wrong?

Just about everything.

47: Dark haven Illusion

Welcome to Safe Haven, where not everything is what it seems.

On a quest to process personal pain, Anastasia joins the Safe Haven Spiritual Retreat.

Through meditation, self-reflection, and hard work, she hopes to make peace with the voices in her head.

This is where she belongs.

Except, membership comes with a hefty price, doubts are sacrilege, and leaving is not as easy as walking out the front gate.

Is living in utopia worth the sacrifice?

Anastasia believes so until the arrival of a new acolyte changes everything.

Apparently, the gods of old were not a myth, their immortal descendants share the planet with humans, and she might be a carrier of their genes.

48: Dark Haven Unmasked

As Anastasia leaves Safe Haven for a week-long romantic vacation with Leon, she hopes to explore her newly discovered passionate side, their budding relationship, and perhaps also solve the mystery of the voices in her head. What she discovers exceeds her wildest expectations.

In the meantime, Eleanor and Peter hope to solve another mystery. Who is Emmett Haderech, and what is he up to?

TRY THE SERIES ON

AUDIBLE

2 FREE audiobooks with your new Audible subscription!

THE PERFECT MATCH SERIES

PERFECT MATCH 1: VAMPIRE'S CONSORT

When Gabriel's company is ready to start beta testing, he invites his old crush to inspect its medical safety protocol.

Curious about the revolutionary technology of the *Perfect Match Virtual Fantasy-Fulfillment studios*, Brenna agrees.

Neither expects to end up partnering for its first fully immersive test run.

PERFECT MATCH 2: KING'S CHOSEN

When Lisa's nutty friends get her a gift certificate to *Perfect Match Virtual Fantasy Studios*, she has no intentions of using it. But since the only way to get a refund is if no partner can be found for her, she makes sure to request a fantasy so girly and over the top that no sane guy will pick it up.

Except, someone does.

Warning: This fantasy contains a hot, domineering crown prince, sweet insta-love, steamy love scenes painted with light shades of gray, a wedding, and a HEA in both the virtual and real worlds.

Intended for mature audience.

Perfect Match 3: Captain's Conquest

Working as a Starbucks barista, Alicia fends off flirting all day long, but none of the guys are as charming and sexy as Gregg. His frequent visits are the highlight of her day, but since he's never asked her out, she assumes he's taken. Besides, between a day job and a budding music career, she has no time to start a new relationship.

That is until Gregg makes her an offer she can't refuse—a gift certificate to the virtual fantasy fulfillment service everyone is talking about. As a huge Star Trek fan, Alicia has a perfect match in mind—the captain of the Starship Enterprise.

Also by I. T. Lucas

THE CHILDREN OF THE GODS ORIGINS
1: GODDESS'S CHOICE
2: GODDESS'S HOPE

THE CHILDREN OF THE GODS

DARK STRANGER

1: DARK STRANGER THE DREAM
2: DARK STRANGER REVEALED
3: DARK STRANGER IMMORTAL

DARK ENEMY

4: DARK ENEMY TAKEN
5: DARK ENEMY CAPTIVE
6: DARK ENEMY REDEEMED

KRI & MICHAEL'S STORY

6.5: MY DARK AMAZON

DARK WARRIOR

7: DARK WARRIOR MINE
8: DARK WARRIOR'S PROMISE
9: DARK WARRIOR'S DESTINY
10: DARK WARRIOR'S LEGACY

DARK GUARDIAN

11: DARK GUARDIAN FOUND
12: DARK GUARDIAN CRAVED
13: DARK GUARDIAN'S MATE

DARK ANGEL

14: DARK ANGEL'S OBSESSION
15: DARK ANGEL'S SEDUCTION
16: DARK ANGEL'S SURRENDER

DARK OPERATIVE

17: DARK OPERATIVE: A SHADOW OF DEATH
18: DARK OPERATIVE: A GLIMMER OF HOPE
19: DARK OPERATIVE: THE DAWN OF LOVE

DARK SURVIVOR

20: DARK SURVIVOR AWAKENED

21: DARK SURVIVOR ECHOES OF LOVE

22: DARK SURVIVOR REUNITED

DARK WIDOW

23: DARK WIDOW'S SECRET

24: DARK WIDOW'S CURSE

25: DARK WIDOW'S BLESSING

DARK DREAM

26: DARK DREAM'S TEMPTATION

27: DARK DREAM'S UNRAVELING

28: DARK DREAM'S TRAP

DARK PRINCE

29: DARK PRINCE'S ENIGMA

30: DARK PRINCE'S DILEMMA

31: DARK PRINCE'S AGENDA

DARK QUEEN

32: DARK QUEEN'S QUEST

33: DARK QUEEN'S KNIGHT

34: DARK QUEEN'S ARMY

DARK SPY

35: DARK SPY CONSCRIPTED

36: DARK SPY'S MISSION

37: DARK SPY'S RESOLUTION

DARK OVERLORD

38: DARK OVERLORD NEW HORIZON

39: DARK OVERLORD'S WIFE

40: DARK OVERLORD'S CLAN

DARK CHOICES

41: DARK CHOICES THE QUANDARY

42: DARK CHOICES PARADIGM SHIFT

43: DARK CHOICES THE ACCORD

DARK SECRETS

44: DARK SECRETS RESURGENCE

45: DARK SECRETS UNVEILED
46: DARK SECRETS ABSOLVED
DARK HAVEN
47: DARK HAVEN ILLUSION
48: DARK HAVEN UNMASKED

PERFECT MATCH

PERFECT MATCH 1: VAMPIRE'S CONSORT
PERFECT MATCH 2: KING'S CHOSEN
PERFECT MATCH 3: CAPTAIN'S CONQUEST

THE CHILDREN OF THE GODS SERIES SETS

BOOKS 1-3: DARK STRANGER TRILOGY—INCLUDES A BONUS SHORT STORY: **THE FATES TAKE A VACATION**

BOOKS 4-6: DARK ENEMY TRILOGY —INCLUDES A BONUS SHORT STORY—**THE FATES' POST-WEDDING CELEBRATION**

BOOKS 7-10: DARK WARRIOR TETRALOGY
BOOKS 11-13: DARK GUARDIAN TRILOGY
BOOKS 14-16: DARK ANGEL TRILOGY
BOOKS 17-19: DARK OPERATIVE TRILOGY
BOOKS 20-22: DARK SURVIVOR TRILOGY
BOOKS 23-25: DARK WIDOW TRILOGY
BOOKS 26-28: DARK DREAM TRILOGY
BOOKS 29-31: DARK PRINCE TRILOGY
BOOKS 32-34: DARK QUEEN TRILOGY
BOOKS 35-37: DARK SPY TRILOGY
BOOKS 38-40: DARK OVERLORD TRILOGY
BOOKS 41-43: DARK CHOICES TRILOGY

ALSO BY I. T. LUCAS

BOOKS 44-46: DARK SECRETS TRILOGY

MEGA SETS

THE CHILDREN OF THE GODS: BOOKS 1-6—INCLUDES CHARACTER LISTS

THE CHILDREN OF THE GODS: BOOKS 6.5-10 —INCLUDES CHARACTER LISTS

TRY THE CHILDREN OF THE GODS SERIES ON <u>AUDIBLE</u>

2 FREE audiobooks with your new Audible subscription!

FOR EXCLUSIVE PEEKS AT UPCOMING RELEASES & A FREE COMPANION BOOK

JOIN MY *VIP CLUB* AND GAIN ACCESS TO THE VIP PORTAL AT ITLUCAS.COM

CLICK HERE TO JOIN
(OR GO TO: http://eepurl.com/blMTpD)

INCLUDED IN YOUR FREE MEMBERSHIP:

- **FREE** CHILDREN OF THE GODS COMPANION BOOK 1
- **FREE** NARRATION OF GODDESS'S CHOICE—BOOK 1 IN THE CHILDREN OF THE GODS ORIGINS SERIES.
- PREVIEW CHAPTERS OF UPCOMING RELEASES.
- AND OTHER EXCLUSIVE CONTENT OFFERED ONLY TO MY VIPS.

Printed in Great Britain
by Amazon